NOWHERE

BINK CUMMINGS

Shiloh

The First round's
on Me.

Peace,
Bink

Proofreader/Editor- Kristina Canady & Genevieve Scholl
Proofreader/Beta- Mary Bevinger, Tammy Anderson, &
Heather Hendrickson
Cover Designer- Bink Cummings
Photo provided from: Big Stock

Dedicated to those who should embrace their inner kink… or… those who already do.

BINK CUMMINGS

Chapter One

Turning into the rural lot after dusk, I release the throttle and drop my feet to the ground. The wet gravel crunches under my boot heels and tires as I walk to my spot—the first space in a long row of black and chrome. Kicking my stand down, I cut the engine and dismount my bike. Riding twenty minutes outta town in a micro-mini skirt isn't what I'd call comfortable, but it fits tonight's festivities. My corset hidden beneath my leather jacket is even more apt for such an occasion.

Peeling off my leather gloves, I toss them into my saddle bag and run my hands over my hips to right my skirt so that my bareness underneath is momentarily concealed. Then I remove my helmet and rest it safely on my bike's seat. The fresh scent of spring engulfs my senses. Damn, I love being outside, riding with the wind, my legs wrapped around my bike. It's about flippin' time that winter's wrath has passed. Tonight was the first time I've ridden my Harley since October.

Combing my fingers through my long, chestnut colored hair, I shift on my feet, readying my nerves. A deep inhale steels them a fraction further, even though my heart is nearly beating out of my chest and my palms are clammy.

You'd think after two-plus years of these monthly visits that I'd be immune to this by now. That the mixture of tension, and anticipation simmering underneath the surface would vanish. That I wouldn't chew my glossed bottom lip as I move toward the entrance of *Nowhere,* a bar. That my heart wouldn't flutter, then almost bottom out when I take the first step. Another gulp and I set my shoulders back, holding my head high as the thumping of music draws me nearer. Three more wooden steps and I'm on the bar's wraparound porch.

Stalling, I scan my surroundings. If you've ever driven by this place, you'd swear that from the Wild West exterior it would have horses tied to posts outside. Instead, there are tons of motorcycles lining the bar's front. Across the gravel lot, alongside the butting forest, cars and trucks mark their own parking spots. A dim light attached to the bar's roof illuminates them in the distance like something out of a bad horror movie.

One more step toward the door and my legs turn to lead. I don't know why it's always this way. Why it's so hard for me to succumb to the choice that I made years ago to feed this hunger that gnaws at my deepest self. It's insatiable. And tonight, it's going to be fed. It'll gorge itself until next month when the recess is empty, and the bottomless ache awakens my appetite yet again. My logical mind tells me this is wrong. That I shouldn't be walking into the lion's den of a biker bar. What if my students knew I visited here for this reason? God, I'd be fired for sure.

My fingers curl around the cool handle of the squeaky screen door. *It's time.*

NOWHERE

Just as I pull it wide, the interior door swings open and there stands Price, wearing his cut and signature bowtie. "Well, lookie who the cat dragged in."

He winks at me and steps away, so I'm able to come inside. The potent scent of leather and alcohol hits my nose full force. My heart lodges in my throat as I wade further into the space, my heels clicking on the wooden floor.

Men—the men that I've known for over a decade—are milling about. Some are playing pool in the corner, taking shots of Jack from a bottle. Others are preoccupied with club whores. This is the Crimson Outlaws' watering hole—their domain. Club whores are always here in abundance, their scantily clad bodies continuously in a state of undress. There's rarely an occasion that I don't arrive to see a man balls deep in some pussy. These girls are pros. They put on award-winning shows of hedonistic pleasure that make me weak with envy. I'm no professional. No whore. I'm just … me. Gwen Donovan, thirty-three year old mother of one. An average, every day, high school teacher with a taste for bad boy dick, who also happens to ride a motorcycle. And...

A catcall is whistled severing my thoughts. The music is lowered, and all eyes swing to me. It's like being center stage when you don't want to be. Heat burns my cheeks as I smile, raising a tentative hand in hello to the men I'm here to have service me.

"Gwennie-bee, get your fuckin' ass over here!" a familiar voice yells from behind the bar.

Not wasting any time, I unzip my jacket to hang it on the rack by the door. My bare shoulders and cleavage are on display as I purposely saunter over to the bar, and slide onto a black stool. The heat of eyes searing into my back sends a shiver through me. I know they're watching. The distinctive grumble of the whores is indication enough. They don't like me. I'm not an old lady, which is biker code for a wife or serious girlfriend. And I'm not a club whore. I'm the sister to the club VP, Nash. Or, to be more accurate, his step-sister. Although, we've been in each other's lives since I was nine. We have a unique relationship to say the very least.

Across the worn bar top, Nash stands in his usual badass fashion—arms tucked across his broad chest, making his inked forearms stand out. His jade green eyes are fixed on me, one brow raised in question. Tonight, his long, jet-black hair is tied into a low man-bun. The thick stubble on his jaw tells me that he's not shaved in days. With the strong lift of his chin, he silently asks for my order. Some may not understand his subtleties, but I've known this man so long I often wonder if we can't read each other's minds.

"The usual," I say, laying my palms flat on the bar, one red fingernail nervously tapping the varnished top.

Without delay, Nash pours my usual double of Jose, then slides it over to me. I catch it between two fingers, raise it to my lips, and give him a tiny grin before tossing it down the hatch. No lime, no lemon, no salt for me; just the powerful burn of tequila as it settles in my gut, warming me from the inside out.

Damn, that's the good stuff.

Savoring the taste, I lick my lips, and he smiles, flashing me a set of pearly whites.

"You almost had a panic attack on your way inside, didn't ya?" he asks.

Frowning, I give him the hairy eyeball. "No," I lie, shifting guiltily on my seat. I hate that he knows me so well.

Nash steps forward and lays his big paws on the bar as he closes the distance between us, his body arching over the edge. Those all-knowing eyes meet my blue ones. The corner of his lip twitches. "You know the brothers would understand if ya decided to break tradition."

I'm not sure why he's mentioning this again. We've had this heart-to-heart before. A year ago, I went cold turkey to try and screw my head on straight. To fuck normal Joes and cleanse my dirty conscience. Regrettably, the void couldn't be filled, and my conscience can never be power washed. The hole inside of me just grew bigger and bigger until I went mad with need. And the only way to fix myself was to sell a piece of my soul. I was a very bad bad girl that night.

Just like I'm gonna be tonight when my pussy takes on a mind of her own. Nash gets it. The club brothers get it. It's how I'm hardwired— I can't explain why I am the way I am. I just have to live with it. The sane part of me hates the kinky darkness. While the other bitch residing in the twisted parts of my soul rejoices in it. I know I sound crazed talking this way. Perhaps this is how men feel when their dicks and brains work apart from one another. My pussy and my mind rarely agree. She's over here being a relentless slut while I'm dousing holy water on my soul to cleanse it of sin.

"I'm fine with it." Another lie.

Nash shakes his head, expression disbelieving. "Uh huh," he mumbles as his eyes cast to the side, where a topless club whore plops onto the seat beside me. Throwing a dirty look my way, her tits jiggle as she flings her blonde hair with attitude. Then she dismisses me and taps the bar top with her fake, pink nails.

Yep. Fuck you, too, bitch.

"The girls and I need some more tequila and limes for the body shots," she addresses Nash, unmistakably checking him out.

To add insult to injury, she licks her pouty lips, openly flirting with him. The sudden desire to slap her upside her head rides me hard, but I ignore her. I'm not up for a round of cat fighting tonight. Not that it hasn't happened before. It has. I can throw a mean hook. Nevertheless, I'm not in the mood for BS.

Nash jerks a nod, setting a bottle of cheap tequila on the bar along with a few lime slices atop a napkin.

"Thanks, doll," she purrs, grabbing the liquor and limes. But not before shooting me another disgusted look over her shoulder as she hops off the stool.

A warm hand settles on my arm as the scent of spice and coconut hits my nostrils. It's Toa, the club president. I'd know that smell anywhere. Without looking back, I lift my hand from the bar to rest over his.

Shifting a step closer, Toa's hard front meets my back, eliciting a shudder down my frame. "Hey, Gwen," he rumbles, sliding his other hand around my middle, palm lying flat on my stomach.

Irrepressibly, my breathing takes a turn for the worse, pumping erratically in and out of my lungs, bathing the air in palpable anticipation. I squirm in my seat, eyes glued to Nash's massive chest, illuminated by the dim bar lights. The thumping beat of '*Closer*' by *Nine Inch Nails* booms over the speakers, as if it's spotlighting what's about to happen. It seems to grow louder, pulsing in my ears, along with my blood as it rushes through my veins. Sweat dampens my forehead.

"Gwennie-bee," Nash tears me from staring aimlessly.

Lifting my gaze to meet his, I mumble, "Uh?"

"Toa just asked ya a question."

What? When?

"He … ummm … did?"

My nerves are starting to get the best of me. It's pathetic. I was here two nights ago, bringing Nash a plate of spaghetti and garlic bread. Ever since Trish moved out, I've been cooking for one. Too many leftovers left uneaten makes me cringe. It's bad enough the reality of being alone has just begun to set in; the extra food makes it worse. So now I drop off dinner whenever I get a chance—twice this week, and three last. So, yeah, you'd think I'd be chill here, with this … with Toa as his hands settle on my waist. Especially since I talk to everybody whenever I drop by. We're friendly. We drink. Shoot the shit. And they treat me like family.

Then you've got nights like tonight. You'd think I'd be flattered as Toa's hot breath fans my neck, erupting goosebumps just before his lips connect below my ear, dousing my libido in gasoline. Hell, maybe I am. He is gorgeous with all of that tan skin and tribal ink. Those big hands and juicy lips. Yeah … he's…

"I was just wonderin', baby, if you're ready for me," Toa rasps against my skin.

My pussy clenches at his words. Nipples aching to be sucked.

Oh … yes … I'm…

My mind short circuits as those lips trail across my shoulder to lavish the opposite side of my neck with attention. A throaty moan erupts from me as teeth move to gently nibble my ear.

"Gwen." He groans his need, hands clawing at the front of my corset like he wants to rip it away. Yet, shows restraint. "Are you wet for me?" he adds.

Yes … yes, I'm wet for him. If only I could voice my excitement. But I can't. Instead, I swallow thickly and nod as I lock eyes with Nash. He'll know what I need. He'll take care of this. He's my rock. My center. My protector. He always knows what to do.

Emotion passes between us, his eyes conveying that he's got me. A grin sprouts at the corner of his lips. It's calculated—devilish. Then it's gone as quickly as it came when he dips behind the bar, retrieving a long strip of condoms. He slaps them on the counter, along with a small bottle of lube. Not missing a beat, Toa rests his chin on my shoulder and lifts a hand from my middle, silently requesting one.

A shot of anticipated arousal races through me. God, he's gonna be inside me soon. That cock…

Nash rips a condom off the strip and dangles it above Toa's opened palm. "You gotta eat her pussy first and make her come. Then you can use this." He drops the packet into his president's hand. Toa wraps his fist around it, then briefly kisses my neck before standing.

A knot forms in my throat as I hear him unfasten his pants. Suddenly, Toa's erection pokes me in the back. He's already hot for me. Fuck, I can hardly believe it.

My needy gaze meets Nash's once more when Toa's hands curve around my middle. He's watching me—us. Those green eyes tender around the edges. Leaning over the bar top, he winks as his fingers drop to the top of my corset. I become frozen in shock as he unfastens it with expert precision and doesn't stop moving downward until my breasts spill from the tight garment, landing in Toa's awaiting palms. Groaning his delight, Toa squeezes my tits in his large hands.

Resting back against his big chest, I let him play. I need him to play. Deft fingers pluck at my nipples, sending a spike of pleasure to my clit. I moan, brazenly. As if on cue, the good girl inside me crawls into her hidey-hole as the bad girl makes her appearance. It's about damn time.

Helping me off the bar stool, Toa places his palm in the middle of my back. Wrapped in lust filled silence, he bends me forward until my arms and shoulders rest on the bar top, leaving my tits to hang freely below me. My back arches, pushing my ass into the air as he shimmies my skirt upward until it pools around my waist. Toa kicks my feet apart, leaving my pussy open to the cool draft, as his eyes burn into my wanton flesh. Almost painfully, his fingers grip my hips as his dick bumps my wet folds. My legs tremble on their own accord.

Leaving only one hand on my hip, he uses the other to run his cockhead through my pussy lips, nudging my throbbing clit. An unabashed moan tears from my lungs as he begins to fuck my little bud. My hands fist on the bar top, heart slamming in my chest.

"That's a sweet little pussy, Gwen," Toa finally speaks. "All wet for me."

Yes … Wet…

Standing across the bar in front of me, Nash unfolds his arms from over his chest and rests his elbows on the counter, his face mere inches from mine. I can smell the scent of beer on his breath as it wafts across my cheeks and nose. "Are you wet for Toa, Gwennie-bee?" he prompts in a low, sexy tone.

I nod, then accidentally moan as Toa's cock fucks my little clit harder.

"Tell us," Nash requests.

God, I hate when he does this. I don't want to tell him anything.

Defiantly, I shake my head and Nash scowls. "Stop touching her pussy, Prez," he orders, and Toa doesn't hesitate to comply.

No!

"No," I groan my plea, driving my hips back to regain friction. Sadly, I find nothing but cool air. Damn it.

Nash traps my chin between his fingers, holding my stare. "No, what? You're not wet? Or you don't want him to stop?"

I don't want to look at him like this. It's too much. Why can't I just enjoy my gluttonous need? Why do I have to admit how it makes me feel? How wet I am? How much I love it when he looks at me this way, his eyes heavy, lips inviting. God, it's so sick. I'm sick. Yet, I can't help that I fucking love it.

Trying to turn my head away, Nash holds it in place, not letting me budge. "Tell me," he rumbles. "I wanna know."

"Yes," I croak, humiliated. "I'm excited."

Nash won't let up as he moves closer, his lips a hairsbreadth from mine. "What do you want him to do?"

Steeling myself, I swallow down the rock that's lodged itself in my throat. "I want him to lick my pussy." It comes out barely above a whisper.

Nash's lips brush mine in a 'thank you'. As much as I should hate it, and think it's gross, I don't. It's something I live for. It's a feeling that centers me and makes everything alright. It ignites a soothing ball of happiness in the depths of my soul. My anxiety fades into oblivion, leaving only warmth and ecstasy to indulge in. Everything switches from insecurity to strength, to want, to will. Nash makes it all okay.

A body moves behind me, and warm hands spread my ass cheeks just before a tongue lashes my pussy. My knees nearly give out as I wail my desire, squeezing my eyes shut at the insurmountable pleasure. The tongue runs along my center, dipping into my eager core, then runs up to nibble and lick around my clit. Toa draws the little bud into his mouth at the same time Nash's lips brush mine once more. The fire in my veins turns volcanic as the building pressure sinks its claws into me, leaving only raw emotions to govern my will.

Continuously, Nash's mouth softly teases and taunts me as Toa sucks my clit. Then his thick finger breaches my core and I whimper.

"That's it," Nash urges. "Let yourself go."

Unable to show restraint, I heed his request and reach back with one hand to shove Toa's face harder into my pussy. My hips take on a mind of their own as they undulate against his mouth and tongue. Sounds of starvation erupt around us as he eats me like a savage, his finger plunging in and out of my depths as his other hand grips my ass cheek so hard, I know I'll bruise in the morning. I'm acutely aware of the sounds of other zippers retracting, and the music lowering as the flutter of my impending climax sails through all thought and reason.

A sudden mouth latching onto my nipple rips a moan from my throat, and Nash slams his lips to mine, swallowing my pleasure. They're scorching and hard for an agonizing moment, before he wrenches them away. "That's it. Let him lick that pussy. Does it feel good? Do you like Toa's tongue on your clit? Do you want his dick inside you? Do you like Merrick sucking your tits?"

Yes, yes, yes. I want to scream, and then force his lips to return to mine. Instead, my eyes flutter before they roll into the back of my head. My insides coil tighter, and my legs shake uncontrollably. Nash's mouth rubs mine, sending a perfect jolt of naughtiness to my center. Heat builds between my thighs, feeding a wetness that drips from there. Toa doesn't relent as my seams begin to fray and my pussy clenches around his digit. Another mouth latches onto my other nipple. Whiskers from the new man's face scratch my sensitive skin, and that's all it takes. The lava runneth over, and my back sharply arches as I wail my climax. White-heaven explodes behind my eyes as those mouths pleasing me continue their ministrations, drawing out every single fiber of my being. I vaguely feel myself threading my fingers behind Nash's head and taking his lips with mine. Then everything turns hazy as my entire body runs molten and sparks of endless rapture flitter through me like bursts of fireworks. Another orgasm peaks and fizzles. My tongue breaches and tangles with something wet and delicious. Whimpering moans unfurl from the darkest parts of me, emptying into the heat of someone's mouth.

The hand clawing my ass is the first to release; then a final nibble teases my clit. All of my senses are left inside out, and my legs turn to overcooked noodles. Before I nearly collapse in a heap of mush, Toa scoops me into his arms.

Breathing heavily, little jolts of post-climatic tremors spring to the surface, making me twitch. I rest my head on Toa's shoulder, barely prying my eyes open enough to see him carry me over to the pool table, where some of the brothers are already standing with their cocks out, condoms stretched over their members. Beside us, Nash walks, his loving hand resting on my arm. He moves ahead of us and climbs, fully clothed, onto the pool table. Lying flat on his back, he gestures for Toa to bring me forth. I don't resist as Toa kisses my forehead before depositing me onto the table

"Straddle him and let him hold you while we fuck that pussy." Toa's sweet voice registers through my muddled brain, and I comply without protest.

On my knees, I crawl over to Nash and straddle his waist, sitting upright, my palms lying flat on his pecs to keep myself from falling over. He unfastens the rest of my corset and hands it to one of the brothers for safe keeping. Then he pulls me until my breasts are flat against his chest, our faces lining up, lips merely an inch from colliding. My eyes flick down his features, settling on his mouth. I lick my lips at the thought of kissing him there. It's the most he's ever sexually touched me. Yet, it feels like he's caressing my very soul when he does. For years, it's been his mouth that brings comfort. His mouth that, somehow, makes all the fucked up shit right again. It's my own personal home. No matter how sick or twisted that may be, it's my reality. We've never discussed how it affects either of us. Most of the time, I feel he does it out of duty and love. But for me, it's far more than that. There's a tangible feeling that it elicits—a need. I would never tell him that. Not ever. Then again, that doesn't keep it from being the truth. One of my dirtiest, darkest secrets.

Behind me, a set of palms rest on my backside as a thickness nudges my core. The scent of coconut mixed with spice tells me it's okay to trust who's there.

"Go easy," Nash warns, wrapping his arms around my middle, securing me in place. Turning my head to the side, I rest my cheek against his shoulder, my face stuffed into the crook of his neck. On my knees, I lift my ass a little higher into the air.

"I've got it, brother," Toa replies, thrusting forward, his thick cockhead breaching my pussy.

Slick with my juices, he glides in effortlessly until his balls settle against my clit. Stretching around his girth feels magnificent; having him deep is even better. My walls contract around him, begging him to move.

Below me, Nash whispers, "How ya doin'? Does it feel good?"

I nod. "Yes. So good." The words flutter from my lips in a dainty moan.

Sliding out, Toa leaves just his crown nestled inside. His hands on my hips dig into flesh, sending a tremor of pleasured-pain through my pussy. Powerless to control myself, or wait another second, I drive my hips backward, impaling myself on his cock. He takes this as an open invitation to snap his hips in succession with my downward thrusts.

Over and over, he fucks me deep, his dick hitting my sweet spot every damn time. Resounding moans belt from my lips, only to be muffled as I press my mouth to Nash's neck. Air pumps from my lungs in a frenzied pace as sweat dampens my body.

Grunting in satisfaction, Toa then curses as he bottoms out, only to draw his hips backward to pound into my pussy even harder the next time. My frame pitches atop Nash's, stimulating my aching nipples as they rub against the fabric of his shirt. Everything burns in ecstasy, leaving me to feel nothing but the delicious maelstrom of each thrust.

My mind blanks as a finger breaches my asshole, and I cry a wanton moan.

Oh … God.

Toa pushes his digit deeper, driving me to the edge of no return. With another slam of his hips, I shatter into a million pieces. Biting into flesh, I silently scream through my climax as my body turns rigid for a moment before trembling wildly in Nash's strong embrace. Every single cell of my body flicks on, as the rapid fire of shameless satiation skitters through me. My hips hump on their own accord, needing more, wanting more. And Toa doesn't disappoint as he continues to fuck me from one lush orgasm into the next.

"Oh, shit!" I scream, arching off Nash's chest as yet another crescendo peaks.

His hand locks around the back of my neck, bringing my lips to his. Without a moment's pause, he kisses me hard and without remorse, delving his tongue into my willing mouth. Our tongues battle for dominance, as we groan and claw at one another. Losing myself in him, my breath falters. Yet, he doesn't let go as his possessive hand tightens on my neck and his other grabs my side, acting as my anchor.

More and more, I come, unable to stop it as one rolls into the next. Even when Toa finishes, his dick is replaced with another and then another. It doesn't take long for my body to give in to its basic carnal urges. Moans and rapturous groans that I never knew existed explode from the deepest parts of me. Through my wails of raw hunger, my fingers clutch anything that I'm able to, as I lick and bite whatever my mouth settles on. Including Nash's lips that I can never get enough of.

Once another orgasm passes, a new one replaces it, and my mind goes from blank to floating. Every muscle turns to goo as I melt into Nash's heaving chest. Both of his arms lock around me, his lips pressing kisses into my soaked hair.

"That's enough," he orders gruffly. "Beau, she's done. Take your dick outta her pussy right the fuck now."

Listening to his VP, the cock pounding my center slides out, leaving a vacancy that makes me want to beg for more. For them to fill me up again. To ease this need just one more time. In place of whining, I fall deeper into this heavenly plane where I can drift and everything is warm, soft, and utterly perfect. Nothing can touch me here. Nothing can breach this ethereal fog to fuck with my head.

As exhaustion plays heavily on my body, a further calmness settles over me, and my eyes shut. A few beats later, my breathing begins to even out. My limbs turn boneless.

I'm vaguely aware that Nash is speaking to me, or someone else, as the vibrations in his chest break like tiny waves into my dream world. I feel my weightless frame being shifted off his muscled one, and then I'm being carted away, drifting through the cold air. My legs dangle freely, with a sense of heat enveloping my left side. My cheek rests on a soft, yet firm cloud that smells of *him,* and I release a sigh of contentment. This is my heaven.

The floating halts and my legs swing as the distinct smell of cinnamon and cloves invades my brain, briefly flashing a picture behind my eyelids of the only place this scent lingers—Nash's bedroom. Ever since I was a little girl, his rooms have always smelled of this. From place to place, year to year, it remains untouched.

A deeper sense of infallible comfort spreads through my limbs, and I wrap that feeling around me like a cape to keep me safe for always. I try to pull my knees to my chest, but I'm not sure if I'm successful.

Descending through air, the strong firmness is torn away when I melt into a long pillow of *Downy* scented paradise. A silky blanket of warmth settles over my body. Indistinguishable words are uttered. The tightness around my calves is released. And a delicate softness is pressed firmly against my forehead, as thick prongs sift through my hair, driving me deeper into this divine plane of absentminded nirvana. In the only place that feels like home—a place where cinnamon, clove bedrooms, and the man who protects me against all odds lives.

Goodnight.

Chapter Two

Bounding up the front steps of my parent's house, I don't pause to knock before seeing myself inside. Out of habit, I kick my boots off after I shut the door. They fall alongside Nash's, and two pairs of women's tennis shoes. They're all the evidence I need to know that I'm the last person to arrive for our Sunday lunch. It's a tradition in the McQueen household. Even though I'm not technically a McQueen I've been raised as one. My mother has forced this on Nash and me since we were little. If we don't attend every Sunday, the wrath of guilt she thrusts upon us is way more than I can bear. So we make it as much as possible.

"Gwen is that you?!" Mom hollers from the kitchen. I drop my purse beside my boots before following the voices in that direction.

Turning the corner, I get a full view of the open kitchen that flows into the dining room. At the island, Nash sits with his tatted arm draped across the top of his long-time girlfriend's chair. Both of their backs are to me, as is my daughter, Trish's, who's busy fiddling with her damn phone.

"Yeah, Ma, I'm here." I pad my way across the old hardwood floors, my socks slipping over the surface just like they used to when we were kids.

For a second, I stop behind Trish's stool and kiss the back of her head in greeting.

"Hey, Mom." She glances over her shoulder, giving me a sweet grin.

"Hey, back, stranger." I poke her arm. "You were MIA last night when I texted you. You move out, and now you won't even text your poor mom back," I tease, only half-serious with the guilt I'm laying on her.

When she started school in the fall, Trish moved out of my house in Carolina Rose and into the apartment above my parent's garage. It's sort of a family tradition to live there at least once in your life. I have, Nash has, and now Trish is carrying the torch. Honestly, I hate it, since I don't get to see her every day. At the same time, I understand that it's more practical. The drive from Carolina Rose to Charlotteton is at least thirty minutes; and with her attending school here and working part-time for my mom, it only makes sense that she'd live nearby. However, she's still my little girl no matter how big she gets, and that's never gonna change. So I try to keep tabs on her whenever she lets me.

"Sorry. I was out last night. Didn't think you'd want me to text at four in the morning," she replies as I make my way into the kitchen to help prepare lunch.

My frowning expression meets her awkward one across the island. Four in the morning? *Jesus*. What could she have been doing until four in the morning? She's only eighteen. Pretty sure I was already passed out by then. But still… *Four … in … the … morning.* What the hell?

Just as I'm revving up to slip into full throttle mom-mode, Nash intercedes. "You can't leave your mom hangin' like that, Bug." He hooks his arm around her neck, bringing her in for a quick hug.

"I know," she mumbles, ashamed. Then lifts her gaze to lock with mine. The green of her eyes shimmer as emotions below the surface start to rise. *Shit*. I don't want her to cry. "I'm sorry, Mom. I was out with friends and left my phone in the car. I swear I didn't mean to ignore you. Christy was drunk so I drove her home and stayed with her when she threw up. It was after four by the time I got back. Grandpa saw me drive in and gave me hell for being so late. I promise it won't happen again." A tear drips from the corner of her eye, and I reach out to swipe it away. Then I pinch her cheek with affection.

"It's not a problem, Bug. Just be safe, okay? You don't want Nash to have to kick someone's ass, do ya?"

I try to make light of the situation, to keep her from crying. She's always been an emotional girl. Something that most women can relate with. But it tears my heart out every time she cries. And I know for a fact that it rips Nash apart, too. He's told me that on many occasions.

Sadness quickly dispersed, she offers me a tiny giggle, tucking a strand of her black hair behind her ear. "No. I suppose I don't."

Interrupting our moment, my mom bumps her hip with mine and drops armfuls of sandwich fixin's in front of me. "Put those lovely hands to work. The sandwiches aren't gonna make themselves." She playfully knocks my hip again.

"Yes, Mooommm," I drone with a smirk, winking at Trish, who stifles a laugh with her hand. "I still don't think it's fair that you don't have *Nath-an-iel* helping, too." My

24

words flow like a childish whine. It's fun getting under my parent's skin, and this is the sure fire way to do it.

Chuckling, my mom slaps my bottom with a damp dish towel as she turns to hand wash whatever mess she's made in the sink. It stings, making me suck in a pained breath. Even the most playful of touches piss off my budding bruises, but she doesn't know that and I'm not about to tell her. "Stop talking that way, young lady. Men do not work in the kitchen. They work in the yard." Being a pain in the butt, I mouth the last of her sentence right along with her, making Trish all-out giggle and Nash roll his eyes with amusement.

It's my mom's mantra and has been for years. However, that doesn't stop me from picking on her about it any chance I get. My mom is very old fashioned when it comes to household chores, yet, she's pretty open-minded about everything else. The funny thing is, as much as I love my dad, he is not a typical man's man. He sucks at mowing the grass—so much so that Nash has to do it. He couldn't fix a car to save his life. Which forces Nash to come to the rescue whenever Mom, Trish, or I have any type of car problems. I'm pretty sure the only manly thing my dad can do is grill. And if Mom would let him, he could probably cook as well. Nevertheless, she's still too stubborn to allow any man into her kitchen. And, truthfully, I wish she wasn't always that way. Then maybe Nash would have learned to cook more than frozen dinners.

As requested, I fall in line and start fixing the sandwiches for lunch. Trish plays on her phone as I do, and when I finally get a second to glance up, I see Nash immersed in small talk with his girlfriend, Kelly. His head is turned to the side, hand flat on the counter, body language showing he's engrossed in whatever they're chatting about. From this angle, I catch sight of his corded neck, and I gasp. It's loud as it bounces off the walls in the kitchen, even though I try to suck it back in. Fire burns at my cheeks as my eyes fly wide in shock. Penetrating guilt slithers its way through my body like venom from the most poisonous snake. I feel like I'm going to puke.

A sudden hand touches my shoulder, causing me to jump outta my skin. It's my mom. "Nasty lookin' bruises he's got, huh?" she comments.

No shit, they are. I did them! Oh, my god! That's the worst yet. Month to month, as these sexual urges strengthen, I become more aggressive when I get off. I don't know if it's because I'm finally allowing myself to embrace the dark side and let it fly freely. Or something else entirely. But, that … shit … it looks awful. Ugly bruises scatter the entire left side of Nash's neck from where his collar begins all the way up to the sharp edge of his jaw. Even the extra day of hair growth does little to mask it.

Nash, now realizing we're staring, cups the side of his neck and meets my eyes. I'm not sure what they're trying to convey, but they don't seem angry. If anything, I'd say they appear to be the opposite. That's a relief.

I exhale the breath I didn't realize I was harboring.

The first time I scratched Nash during the heat of the moment, he came unglued. That is one of the reasons I tried to quit these monthly sessions cold turkey. The guilt from it all became too much, especially when I started to injure him as well. Kelly had even threatened to leave him because she thought he was cheating on her. He'd never do that. Not with anyone. Sure, our relationship is quite unconventional, but he's never so much as touched me inappropriately. Except, maybe, when he plunders my mouth. I know that's probably cheating and I should feel like shit about it. However, I don't. It's something I physically need, and he provides. It's nothing more than him tending to his sister in the one way that he probably shouldn't. You can judge us all you want. I understand how this looks—that it's fucked up, and I shouldn't like to kiss my step-brother. Especially since he's in a committed relationship. I should feel like hell for even doing it. I've tried to feel remorse for the way the soft pillows of his lips fuse against mine, easily filling the void that often consumes me. Perhaps, I would feel like hell if he detested our actions. Thankfully, he doesn't. Nash has been nothing more than attentive and caring since the very first time it happened. That's a story for another time.

Possessively, Kelly lays her hand atop Nash's. "Oh, I know, Susan. You should see the rest of his body. It's like a bear tried to maul him." Annoyance hangs from her every word.

"No, Kelly. I mauled him!" I want to yell. Instead, I clamp my mouth shut.

This is fucking bad. The sudden itch to run away, and never look back eats at me. I can't believe I hurt him like that. I'm a monster!

This morning, I woke up like I do every night I stay at Nash's—alone and dressed in one of his t-shirts. It's nothing, if not repetitive. Some time after he carries me to bed he undresses me, washes me, and then slips me into one of his many shirts. In the morning when I awaken, he's nowhere to be found. On the nightstand beside his bed sits a bottle of water, Tylenol, and a pair of sweats in my size. A note hangs from his lampshade.

This morning's one read…

See ya at Mom and Dad's for lunch.
Xo- N.

In no way, shape, or form did I expect to see him in that condition when I arrived. I knew that I'd be sore. That my pussy would be tender, yet delightfully so—just like a night of hard sex always leaves you feeling. I also figured I'd bear the mark of many bruises. Most of them on my thighs and ass. It's something I've grown accustomed to; finding bruises in places I didn't even know you could get them. After about a week, they'll be gone, and in my own twisted way, I'll miss them. Sadly, I enjoy the constant reminder of the pleasure I felt, even if I know it's sick. But, hey, at least I found something to embrace about the aftermath that doesn't include stifling shame.

Nash rubs the side of his neck, looking a bit sheepish. "It's not a big deal, babe," he grumbles, eyes staring at the countertop. Fuck, he's gotta be feeling the heat right about now. I know I am.

"The hell it isn't. Those stupid club whores need to leave without biting and scratching at you like that. That mark on your chest … I'm surprised it didn't bleed." She's full of fire and ice, having none of this.

Club whores biting and scratching him? God, he sucks at lying. At least this one is plausible, though. Last month, he told her he'd gotten hurt working under someone's car. Not sure if Kelly is that gullible, or trusts him wholeheartedly. I guess if I'd ever dated a man for nearly three years I'd have to trust him, too. And Nash is a pretty trustworthy man, even if he's rough around the edges.

Avoiding a conversation that is going to leave me more upset than I already am, I ignore them and continue with my meal preparations. Twenty minutes later, my dad emerges from his office and takes the seat at the end of the table. The rest of us filter over, carrying enough food to feed a small army. It's time for lunch.

Chapter Three

Taking a gulp of ice water, I silently listen to Dad and Nash hashing out a flower purchase my mom wants. Something about annuals that he's trying to force my brother into planting. At the same time, Nash is shaking his head in a *'hell no, old man'* gesture.

"Dad. No." Nash finally puts his foot down, literally stomping on the floor.

Glowering at him, Dad tucks his arms across his chest—like father like son.

Ya see, even though Patrick isn't technically my birth father, he's the only man I've ever had in my life. My real dad died in a car wreck when I was six months old, leaving my mom a widow and single mother for many years to come. During that time, instead of dating, she became a seamstress and started her own small business. It's a cute little shop in downtown Charlotteton. It's become a place where the Crimson Outlaw brothers go to have patches sewn on their cuts, as does the neighboring club, Corrupt Chaos.

When I was nine, my mom and a few of her seamstress girlfriends attended a convention for crafters in

Las Vegas. That weekend, she left a single mother and returned with a brand new husband and son.

I'm sure you can already guess where I'm going with this.

To hear Mom and Patrick tell their story, it was love at first sight at a craps table inside the *Golden Nugget*. She blew on his dice, probably something else a little more south, and then twelve hours later they were hitched. It was way out of character for my mother, who's always been the sensible one. Nonetheless, it must have been dumb luck, or a strike of fate because those two, love-sick fools have been together ever since. Patrick and Nathaniel packed up everything and moved from their tiny apartment in Virginia into our old Victorian home in Kentucky. The same one I'm seated in right now.

Like me, Nathaniel's only ever known my mother, Susan, as his own. From what I've been told, his birth mom skipped out on them when he was five, and never looked back. Maybe a bit more of that dumb luck sprinkled over our lives, so we were able to come together like we did. Nash needed a mom while I needed a dad. And unlike many other blended families, ours doesn't feel off balance. We're all each other has.

"Come on," Dad grumbles, trying to wear Nash down with his fatherly stare. You know the one I'm talking about. The *'I mean business'* one. It works on me, but he should know by now it's not going to work on Nash. It never has.

Seated next to him, Kelly elbows her boyfriend in the side. "Yeah, Nash, come on. It's just a few flowers."

Why can't she stay out of it? I'm all for Nash helping our parents, but he's not unreasonable when he does say no. As much as I try to like Kelly, this is none of her business.

"Try two fucking truckloads," he growls under his breath, making the hairs on the back of my neck stand on end. He sounds oddly erotic when he does that. I shouldn't feel that way about it, but I do. It's kinda hot. Don't deny it, you think so, too.

"Can't some of the brothers help?" she suggests, and I ignore anything further she says, in fear that I'll blurt something rude in retort.

With those marks adorning Nash's neck and under his shirt, I don't need to come across any more overprotective than I already do. Not against his girlfriend, at least. He can handle her just fine. No need to raise possible suspicions.

Trish returns to the table from helping her grandma in the kitchen. As usual, I help prepare the food with my mom, and Trish cleans up afterward. Not sure why, after nearly three years of this, Kelly hasn't been given a duty as well. But Mom hasn't delegated one. Perhaps she realizes that Nash will eventually get bored and dump this chick like he did the last four. One of which he'd dated almost two years before she gave him the marriage ultimatum. That was when he finally told her to kick rocks.

Seriously, you'd think being an attractive biker, that he'd fuck a bunch of women. Oddly enough, he's not that type of man. He's what I'd call a serial monogamist. Bouncing from one serious relationship to the next, until one of these chicks finally pins him down. At thirty-eight, he hasn't taken the plunge. I'm not sure if he ever will.

Beside me, Trish clears her throat like she has something to say. Except, nobody is listening as Nash continues to fight with Dad about these stupid flowers, and Kelly won't shut up. It's starting to get heated in here, the air clouding with masculine energy. When those two thick-headed men go at it, it's nearly impossible to break them up. Most of the time, Nash ends up storming from the house, and I'm sent to calm him down. It's a vicious cycle.

Trish clears her throat once again, slapping her hand on the tabletop. "Hello!" she raises her voice. Still, Dad and Nash continue their bullshit, and I've had enough. They're ignoring my daughter.

"Hey, you two assholes, will you stop your bickering for just a minute?!" I yell, cupping my hands on either side of my mouth to funnel my voice like a makeshift megaphone.

It seems to work when both men freeze and swing their gaze my way as Kelly glares. If I weren't as nice as I am, I'd reach across the table and slap that attitude right off her fucking face. She's really starting to get on my nerves today.

Calming myself with a much-needed breath, I look to Trish and offer her a sly wink. "They're all yours."

"Thanks, Mom." She smiles at me before turning her sights on the three idiots. "So, I wanted to talk to everyone about this together." She pauses, and tension rises within me, gurgling beneath the surface. Talk to everyone about this together? Shit. I hope it's nothing bad.

Nash's attention glues to Trish, and he smiles kindly, gesturing with his hand for her to continue. Kelly leans on him as he does this, laying her stupid head on his shoulder.

God, what is my problem today? Generally, I like Kelly. Even if she is almost six feet tall, lean, with big, cosmetically enhanced boobs, and has an abundance of long, stick-straight, platinum blonde hair. I've always thought she looks like a Barbie doll, or maybe a Bratz doll since her lips have been injected one too many times. Regardless of her semi-fake appearance, I've always been taught not to judge someone by their looks. Nash has always been known to date exceptionally beautiful girls. The last one was a Playboy Bunny. So, Kelly wasn't a surprise when he met her at a club rally years ago. She's honestly a nice person. One who loves my brother with her whole heart. The only thing that's ever bothered me about her, which has nothing to do with her looks, is the fact that she has zero aspirations in life. She's content being a strip club waitress here in Charlotteton. She doesn't dance at the club since I know she has two left feet. But at thirty, she doesn't seem to want to do much else with her life. I've never heard her talk about kids. Getting a better job. Going to college. Nothing, but working at the strip club. Which is fine for now, but those looks are going to fade and then where's that going to leave her? My brother's sole responsibility, that's what- and I'm not cool with it. Even though that's none of my damn business.

Shifting uncomfortably in her seat, Trish rubs her palms together in her lap. To give her a boost of confidence, I lay my hand on her shoulder for moral support.

"I have a boyfriend!" she blurts exceptionally fast. "And I want him to come to lunch sometime soon."

Mom must hear the news from the kitchen because she silently takes her seat at the table. Everyone's eyes are not fastened on Trish. They're on Nash, who went from okay to pissed in two seconds flat. I knew this day would come, and I knew he'd flip. Apparently, Trish knew this as well and timed it accordingly. Smart girl.

Nash takes a deep breath, his jaw working. You can hear his molars grind as he stares at Trish with pinched brows.

Undeterred, Trish continues, those hands still working in her lap. "His name is Joshua."

"What kind of fuckin' name is that?" Nash snarls, sitting forward, laying his fisted hands on the table.

Jesus, you'd think that being her mother, I'd be the one worked up. But I'm not. I'm very happy for her. She's responsible, still a virgin as far as I know, and is growing into a wonderful young woman. What more can a mother hope for?

"I-it's his name," she stutters, her voice shrinking to a quivering murmur. "He … um … goes to college with me. He's a … um … freshman. He … um … asked me out for coffee a month ago, and we've been … um … dat—"

Nash slams his fist against the table, making us recoil. "You're not dating anyone!" he roars, eyes moving to mine to back him up in this. No way in hell. I'm not doing that. He can have his overreaction. Then we'll talk in private. A place where I can kick his ass for scaring the piss outta Trish. I've never fought in front of her before, and I'm not about to start doing that now.

"I'm … I'm…" Trish blubbers.

Son of a bitch, he's making her cry. That's it! Powerless to control it, furious mama bear rises within me, and I stand from the table, pointing directly at the dickhead.

"Spare bedroom. Now!"

I don't pause for him to respond when I huff my way down the hall, into the room at the very end. Leaving the door open, I wait for him to join me. Only, it takes him a minute as I watch him argue with Kelly, who apparently thinks this is the time to be clingy. This is none of her business. This is my fucking daughter he made cry. *Not hers*. She needs to stay the hell put!

Down the way, I see him grab her shoulders, forcing her to stay back as she tries to slip past him. I'm unable to hear a thing he says through the pounding in my ears as my heart races, I fist and unfist my hands at my sides, wanting to hit something. Shit, between him and Kelly, they're working my last nerve.

Inhaling deeply, I attempt to regain my wits. It does nothing to help.

Ten more seconds tick by, as Kelly continues to fling her hands in the air, causing a big show. That's it.

Incapable of waiting another second for him to convince *the baby* that he needs to talk to me, I pause inside the open door, cuffing my hands on either side of the frame as I lean forward. With nostrils flaring, and adrenaline coursing through me like a freight train, I lose it. "Kelly, this is none of your fucking business. Three years with someone doesn't make it your business. I need to talk to Nash. So you better sit your ass down or leave. Make a choice!"

In my direction, her eyes blaze like liquid fire, and just as she opens her mouth to argue, my Dad grabs hold of her shoulder, steering her away from a fight she was about to lose. Taller than me or not, skinnier than me or not, I would have put her on her ass. I have no tolerance for this shit when I'm furious. It might take me a lot to get there, but fucking with my daughter and making her cry is the first way to push me straight into crazy bitch mode.

Now that Kelly's under control, Nash pivots on his heel and thunders his way down the hall. He's just as angry as I am. Good. It'll make for an interesting fight.

I back away from the door when he enters, and it slams shut in his wake. He flicks the lock. For a moment, we glare at each other, circling in the middle of the room like lions in the wild, ready to pounce. Out of habit, I bounce on my toes, shaking my hands loose at my sides, ready to sucker punch him if the need arises.

Thankfully, he's the first to carve through the mounting tension. "She's not fuckin' dating." His tone is low—menacing, as his lip curls in aggression.

"You made her cry," I growl my frustration at him as we continue our little dance. "It's none of your business who she dates. She's eighteen. You're just gonna make her close up, and not tell us a damn thing ever again. Do you want that, asshole?"

Nash's face falls at my words, and his shoulders deflate. He stops moving. Lifting his head, those tender green eyes reach in to fuse with mine. Every part of me wants to melt with just one look. *That look.* I've seen it before. It's not often that his vulnerable side surfaces. That he exposes these kinds of emotions. He's lost, and looking to me for direction. Fuck. I can't stay mad at him anymore. I wish I could. But those eyes, that face, and how he tugs the band from his hair, letting it fall to his shoulders. I know what he needs.

My stomach clenches as I walk toward him, opening my arms wide.

"Oh, fuck, Gwennie-bee," Nash murmurs, bursting with pain as he steps forward into my embrace and wraps his arms around my middle.

His massive body jostles me, forcing me to take a wobbly step backward, then another and another as he tries to crawl into me. To hold me tighter. To get the comfort he desperately seeks. As my back collides loudly with the door, I'm finally able to brace myself for his intensity. His head tucks into the crook of my neck, and he sniffs me as his body trembles in my arms. My breasts smash against his ripped abs. I can feel his pulse throbbing through them, blending with my own manic beat.

Knowing exactly what he desires most, my fingers slide up the planes of Nash's muscled back, and he groans. It's so sexy to hear as it vibrates on my neck, sending a tingling sensation through my skin where it catches my bloodstream and stops to pool in the juncture between my thighs. With considerable effort, I suppress a shiver.

Mother-shit-fuck. This isn't how things were supposed to go down. Then again, the hankering to lash out at Nash has vanished and has been replaced with this deep-seeded need to take care of him like he's always done for me.

Slipping my hand underneath Nash's hair, the tips of my fingers brush along his neck until they glide into the base of his thick mane. He breathes a sigh of weighted relief as I comb through, feeling the silky strands caress my sensitive flesh.

Nash's nose nuzzles the edge of my jaw. "I don't want her to end up like you," he finally expresses.

Of course, that's why this is bothering him. Why he's acting this way.

"She's an eighteen year old adult, Nash," I soothe. "She's not some innocent, fifteen year old girl at a party she shouldn't be at. Acting like she's older than she is."

"Fuck. I know. But…" His mind seems to drift into darkness, following the same path that mine is headed. I didn't want to deal with this today. Sometimes, the past is better left buried.

My fingers continue their job, and I dampen my lips with the sweep of my tongue before speaking. "Yeah, I know." A sigh escapes me. "I lived through it. I survived. And now I've got a beautiful daughter to show for it."

For a moment, his body stiffens. "I know that," he grumbles. "But you were raped."

Yes, I was, and I'll never be able to forget it.

"Not by my boyfriend," I remind, so he realizes Trish and I are not the same. "You wouldn't let me have a boyfriend then either." Weighed down by painful memories, I exhaust another sigh.

It's true. Nash never let me have a boyfriend. Then again, that didn't stop what happened from happening. It was a Friday night, and our parents were out of town for a weekend getaway. I was barely fifteen when Jenny, an older girl in school, invited me to her cousin's Frat party. At that age, I knew I could easily pass for a senior. Like most kids, I ached to be one of the popular crowd, so I agreed to go. It's not that I was a social outcast. I wasn't. But I was tired of being labeled as Nathaniel, the bad boy's, younger sis. It gave me a certain credibility by the time I entered high school, which kept me from being picked on. And I should have appreciated that. Instead, I hated it. Hated the way my peers eyed me warily in the hall. The way boys refused to flirt with me. I desperately wanted my own identity; not one Nathaniel had constructed to keep the guys away. In the end, it hadn't worked anyhow.

That very night when Nash was making out with Jessica Simmons on the couch, I snuck out the back door and walked to Jenny's house, which was only three blocks away. From there, she drove us in her blue, souped up

Mustang to Charlotteton's infamous college campus where the fraternities were housed.

I can remember that moment like it was yesterday. We cut the engine and parked down the block, at the butt end of about fifteen rich-kid cars. Stepping onto the curb, I smoothed my hand over my skirt and followed Jenny to the two-story, white Victorian that looked larger than life as music pulsed from the inside, rattling the tall windows.

Up the broad front steps, a set of college students were making out against the banister. Higher, on the wraparound porch, a group of guys played quarters. Walking too slow for her taste, Jenny grabbed my hand and hauled me into the massive house. It was flooded wall-to-wall with people of all shapes and sizes. I could almost taste the sexual energy floating in the air. It was sweet and tangy.

Forever the outgoing one, Jenny tugged me behind her, hand-in-hand, through a throng of gyrating bodies, until we stopped in the kitchen by a row of kegs. Without missing a beat, she poured two cups of the tart trash and handed me one.

"Drink up!" she hollered over the crazy music, and that was how the rest of the night went.

We danced, drank, and she flirted with as many college men that'd give her attention. Being a curvy blonde had its merits because the men ate her up as I watched with green envy, wishing I had those luscious curves, her petite frame, and bright blonde hair. Which was natural; not from a bottle. Not only was she adorable, but she also had a great smile and flirted without an ounce of teenage awkwardness.

Pressed against the far wall, next to a window, I intently watched Jenny as I drank my fifth cup of disgusting beer. Suddenly, a shoulder bumped into mine, startling to me so much that the beer sloshed out of my cup and onto my white top. I cursed, and the man chuckled. It was a deep, sensuous baritone that went straight to my virginal nether regions.

"Be careful, little one!" he cooed loudly, pinching my chin and lifting it to garner eye contact.

The jolt of his touch did funny things to my insides, and for the first time in my life I was genuinely attracted to a man. A man with green eyes and short black hair, who stood a good foot taller than me. He was gorgeous in every sense of the word, striking me speechless with his simple presence. My tongue felt too big for my mouth. Which he didn't seem to mind as he talked nonstop and I attempted to listen, barely catching a word thanks to the ear-splitting tunes.

Guys I didn't know kept passing us, and slapping him on the back like they were good friends. They seemed to admire him, which I found even more attractive. Not to mention his designer duds that I would have never been able to afford. My parents were middle class, and he was obviously not. But all that mattered was that he was there, talking to lowly ole me, his hand brushing over my shoulder from time to time. I couldn't have been giddier.

As the night wore on, he kept refilling my drink, shifting from beer to liquor, until my head began to spin. That was the moment he guided my stumbling frame up the wooden staircase and into his blue and white bedroom, where he locked the door—turning a night of fun into the scariest pits of hell.

The rest of the evening became a blur of horrific events. With my brain incapacitated, my body fell at his mercy, and he gave none. Not wasting any time, I was thrown onto a twin sized bed, and my skirt was lifted, panties torn from my body. I remember trying to cover myself with my hands, telling him, "No. Stop." But he shoved a pillow over my face, and that was when the panic set in. I screamed into the dense cotton, kicking and thrashing on his mattress. Something tight restrained my wrists in the darkness of my worst fears. I wouldn't stop fighting as something hard and painful penetrated the most intimate of places. Twisting my head side to side in agony, I wailed, trying to make him stop. But he didn't. He just kept going, thrusting himself into me, hard and fast, with no remorse. My insides were on fire, and everything hurt. My wrists burned from being restrained. My throat ached from screaming through my wails of desperation. It seemed to drag on and on, lasting forever. I thought I was going to die. That the pain would consume me, turning me inside out. I nearly begged for him to knock me unconscious at one point. Then, it suddenly ended; a liquid heat flooded my channel, and the room went eerily quiet.

Over the next day and a half, the man I came to learn was Josiah Bower continued to rape me repeatedly until I was raw like fresh hamburger meat. Blood stained his sheets. My eyes were nearly swollen shut from crying. He'd decided to gag me after the first time, and held a bowl under me so I was able to pee. The one instance that I couldn't hold it, I wet the bed and his fist met my face. Then a second hit broke my nose when I kicked him. A third smashed into my stomach when I tried to untie myself from the bedposts as he left me to go hang with his buddies. For hours that felt like years, I continued to fight for my life, my sanity, as he ripped it away bit by bit. My ass was the next to become violated. My breasts sucked raw. Everything was taken from me to feed his sick, sadistic pleasure.

Fifty-two hours after walking into that party, my life changed forever. I woke up in a dumpster behind *The Diner*, a restaurant over thirty minutes away, in a neighboring town called Carolina Rose. A woman named Teena found me there, battered and bruised. My skin was burned in the spots where Josiah had dumped an entire jug of bleach on me, to try and mask his DNA. The empty container was tossed beside me on top of the rancid pile of black garbage bags.

People from all over the small town came to my rescue. A tall, lean, Native American man named Sniper was the first to climb into the dumpster.

Cops came, taking my brief statement to clear a missing person's case that had been filed twenty-four hours prior. They even told me they'd began interviewing those who were at the party that night, but nothing came of it. An ambulance arrived and took me to the hospital. For the very first time in my life, I begged *not* to see my parents. All I wanted was Nathaniel. I needed him. By the grace of God, I was given that small gift, as my parents waited anxiously in the waiting room, allowing him to see me first.

Throwing the white curtain back in the ER bay, Nash's eyes rounded as he took in my weak, colorless, condition. A heartbeat later, he saw every ounce of me shatter into a million pieces when my glassy eyes met his. It was like a tiny string was holding me together, and when *my rock* was there, it snapped. Emotions poured from me as I lifted my arms, begging to be held.

Nash rushed to my bedside, sitting on the edge, and crushed me to his chest, where I sobbed until my eyes burned and my throat nearly swelled shut. In the most painful moment I'd ever experienced, he comforted me, as he kissed the top of my head, telling me that everything was going to be alright. Even if I didn't believe him.

Soft lips caressing my jaw tears me from my horrid past, and I try to refocus on the here and now. My sight slowly scans the expanse of the room before me, or the portion that I can see with a massive man still locked in my arms. This is my parent's spare bedroom, where I'm safe. There's my old, full sized bed now draped in a cream duvet. Pictures of Nash and I as kids are scattered in gold picture frames atop an oversized dresser. Centering myself further, my fingers comb through Nash's hair. I inhale sharply, getting a heady burst of his scent invading my nostrils, which serves to further comfort my rampant emotions.

"You okay?" Nash mutters, stroking the same spot on my jaw once more.

Clearing my throat, I keep it from wavering. "Yeah, I'm okay. But, Nash, if Joshua is a nice guy, which I'm sure he is or Trish wouldn't give him the time of day, then I think you need to stop going all," I drop my voice to a low manly grumble, "*I'm a macho biker* on her, and let us meet him first. Then you can decide for yourself."

Nash grunts his potent disapproval, teeth scraping gently along my neck. "I'm not gonna like him. I don't give a fuck if he's a bible-toting, good ole' boy. It's not gonna fuckin' happen."

Damn, he's stubborn.

"Maybe not. But she's got you to protect her regardless of the kinda boy he is. You can't expect her to be single forever." Once again, this is case in point as to why Trish is nothing like me. She actually wants to date.

44

Nash groans. "I know. But, fuck, this is too soon."

"For who? You or her?"

"Me!" he yells, ripping out of our embrace to stand. With his expression sullen, he rakes his hands through his hair, tugging it a bit. "It's way too soon. That's my girl out there." Nash nods toward the door at my back. "I took care of the fucker who did that shit to you, and I'm gettin' way too damn old to worry about that again. If she's single, and you're single, I don't have to worry all the goddamn time. But now I have to. She's got a boyfriend. A stupid, little, measly boy fucktard. I don't wanna do those things again, Gwen. Not unless I have to." He begins pacing the room, lost in thought.

I reach out to him, grabbing his bicep to yank him back into my embrace. Thankfully, he doesn't fight and willingly falls against my chest, arms around my center, anchoring us together. My fingers lift once again to sift through his locks, just like he needs. "I know ya don't, Nash," I coo. "And I don't think you'll have to go through all of that again, either."

That very night in the hospital, when I had been found, Nash laid awake in the bed next to me as my parents slept in chairs. Sometime before morning, after I'd finally passed out, he disappeared, and none of us saw him again for six months. Six months for me to grow bigger and bigger each day as the baby implanted inside of me sucked nutrients from my body. I wanted to hate being pregnant. To hate the baby because it was a constant reminder of what I'd gone through. But I couldn't seem to allow myself to feel that way. Even at fifteen, I loved my bump, regardless of what I knew would happen when she came into the world. That I'd give her up for adoption, to have a better life without a teenage mother.

It was a chilly February morning when Nash returned home. I can remember the shock I felt when I woke up to see him seated at the foot of my bed, a newspaper rolled in his grasp. "Good morning, Gwennie." He smiled cheerfully, slapping the paper atop my comforter-clad legs.

Securing my bump with my hand, I shuffled upward until my back rested against the headboard. Nash's eyes rounded as he took in the size of it. "You're gettin' big." He reached out to pat the top affectionately.

Swallowing hard, I nodded, dumbstruck, unable to believe my brother was seated on my mattress, looking like himself, yet not. He was gruffer. His arms tattooed, face unshaven, hair longer. His eyes were wiser than I last saw him, and at twenty, he looked nearly thirty. It was as if the past six months had aged him an entire decade.

"Not sure if that face means you're happy to see me, or not." He grinned, sliding that damn paper against my stomach. "Read it," he added, flicking those beautiful eyes from the paper to my face and back again.

I wanted to comply, I truly did, but I couldn't stop staring. Nash had gone from attractive boy to hot man overnight. It took me a moment to realize even his clothing was different. He was wearing a leather vest with patches on it, as worn jeans encased his long legs.

Minutes later, when I was finally able to compose myself, and Nash and I stopped staring at one another, I picked up the paper. On the front page in bold letters, it read *Josiah Bower injured in a car crash.* My heart lodged itself in my throat as my fingers shook, making the paper rattle loudly in my grasp. Josiah had been hurt, and I wasn't sure how to take the news. Mostly, I was thrilled to hear what had happened, because Josiah was never convicted of raping me. Evidence came up missing. My statement forged. It was a cluster fuck. But that was the treatment I should have expected when we found out that his father was a judge and his brothers were sheriff's deputies. I didn't matter to them. They just wanted the mess cleaned up. So they power washed the entire situation, making me look like the lying whore who got off on some serious kink.

As I read further down the detailed and somewhat gruesome article, the words traumatic brain injury, fractured femurs, spinal cord injury and a list of about ten other things made me smile victoriously. I shouldn't have found pleasure in his unfortunate pain, but I did. And when I looked into Nash's eyes with that permanent smile on my face, those green orbs shone with pride, love, and a whole lot more I couldn't decipher.

Reaching into my lap, he folded his fingers through mine. "All for you, Gwennie. And I'd do it again." That was all he said, gaze delving into mine, speaking truths I couldn't yet comprehend. Then my door was thrown open, and our parents stood there in just as much shock as I had been, holding a newspaper in their hands. Tears shone in my mother's eyes.

"Mom. Dad. I'm home," Nash announced, and for the rest of the day we celebrated his return, as we silently rejoiced in Josiah's karmic justice.

In the end, they removed him from football, and he now lives his days as a paraplegic, here in Charlotteton. Three years after Patricia was born and Nash talked me into keeping her, Josiah's father was tragically murdered. When Patricia was five, one of Josiah's brothers was killed in the line of duty. And just last year, his other brother was imprisoned for being a dirty cop. Justice has been served, even if it's taken me eighteen years to get it.

Turning my head to kiss the side of Nash's, I mutter, "We're gonna get through this together like we always do."

Nodding, he nuzzles his nose to my neck. "I know. But I've taken care of that little girl since she was born. Treated her like my own. Was there the first day she walked, talked, and peed in that stupid princess potty." We both chuckle at that memory. Trish was so proud of herself that day. And so were we, as we clapped from the bathroom door.

"You've been good to us." I hug him a little tighter to convey how much he truly means to our family. It warms me from the inside out to know he's always been there to have my back. Even if that meant living with me for five years in the apartment above Mom and Dad's garage, to help raise Trish.

"You're good to me, too, Gwennie-bee. I'd be lost without you. Anytime I'm in a dangerous place you pull me back. Just like today."

He's right. I have.

"Yes. That's what family does. We love each other and forgive each other. Just like I hope you'll do for me."

Expelling a grunt, Nash pulls away, standing upright as he meets my gaze with a strange expression. "For what?" he growls.

Reaching out, I dust the tips of my fingers over his damaged neck. He groans sensuously as a shiver visibly passes through him. It does something funny to my belly as the presence of butterflies make their strange appearance.

"This is not a problem," he says, wrapping his hand around mine, holding it to his bruised flesh. Stepping closer, until we're flush, body to body, heat to heat, he tips his head down to brush his lips softly over mine. "No problem at all," he whispers.

Pausing a moment, I inhale a shaky breath.

"What about Kelly? I'm sure it bothers her," I rasp, feeling the warmth of his skin under my palm, and the way his pulse thumps against it.

My thighs tremble, making me weak in the knees. Not wanting to fall, I grab hold of his thick bicep, and he takes it as an invitation to step even closer. Skating his hand behind me, he rests his searing palm against the curve of my back, just above my butt. The air in my lungs seizes in my throat as his fingers begin to dance there, stroking me in tiny, heart-thumping circles.

"And do you see me giving a flying fuck?" he mutters against my mouth.

"No?" I shudder, goosebumps rippling down my arms and legs.

In reply, his tongue runs along the seam of my lips, making me dizzy. On its own accord, my pussy clenches, aching for affection.

"Nash…" I breathe.

"Open for me … I need in that mouth."

Giving in to my innermost desires, I comply by parting my lips with a tiny moan.

"That's it," Nash praises, before he slips inside, languidly caressing the top of my tongue with teasing strokes. It sets my blood on fire as his hand on my back slides lower, palming my ass. Boldly squeezing my tender flesh with his digits, my bruises scream in protest while my body begs like a greedy whore, seeking more pain, more touch, more of anything that he'll give.

Some part of me knows that I shouldn't revel in this. That I should push him away. But my brain has misfired and is now forcing my body to navigate on autopilot—in the most basic of ways; my pussy is giving my mind a big F.U.

Clashing his thick tongue with mine, Nash releases a ravenous groan, rendering me helpless. Every cell in my quivering body burns with unspent desire. I become a slave to my needs, as Nash's onslaught invades my senses, persuading all of the walls I've masterfully built to come tumbling down. I cling to him, my hands fisting in his hair, holding him to my lips. He grabs my thigh, wrapping it around his hip. A thickness I've never felt before prods my stomach through his jeans. Just the feeling of it grinding against me, unfurls this coiled knot of pleasure in my belly. Making me want to come, to give in to temptation, to shatter into a billion pieces of sated rapture.

Cuffing his hand around the back of my neck, Nash deepens our blazing battle. His tongue lavishes mine, hard and impatient. My toes curl as I melt into a ball of breathless goo. Desperately, I try to keep pace, to let him guide the moment, but I can't. I get lost, falling deeper into ecstasy that I vaguely remember I shouldn't be feeling. Moans are passed into each other's mouths, swallowed by one another. He lifts my other leg, so I'm forced to wrap myself around him. My pussy settles on his thickness and Nash bucks his hips, slamming my back into the door. The noise echoes in the room as he does it again, trying to fuck me through our clothes. My clit pleads for him to continue, as my mind focuses on those big lips. That hot mouth sinfully moving over mine. Those hands dominating me. The way he smells. Everything is deliriously perfect.

Unfastening his hand around my neck, Nash slips it between our bodies. I gasp as it brushes my pussy on his way to unbutton his jeans. His zipper rips down at warp speed. "I'm … fuck … I dunno…" he mumbles to my mouth, unable to catch his breath. Nash's trembling fingers move to my pants, and he fumbles with the button. "I need in … fuck … I don't know what I'm … But I … need … *shit*."

Swallowing thickly, I stroke my lips over his. "I don't know if this—"

A violent pounding on the door snaps us out of our fog and into the present.

"Fuck," Nash curses in a harsh whisper, letting my feet down and stepping away, but not before he pecks my lips one last time. I smile shyly at his sweetness, and try to right myself as he readjusts the thickness in his jeans, then runs his hands through his messy hair.

I can't believe that just happened!

The pounding ensues again, this time, followed by Kelly's enraged voice. "Nash! I'm not going to sit out here all fucking night, while you play house with your damn sister, talking about shit that doesn't even pertain to you. I want to leave! Now! Your strange little codependency will not interfere with our time. Do it on your own!" Pausing for a moment, her tone drops to a menacing snarl. "Gwen, you better let him out of there or I'm beating this damn door down."

Her words sober my fuzzy brain right up.

Oh, hell no! She did not just say that to me!

"I'd love to see you try, bitch!" I yell at the same time Nash replies calmly, "I'll be out in a minute, Kelly. "

51

"Oh no. You are *not* going to let your sister call me a bitch, are you?!" Kelly screeches like trailer trash from the *Jerry Springer Show*.

I look to Nash, who's shaking his head and smiling hugely, as his fingers ghost over his swollen lips. It's sexy to see him still affected by what just happened. I know I am. God, he looks so fucking hot like this, doesn't he? That heaving chest pumping beneath his t-shirt. Even those flush cheeks are hot. And the way he keeps swaying on his feet like he can't stand still.

Kelly makes an agitated sound outside the door, snapping Nash out of whatever's going on in that head of his.

"You chicks never make shit easy, do ya?" he whispers so only I can hear.

Following by example, I run a shaky finger across my lips. They're tender to the touch, and I can still taste him in my mouth. Jesus! That has never happened before. *Ever.*

Shrugging nonchalantly, I reply, "What do you expect me to do when she acts like that?" I thumb point to the door at my back. "She's not usually *that* much of a bitch."

"I don't hear you coming!" Kelly screams, cementing my statement.

The itch to tell her that he was close to *coming* when she interrupted us crawls under my skin, but I remain quiet, not wanting to make shit worse for Nash. Part of me realizes that I should probably be freaking the hell out about what might have happened. The other part doesn't give a rat's ass. Right now, I'm concentrating on the open-minded part of myself and staying away from the self-loathing, overthinking portion. It's better this way. No need for overreacting. It's not like we haven't kissed before. I mean, he does have those damn bruises all over him thanks to me. So I shouldn't be surprised that in the heat of the moment when we're both emotional and needing a little comfort, that it might get carried away. That makes sense, right? I'm not insane for thinking that way, am I? Fuck … I don't know.

Nash takes a step in my direction and tucks an errant strand of my hair behind my ear. "She's on edge 'cause someone—*you*—left some deep scratches on my…" Instead of finishing his sentence, Nash lifts his shirt so I can inspect the damage.

I gasp.

Shit. It's worse than I thought. Deep gouges from my nails mar his slightly hairy chest. I take a step forward, laying my hand over his skull inked pec. It's soft and warm under my palm, as the rough scabs from my abuse graze my skin. Lower, where his thick six-pack ripples, tinier bruises sprout beneath the surface. I'm not sure how they got there, and I don't want to ask, just in case I don't want to know. On his shoulder, underneath the protection of his shirt, is the worst of it all. Sunken teeth and claw marks are embedded in his flesh. It's like a wild animal inflicted the worst of its attack there. Kelly was right when she said he looked as if he'd been mauled. He does. Everywhere. And if it weren't for his tattoos masking some of the darker bruises, I'm sure he'd look a helluva lot worse.

Wincing at the sight, I scan the destruction one more time. Then I raise my eyes to Nash's. "I'm so sorry." It doesn't matter how many times I apologize, it won't repair the havoc I've already wreaked. Now, I really do feel like a monster.

Nash peels my hands from his chest and brings them to his lips, giving them a tiny kiss. "I." –Kiss— "Don't." –Peck— "Fucking." –Nip with his teeth on my thumb. — "Care." –Kiss— "How they look," he finishes by kissing each pad of my fingers one by one.

I lose all ability to speak as one kiss lingers longer than the next. Then he reaches my pinky, and I gasp a noiseless breath as he sucks it into his mouth, swirling his hot tongue around it before pulling away with a cunning smile. Releasing my hands, Nash carefully escorts them to my sides, his pleased eyes still glued to my dazed ones.

"You were saying?" he prompts with a knowing wink.

Christ almighty, what has gotten into him today? I've never seen him like this. How's he acting playful and sexy when his girlfriend is standing right outside the door?

Clearing my throat, I force myself to speak. "I'll … I'll bring over some first aid stuff later. To keep your scratches from getting infected."

He dismisses the notion with the wave of his hand. "Don't bother. Kelly already took care of that."

She did?

Speak of the devil. "Hello! I can hear you two whispering in there!"

"Please go sit down, babe. I'm about done." His tone is sickeningly gentle. I wanna puke.

"Promise," he adds.

"Fine!" Kelly huffs in retort. "But I'm not sucking your dick tonight."

Great, that's just what my parents need to hear.

"That's fine, babe. Now go sit down."

I can't believe he's still so patient with her when I'd like to ram a two-by-four down her throat.

"And I want a new pair of earrings," she demands.

"Fine."

"And a necklace to match."

"Okay. I'll throw in a bracelet if you just go sit your ass down," he snaps. It's about damn time he's starting to lose his cool.

"Yes, baby. Anything for you." Kelly's tone is anything but sweet. She sounds like a sarcastic cunt.

The sound of feet stomping away are music to my ears as I turn my attention back to Nash. He's re-securing his hair into a low man-bun. "How in the hell do you put up with that? How much did you have to promise to buy her, for her to clean your cuts?" I sass.

In all my life, I've never heard of a female blackmailing a guy into buying them stuff when they're the ones acting like a gold digging thundercunt. Who does that?

"It's not like that," Nash defends. It's weak at best.

Swelling with attitude, I cock my head to the side, hitching my hand on my hip. "It sure sounds like it. You hold me while a group of men pound my pussy like a punching bag and I tear into you like a savage. Yet, you never ask—"

"Don't even go there, Gwen," Nash interjects, raising his voice. "I got your back when my brothers pound that pussy. There's no shame in it. And the marks are a sweet reminder of all that pleasure you felt when you finally let yourself go. That makes me happy as hell. You gettin' outta that head of yours," he gestures to my noggin, "and succumbing to their dicks. There ain't nothin' more beautiful than that."

Uh huh. If it's not shameful, then I was born yesterday as *David Beckham* and woke up this morning with a sex change.

My brashness kicks up a notch. "So you're tryin' to tell me that there's nothing more beautiful than me being filled by ten different cocks? You can't be serious."

He has to be joking. No one in their right mind would find that beautiful. Slutty? Yes. Appalling? Hell yes. Beautiful? Not unless you're a sadistic son of a bitch. Just thinking about being stuffed by that many dicks makes me oddly turned on and disgusted at the same time. I'm ten ways of fucked up, I tell ya.

Nash shakes his head in palpable irritation. "Your pleasure … happiness, means everything to me. And if it takes ten or twenty or thirty dicks once a month to make you happy, then that's all I care about. You knew that years ago when you first came to me about it."

God, I remember that evening vividly. I'd been drinking at *Nowhere*, and as always, Nash was tending bar. Toa was seated there with us, shootin' the shit. He always seems to chill with me when I'm there. He's a friendly guy.

On that particular night, I'd had a few too many, which inevitably killed any moral reserves I held in place. By the time my head started to spin, Toa had begun chatting about some threesome he'd had with another brother. I was fascinated with the story, so I asked him how it worked logistically. At that time in my life, I was using my vibrator three times a day. Hell. I was buying a new one every six weeks. Nothing was satisfying me. Not any man. Not any toy. Not even my fingers. Nothing. I couldn't be fulfilled no matter how hard I tried. So when

Toa openly spoke about double-teaming this chick, it turned me on to possibilities I'd never considered.

Over the course of those hours, I don't remember much of what I said. But I recall being enamored enough to ask an abundance of embarrassing questions, which at the time, didn't bother me. It wasn't until the next morning when I woke up in Nash's bed with a hangover from hell that I recalled the conversations from the night before— where I had asked to be double-teamed at least once. With a cocky smirk on his face, Toa had slipped behind the bar with Nash to discuss it and came back with a definitive *hell yes*. Three nights later, my very first threesome took place with Nash standing in the room as my bodyguard, while Price and Toa fucked me senseless. It was singularly the most liberating sexual experience I had ever had up to that point. And it unleashed a part of me that's never been tethered since.

Over the months, the escapades grew from a threesome to a foursome. By the time I hit a fiver, I was desperate for Nash to be more involved. Sure, we'd kissed sporadically over the first few months. His mouth gave me that extra shot of thrill that my inner, dirty whore craved. However, as things wore on he started to hold me. To control more and more of my pleasure by dispensing duties for the brothers to follow. Soon, all of them were in tune with my body, and I began to comprehend that nothing would ever be the same. No man could satisfy me on his own. No toy could give me so many orgasms that I nearly went blind. It just wasn't possible for anything to feel as good, even if I knew deep down, it was bad.

Uh. I need to stop thinking about this. About that. It's too much right now.

Blinking rapidly, I clear my head. "It doesn't gross you out to be there?" I ask because we've never discussed this before. After the first night they agreed to the threesome, Nash and I have never expressed our feelings on the matter. Today is a first of many, it seems.

Nash scowls at me, his brows pinched, lip curled. "No. Your body is beautiful. And sex is just sex. I am a man, Gwen. I know the difference between fucking and making love."

I know the difference, too. At least, I think I do. I've never actually been in love before. The desire to be in love, and to have to worry about my heart being ripped from my chest when it didn't work out has never been important. After what I went through raising Trish, it didn't seem logical. I'm too busy with work, anyhow. And yes, I do recognize what Nash said about my body being beautiful. I'm just choosing not to dwell on that, or the fact that it's making those butterflies take flight again. I wish those damn things would just go away. Is that too much to ask?

Done with this conversation, I wave dismissively. "I can't talk about this anymore." Grabbing the door handle, I unlock it, then pry it open just a smidge. "You can go buy your girlfriend some expensive jewelry now." I try not to sound snobby about it. Although, I'm pretty sure I fail when Nash's face screws into an even bigger scowl.

"Don't be like that, Gwennie," he speaks softly, resting his hand atop mine that's holding the knob. The sensation of his skin touching me shoots a bolt of lightning up my arm, yet I choose to ignore this feeling, too. There's just too many damn emotions to go through in one day. I'm all tapped out.

"Just go." Refusing to look at him, I stare at my sock covered feet instead. They're cute with pink, fuzzy giraffes encasing them.

"Alright," Nash sighs, giving my cheek a quick peck that leaves a lasting imprint that I'll feel for days. "I love you," he adds, sullenly.

Damn. Talk about a brutal shot to the heart.

"Uh huh … and I love you, too." I play it up like I'm pissy, instead of how I actually feel right now, which I'm too chicken shit to tell you either.

On the way out the door, Nash doesn't say another word. Lifting my head just after he crosses the threshold, I watch him walk away. An ache in my chest amplifies with each steady step that separates us. Why did Kelly have to come here today? If she hadn't, then none of this would have happened as it had. Or, I don't *think* it would've. I guess we'll never know.

Nash's retreating back turns the corner at the end of the hall. For a second, I listen to Kelly give him hell about wanting to leave. But he scolds her, telling her that he needs to speak to Trish first. Words that I can't decipher are exchanged between niece and uncle. Then my parents say their goodbyes. All the while I stand in the doorway, staring straight into a wall of air. Air that seems to take my breath away as the feeling of loss consumes me. The stifling emotion only seems to swell to a whole new level when I hear Kelly and Nash depart with the slam of the front door.

Why did he have to leave? Why did I tell him to go? Why did we kiss? Fuck! Why did today happen at all?

Dad's tall, lean frame steps into the end of the vacant hallway. There's a sad smile playing on his lips. "They're gone, sweetheart. You can come out now. I'm sorry she acted that way. I tried to stop her," he says, running a hand over his bald head. I know he would have tried to stop her. What little good it did. Nash is gone, I'm sad, and all I want to do is curl up in a ball and watch junk TV with my family for the rest of the day.

Hope your day turns out better than mine.

Popcorn with extra butter, here I come.

Chapter Four

No more school!

Hallelujah!

I've been living in end-of-the-school-year Hell for the past two weeks. Two weeks of nonstop grading, cleaning out my classroom, restless high school students, and end of year exams. It's a special kind of torture. For kids, they love it, because that means school is almost out. Teachers love and dread it in equal parts. Today was my final day, just as Tuesday was the student's last. I've been inputting final grades into my computer before taking a nice, long weekend off. A weekend that I've been looking forward to since last summer. It'll be my very own sweet release. I can't wait to take off and catch some wind. There's nothing better than that.

Although, right now, I guess it's time to tell you that Nash and I haven't been as friendly as of late. After the Sunday incident that took place weeks ago, we've kept it cordial with basic texts. The times we do see each other, it seems strained. I'm not sure if he's mad at me, or if I'm supposed to be peeved off at him. Honestly, I have no clue what's going on between us, and it sucks. We're growing apart. Not closer. Kelly has still attended weekend luncheons with Nash and is clingier than ever. Trish finally brought her boyfriend over last Sunday. It went over better than I expected. Nash kept a lid on his obvious irritation, and nobody had a blow-up. However, as soon as lunch had ended, Nash told Kelly they were going to go *fuck,* and they left. Yup, he said it right in front of my parents, and Trish. He can be such a peach sometimes, can't ya tell?

So, yeah, that's been my past couple of weeks. It's not very exciting. I've been too exhausted to do much more than go to work, come home to my empty house, chat a few seconds with my neighbors Asher and Justin, eat something horrible for dinner, masturbate a handful of times, take a shower, and then off to bed I go—wash, rinse, and repeat. It's rather mundane, I know. But with the summer here, my life's about to change drastically. This weekend commences the illegal street bike racing circuit. It's a bi-weekend event throughout the entire season, here on the East Coast. I fell into it a few years back when I started shopping around for a street bike on Craigslist. The man I bought my souped up *Ducati* from was a former racer and introduced me to a group of his buddies who were still heavily involved in the scene. All of them are men, which appealed to me the most. I've always loved being around dicks more than chicks. Nothing against women, but most of them don't get me. They're too focused on how they look, instead of how they feel. They try to be who they're not. Yes, I guess I do, too, on occasion. However, I still try to be myself, by embracing who I am and what I enjoy. And one of those things just happens to be racing. It's a fucking thrill.

NOWHERE

To keep a very long story short—I joined those men that I'd met for one race, got hooked on the rush, and now I've been running this circuit for almost three years. Just like I get off on fucking a roomful of bikers, I get off on this, too. I've won a few races, and those I haven't, didn't lose much money on. The best part about it is that it's one of the few things I can say is actually mine. Since nobody knows about it, aside from Trish, who I've sworn to secrecy. I couldn't be driving a couple hundred miles on a weekend without telling her what's going on. That's irresponsible parenting. Trish has never seemed to mind, though. As long as I text her while I'm gone. Then again, now that she's out of the house and taking summer classes, I'm sure she'll care even less if I contact her. She'll be too busy with her boyfriend, working with my mom, and hitting the books.

Which is precisely what she should be doing. She should be living her life and having fun with it. Being young is a beautiful thing. I just never got to enjoy it. I was a mom then—worked part-time and even went to school. I didn't get to have boyfriends when I had a baby at home to raise. I'm just thrilled that my daughter gets to experience the life that I never did. I'm beyond grateful for that.

Slamming my car door shut, I grab the bucket of fried chicken out of the backseat before traipsing up the front steps of *Nowhere*. The air is cooler now that the sun is just dipping below the horizon. A gust of wind blows through my ponytail, and it slaps me in the face. I thought I'd noticed when I parked that the beer signs weren't illuminated. They're not. And what's even stranger is when I hit the porch and see Meatball, the club's prospect, guarding the front door.

With the bag of food in one hand and my purse in the other, I stop in front of him. He's a beast of a man with wild brown hair that lays haphazardly atop his head, as tattoos of naked women dance down the lengths of his arms. Which are now tucked over his obscenely large chest. He could easily give professional wrestlers a run for their money.

"Gwen," he greets in that deep bass, eyebrows furrowed.

"Meatball," I return.

Pausing for a beat, his gaze roams my form, up and down then back again. "There's business goin' on inside. You need to go home."

If he thinks I'm going to comply, he's got another thing comin'.

After I had finished working my last day on the job, I drove to this local chain to order some of the best fried chicken in existence. It's Nash's favorite. Since I'll be gone all weekend, I figured now was as good a time as ever to try and mend fences with my stubborn brother. Even if I'm still nursing some hurt feelings from weeks ago. Chicken should do the trick to help repair our problems, or I hope it will.

Slinging my purse onto my shoulder, I use my free hand to pat Meatball on one of his pecs. It makes my hand look like a Barbie dolls. "No can do, amigo. Nash will want to see me…" *At least, I think so.*

Taking a step back, I return my arm to my side, not wanting to crowd him.

Meatball shakes his head defiantly. "I was told to keep everyone out. You know the rules."

Boy-oh-boy, do I. Club business—it's a secretive thing, like FBI, Area 54, hush-hush. This isn't the first time I've arrived to see one of the brothers manning the front door. The back door is a giant metal one, so it's not like I could try to sneak in there. However, what's the point of having rules if they can't be broken? That takes out all the fun. Don't you agree?

Plastering on a sweet smile, I reply, "Yeah, I know the rules, but none of them say you can't call Toa to ask permission." If anyone is going to allow me to enter the premises, it's him. We're kind of tight.

"Fine," Meatball grumbles as he withdraws his phone from the inside pocket of his cut to ring Toa.

Unable to hear the other side of the line, I eavesdrop on the one-sided conversation. "Yeah, I know you're busy." His peeved eyes bore into me as he says this. "Gwen is standing on the porch," he adds. "Looks like she's brought Nash some dinner … Yup … No …Yes…" A few more words are exchanged, and just as Meatball hangs up, the front door flies open. On the opposite side of the screen stands Toa, and he doesn't seem pissed. Thank Christ.

"Come on, little one. Get your ass in here," Toa invites, and Meatball steps to the side as the rickety screen door is shoved wide.

"Thank you for your cooperation," I praise Meatball before seeing myself indoors. The main room is empty aside from Toa and me.

Not wasting any time, I set my stuff on the bar top and turn around to find a suddenly irate Toa pacing in a small circle, his eyes glued to his feet, hands fisted at his sides. Without pause, I shift into mothering mode and approach him. Grazing my hand along his forearm, trying not to spook him, I attempt to garner his attention.

Toa flinches away, then looks up to realize it's me. "Sorry, Gwen. We've got some shit goin' on, and I needed a fuckin' breather."

From the looks of it, he needs more than a breather. He needs a stiff drink. Wordlessly grabbing his bicep, I guide Toa over to one of the ten bar stools, and he climbs on, resting his elbows on the top. Shuffling behind the bar, I take this opportunity to play Nash's roll as I locate the expensive tequila and pour two shots.

Sliding them in front of Toa, he gulps them down, then slams the glasses on the counter while releasing a weighted sigh.

"Penny for your thoughts?" I ask softly.

Toa taps the top of his shot glasses for me to fill 'em up, so I do. He downs those just as quickly as the last. "It's in confidence," he notes, meeting my eyes. They're as serious as a heart attack. I know their rules—club business stays club business. I've grown up around these men long enough to know what I'm allowed or not allowed to share.

"Always is."

Toa nods, accepting my words. "There's a fucker in the cellar that just won't squeal. We've beat him. Left him to starve for two days. And we've even unleashed Price on the asshole, to fuck with his head. So far, the bastard won't break."

"What are you lookin' to get?" I tuck the tequila back into the shelf and pull out the coconut rum. I fill up the two glasses once again. Coconut rum is Toa's favorite. The man's got a severe coconut fetish. That's one of the reasons he smells like it all the time. Just like now. I can smell him from here.

"Thanks." He winks before swallowing the contents and licking his lips with a smile. Expelling another sigh, this time a relaxed one, he continues on. "We're lookin' to get dates, times, and some dirty shit on this guy's prez. They're a small-time club who wanted to fuck with the big boys. So we got called to assist."

"Assist?"

"Yeah. We're doin' a favor for one of the clubs we support. The national prez's old lady is pregnant, and he doesn't have the time to handle shit this small, so he sent one of his men here to help us handle biz. But so far, we've got nothin'."

Interesting…

"Why didn't he just call one of his other chapters?"

If the man is a national prez, doesn't that mean there are other chapters? I remember Nash mentioning they're a support club for one of the bigger clubs. Something about keeping themselves protected since the Crimson Outlaws only have two chapters. The one here is called C.O.C.K—Crimson Outlaws of Charlotteton Kentucky—and I'm not sure about the other. It's on the West Coast. I try to stay a good arm's length from most club related stuff unless Nash or Toa confides in me—like he's doing right now.

"We were the closest for pick up," he replies. "And we're gettin' a cut of the shipment, so it's fine for us to do the grunt work."

"Is that what Nash is doin'? The grunt work."

Toa jerks a nod, skimming a hand over his short, black hair, one elbow perched on the bar top. "Nash and Steel, the VP from the other club, were talkin' strategy when I decided to step out. It sounded like they wanted to bleed the fucker."

Now that sounds disgusting. I've already seen what damage Nash's wallet chain can do to a hang-around who wouldn't leave the bar. And I'm sure this is gonna be much worse than that. Shit, the guy couldn't even walk by the time Nash beat him all the way to his car. The poor man had to army crawl, blood trailing behind him on the gravel lot, soaking into the stones. It was painful to watch.

Blinking, I wash that image from my mind. "And now you're mad?"

"No. I'm sick and tired of dealin' with the asshole. He's got one helluva mouth on him, and won't shut the fuck up. Unfortunately, we can't gag him if we want him to talk. So we're stuck listenin' to the idiot rattle on and fuckin' on about bullshit. He's got a screw loose or somethin', because he's talkin' to us like we're his new best friends. Tellin' us nonsense shit about chicks he's banged and parties his club has had. He's a bragger. It's un-fuckin-real." He rolls his eyes dramatically. "Kinda surprised I haven't broken his jaw, yet."

"Me, too," I muse. "So do you have any idea how long Nash might be? I brought him dinner." Reaching over the bar, I tap the side of the bag, and Toa lifts his chin in acknowledgment.

"Do you wanna head down to the cellar with me to check on the progress? Maybe we can get Nash to break away for a few so you can eat." He raises a challenging brow.

Now, why doesn't this shock me that he's offering me to see this man? When Nash joined the club, Toa was the VP then and only twenty-three. Five years later, he was patched in as president when their other stepped down. That was when he brought Nash in as his VP. And I've grown up around him and the rest of the brothers since. They're an extension of our small family. My dad invites them all over each year for a few summer cookouts. My mom mends their leathers. It's a real sense of comradery and respect here. Even if I'm just a chick and not a club whore or someone's old lady. Most of the brothers don't have women. And those that do don't have a female who's been around as long as I have. Sometimes, it's not rank that gives you seniority; it's time invested. And I've got over fifteen years.

"Are you sure you don't care if I see? I don't want to interfere. I know the rules." I have to ask just to be certain he's thinking clearly and not allowing alcohol to cloud his judgment. He's not a lightweight—thankfully.

"Haven't you seen plenty of violence here before?"

My head bobs. This is true. A lot of it. It comes with the territory.

"So how's this gonna be any different?" he tacks on.

Shrugging, I return the coconut rum to the shelf at the back of the bar. It sits in front of a massive mirror that runs the entire length of the wall. It's used as a backdrop as it rests behind three staggered rows of liquor. The top shelf alcohol goes on the top, and as you go down, the cheaper the poison gets. Etched into the middle of the mirror is the club's emblem. It's pretty badass with its muscled rooster crossing his arms over his big chest as he glares at you. The same design is sewn into the patch on the back of their cuts.

After I finish tidying up, I walk around the bar and join Toa on the other side. "Let's see what those men are up to," I comment as he slides rather deliciously off his stool.

I've gotta hand it to him; he's a damn fine man. All those tribal tats, dark hair, hazel eyes, and caramel skin is enough to make a nun's mouth water. Plus, it doesn't hurt that he knows how to fuck, and has a big dick to boot. Too bad nobody has snagged him up. He's never even had a girlfriend that I know of. Nash said something about being burned when he was a teenager. I never did ask what happened since it's none of my business.

Right on his tail, I follow Toa down the western styled hallway that houses the public restrooms. Then to the left, we turn down another corridor. At the very end, we're met with a steel door. He raps on it three times and a slot slides open at eye level. "Hey, Prez," one of his brothers greet, peeking through the rectangular hole. "And Gwen." The man's gaze shifts to me, and I offer him a small wave.

Without pause, a heavy lock is slid free, and the door is opened. I notice it's Johnny manning the entrance as we pass by to descend a flight of old, concrete stairs. Another door just like the one previously is at the bottom, and Toa has to go about the same knocking routine for a second time before we're welcomed inside.

It's a good twenty degrees colder down here when I cross the cellar's threshold, suppressing a shiver. Immediately my nostrils are assaulted with the unmistakable tang of blood and mildew. I cover my mouth, trying not to gag. This is so nasty!

"What the fuck is Gwen doing here?" Nash barks, stepping away from the naked man hanging from a set of chains that are screwed into the concrete ceiling. His arms are pulled tight, exposing a patch of hair in his pits. Below his colorless feet is a rusted drain, which has already collected a number of vile liquids. Dried blood covers his skin. His nose is unquestionably broken. One eye nearly swollen shut. Lip busted. From head to toe, dark purple bruises deface his ghostly flesh. He's a sad mess.

Shuffling away from the scene, I press my back against the wall closest to the door. The coolness of the surface seeps through the cotton of my shirt. This time, I can't throttle a shiver. It takes over as goosebumps break out down my arms and legs. Toa slides up next to me, and Price takes my other side, acting as if they're my guard dogs. I kind of like it. Their radiant heat is most welcome.

A low, degrading whistle is blown, ringing in the small room "Ooh, look what we have here," the hostage coos. "I knew I was starting to grow on you guys if you bring me that hot a bitch. Mmm … Mmm … Mmm … I think you need to take off that shirt of yours, baby, and show me those tits."

I go stiff at his abhorrent words, my stomach curdling. The room's air suddenly changes, filling with throat clogging fury as Nash takes a step toward the prisoner, his body coiled tight, fist shaking at his sides, jaw grinding. I can hear it from here. Can't you?

"Don't fuckin' talk to her, asshole," he growls, then cuts his eyes my way. They're liquid fire. "Why are you down here? You're not supposed to be around this shit." He's pissed.

I should've known this would happen. But I wanted to see him. I want him to have dinner with me. I'm tired of us being distant, and since I'm leaving this weekend, I don't want to drive a hundred miles away on bad terms. It's not good for me to race if my mind is focused elsewhere. It could mean disaster, and I could end up hurt.

I chew my bottom lip, not knowing how to reply. He's their VP right now. Not my brother. Not my best friend. Not the man who centers my world. He's the man who handles business. I know my place. It's to keep my mouth shut.

"I let her," Toa clarifies in my stead. "She brought you dinner, and I knew your ass wouldn't come upstairs unless you had to. So I brought her down here. Figured if ya saw her, you'd take a fuckin' break."

"I would have," Nash snarls at his prez, "if she'd have asked."

Beside me, Toa shakes his head, emitting a sound of skepticism in his throat. Not knowing what to do with my hands, I tuck them into my front jean pockets. "No, you wouldn't have. You've been a fucking dick to deal with the past two weeks, and you haven't slept since this stupid fuck was brought in." Toa inclines his head toward their detainee.

"Ooooo, pretty boy has been a dick the past two weeks," the shackled dumbass mocks.

A biker I've never met before steps behind him, grabbing a fistful of the man's brown hair. He jerks his head back. "Shut up, shithead," he rumbles lowly.

You'd think the idiot would heed his words, but he doesn't as he continues talking out of turn. "Oh, come on, boys. You know your VP has been a little hormonal the past two weeks. It probably has something to do with that baby over there, don't it? Now, don't hold out on me, brothers. I want all the dirty details. Did he stuff his cock in another hole? I've done that before. Pissed my last girl off. Made her break up with me. I really—"

Tired of listening to him prattle on, Nash slams his forehead into the man's face. There's a deafening crack that echoes, and I cover my ears to keep them from bleeding. The man's head snaps back, and he groans in pain. I watch on as Nash yanks the knife out of his boot and doesn't hesitate a second to slice across the man's chest. He screams in agony as his life-force drips from the shallow cut, which runs diagonally from his right armpit to left hip.

"That's what you get, fucker!" Nash spits on the guy's chest. "You don't wanna tell us shit. That's your choice. You'll give up the goods sooner or later. But you won't be talkin' about *my* Gwen like that." To drive his point home, Nash flicks the man's broken nose, and he winces, tears streaming down his cheeks. I want to feel sorry for him. I really do. Yet, I feel nothing but respect for Nash and his job as club VP. He's amazing. And he called me *his* Gwen. My stomach takes notice as it does a little somersault.

Shit! Now is not the time for warm and fuzzies.

The same man I've never met before, who's wearing a different cut than Nash's, gives him a nod of approval. Then he steps behind the prisoner for a second time. He's busy crying like a baby as bright red blood oozes down the front of his body. Without warning, the older man stabs a knife through the hostage's bicep from behind.

Holy fuck! I can see the tip of his blade from here, poking out of flesh. A flash of shock covers the captive's face but a second before he howls from the pain. The knife is ripped from the wound, and the river runs red. My stomach rolls at the sight, and I choke down rising bile. This is too much. A little punching, a nose break, maybe even a butt to the forehead. I can handle that. But this … this is beyond that. They are draining him.

"You ready to talk now?" the biker who stabbed him seethes. Nothing but a sobbing mess is his reply. "No?" he tests, pausing a second before inflicting the same damage to the other bicep. This time, instead of watching, I turn my head away and glue my eyes shut as I hear the unmistakable shriek of torture. This is too gruesome. Toa shouldn't have let me down here to see this. Nash is going to kick his ass. And mine, too, for agreeing to it.

A warm hand gripping my forearm startles me. It's Nash, and he doesn't say a word as he carts me out of this dank hellhole, up the stairs, through the hall, and into his small apartment on the opposite side of the bar. Just as the lock clicks into place, he starts in on me. I knew it was coming.

"What the fuck were you thinking?!" he booms.

Shrugging out of his tight grasp, I walk over to his brown, ratty couch and drop into it with a sigh. Nash moves across the floor until he's blocking his flat screen that's directly in front of me. I cross my legs, arms folded over my chest, eyeing him warily. "I wanted to make amends. So I brought chicken. It's in the bar." My head nods toward the closed door.

Chest heaving for air, he cracks his neck side to side. Blood stains the front of his shirt and knuckles. He needs a shower. "I didn't fucking give you permission to come downstairs. Thanks for the food. But fuck. That's not a place for any woman."

"I've seen plenty of that before," I defend, haughtily.

"Steel doesn't hold back for no one. For all he knew, you've seen this time and time again. He shouldn't have stabbed him in front of you. That's my fault for not thinkin'. But Toa shouldn't have brought you down there to begin with."

Damn it, this isn't going according to plan. I was supposed to leave work and pick up food. Then eat dinner with Nash before the boys pick me up tonight so we can hit the road. This is not what I want. Why isn't life ever that simple? If I had been talking to Nash, I would have already known about the man in the cellar. Why did I have to wait until last minute to try and take this load off my shoulders? It's been weeks of work hell and emotional turmoil not talking to him. I hate admitting it. It tears me apart inside. I'm not supposed to care this much. But I do. There's something fucked up about me—about this—about us.

"Earth to Gwen." Nash snaps his fingers, and I come to, blinking rapidly.

"What?"

"Stop bein' pissy," he says.

"Pissy? I'm not pissy. You're the one who won't talk to me. You're the one who's been avoiding me for two weeks. I came to get you back into my life. I don't give a shit if it was a bad call for Toa to bring me down there. It's over and done with." My wrist flicks in the air, waving off the event

Some women might be haunted by what I just saw-but not me. There's hardly anything that could permanently disturb me after I was raped all those years ago. Hell, there are still things about that time that I haven't told anyone else. And I never will. Stuff that involves baseball bats and popsicles.

"I'm hungry," he remarks, ignoring what I just said. "I'mma go get the food." Nash doesn't wait for my response before he leaves his apartment. I glare at the door as it's shut in his wake. Minutes later, he returns with the bag of food and a bottle of beer.

Sauntering silently into his galley kitchen, that's directly off the living room, he washes his hands then carries out some plates, napkins, silverware, and a cold bottle of water for me. He sets everything on the coffee table before dropping onto the couch to my left.

Nash opens up the food as I arrange our plates and other stuff. In the company of companionable silence, we dish out our dinners and eat hunched over. The sound of chewing through the crispy chicken skin and dense breaths are the only things to be heard.

Finishing my meal first, I wipe my hands with a wet nap the restaurant provided and lean into the couch, feeling stuffed. "Are you planning on talking to me after you're done?" I ask.

He nods, so I wait.

Once he's through, Nash wipes himself clean, takes a long pull from his beer, finishing it off, and drops back into the cushions with a satisfied groan. Our shoulders bump. "That hit the spot." He pats his stomach. "Kelly doesn't like it when I eat fatty foods, so I don't get it much."

No offense, but I don't want to be talking about Kelly at a time like this, so I keep quiet. She's a mood killer.

He keeps on. "So how's Trish's boyfriend?"

This is *so* not what I came here to discuss.

Staring straight ahead, eyes on the blank wall above the TV, I reply, "I wouldn't know. I haven't asked. So why don't you tell me?"

"He's never even had a speeding ticket."

I guess that's a good thing.

"So you checked in on him, I take it?" This is something I expected, so it's not like I can be upset. He's just looking out for her.

Nash leans a bit closer, his shoulder kissing mine. A calming warmth flitters through me, regulating my crazy nerves. Damn, I've missed him. "You should've known I would. And I texted her yesterday to check in," he states.

Not wanting to waste another second on Trish talk, which is our safe-zone, I cut to the chase, turning my head to face him. "So, are you going to tell me why you've been distant? Last week, you texted three times. That's it. Once about Trish, once about my motorcycle, and another about Sunday lunch. When I replied, that was it. You kept silent. Is this about what happened the other Sunday at Mom and Dad's? You know … the kissing stuff."

God, I really hate discussing this, but it needs to be brought to light. No use in brushing it under the rug.

"I don't wanna talk about this, Gwen." Nash stands and strides hastily to his bedroom door. "Thanks for dinner. It was nice seein' ya. Now I gotta shower and maybe catch a nap before I gotta get back to work. The bar's closed tonight for obvious reasons, but Kelly is supposed to drop by after she gets off at the club."

Leering at him, I remain seated, in fear of what I might do if I get up. I can't believe he's giving me the cold shoulder. He's so fucking hot and cold tonight. One second, he's calling me *his* Gwen, and now he's brushing me off. What the hell?

"What's your problem?" I snap.

"I have no problem, Gwen. I'm busy, tired, and I don't want to fight." He leans his shoulder against the doorframe, looking a bit haggard.

"You're gonna ignore me? Treat me like some second-rate family member? Is that it? I came here to mend whatever it is that's broken." I gesture between the two of us with my hand, trying to keep my voice calm. "Now you wanna blow me off. What the fuck?"

Tugging out his man-bun, he runs fingers through his hair. That's not a good thing. If he combs through his hair, it means he's stressed and needs something to relax him.

"I can't do this, Gwen. Not anymore."

What in the world is he talking about?

"Do what?!"

"This." He does that hand gesturing thingy, too. "I can't do the kissing. The biting. The scratching. I thought I could. But I can't. After I left Mom and Dad's that Sunday, Kelly and I got to talkin', really talkin', and she explained some things."

"What kinda things?!" I can't control it, every word that keeps coming out is high and full of venom.

"That we're codependent. She thinks you need me to breathe. Which makes her jealous."

"She's jealous because I love my brother?! Of course, I need you. Why wouldn't I? You came into my life when I was lonely. We were buds from day one. Since you were fifteen, I watched you work on cars for hours. I used to bake you cookies for Easter because I knew you'd buy me a stuffed bumble bee. I have twelve of those, all from you. All of them on display in my bedroom."

I realize I sound pathetic, but this is just stupid. I can't believe he went from being okay with this for all these years, and now he's suddenly changing his tune. This … Gah!! I dunno … It's wrong! Plain wrong! I need him. I can't do this … live this way. He's ripping my heart from my chest.

I suck in a pained breath and swallow down the lump of emotions that has crawled its way up my throat.

"I know you still have them, Gwen." His tone is flat—sad.

"Then what the hell? Does Kelly expect me not to want to be in your life like I have been? When I was sixteen, when we moved into the apartment above Mom and Dad's garage with Trish, you watched her while I went to school. Then worked nights to bring home money so I could afford diapers. We lived together for years, Nash. Inside of Mom and Dad's, and out. There's nothing that's going to change the bond we share. How could she expect that? It makes no damn sense. I respect Kelly ... or, I did. I get that I need you in ways that are ten degrees of fucked up. I'll be the first to admit that—"

"You need to go, Gwen," he interjects grimly, eyes fixed on the floor. "This'll be the last time I let you bring me food. If you want to continue the monthly weekend fucks, that's fine. I'll watch out for you, but I won't participate anymore. Now, I need to shower. You can see yourself out."

And just like that, Nash spins on his heel, enters his bedroom, and shuts the door. I hear the lock flick into place, and do nothing but stare in stunned silence. What just happened? Did he cut me off? Why would he do such a thing? I don't get it. No communication. No nothing. And now I'm left with this gaping wound in my chest. It literally hurts as I rub my fist there, in the place that my heart is supposed to be. But it's not. He took it with him when he turned his back on me and shut the door in my face.

Tears that I wish to keep at bay give me the big *fuck you* as they stream down my cheeks, dripping off the tip of my chin and onto my shirt.

Oh. My. God. What just happened? Can you tell me? I'm ... I ... shit ... I don't even know what to say as more tears continue their descent. It's like he ... he doesn't love me anymore.

A pained sob rips from my throat, and I cover my mouth, attempting to muffle the noise. I don't want him to hear. He doesn't deserve to know what he's doing to me. That gives the asshole too much power.

I can't stay here. If he doesn't want to fight for me, for our family, then he can kiss my ass. No … I don't mean that. I wish I did. I wish I could hate him, but I don't. In the deepest recesses of my soul, I knew this day would come. The day when I would be cut off. No more soothing kisses. No more hair combing. No more Nash and Gwen against the world. Now, I'm alone. Truly alone. My daughter is busy with her life. Nash is … I can't be sure, but he doesn't want me. What else matters anymore? I have nothing. I'm a thirty-three year old single woman, who's never even been in a relationship. Never been on a date. Never made love to a man. Nothing…

I really am ten ways of fucked up.

Righting myself the best way possible, I hold my head high and see myself out. Thankfully, I avoid everyone besides Meatball as I do the walk of heartbreak. He sees me crying, I know he does, but he keeps quiet as I give him a small wave before climbing into my car. With one final glance, I take in the rustic front of *Nowhere* and pull out of the gravel drive, headed to *somewhere.* Somewhere where I can forget this day ever happened. Somewhere that I can cut away all of this pain and exchange it for the addictive buzz of adrenaline. Somewhere where someone actually cares for me.

Fuck Kelly.

Fuck Nash.

Fuck all of this shit.

It's time to ride.

Chapter Five

AC/DC's '*Highway to Hell*' serenades us along the long stretch of road ahead. It's just past midnight and the stars are out in full force, dotting the clear sky. Seated next to me, Fat Larry is busy strumming his thumbs on the steering wheel to the beat of the music. In the back, Jack and Tony are busy making out. And by the shape of our windows—thanks to them fogging—I wouldn't be surprised if there's a bit of stroking going on underneath the blanket that's covering their laps. Those two are utterly insatiable every time I see them, and rightfully so. Both of them are married, but not to each other. It seems that these summer weekends are the only time they can be together. According to Fat Larry, who's been best friends with them for the past twenty years, Tony and Jack have been an unofficial item for nearly a decade. They all went to college together and stayed close afterward. They were even groomsmen in each other's weddings. Or Tony and Jack's, that is—Fat Larry has never been hitched, because he's never found the right man. Truthfully, it's kind of bittersweet to see the love these men share—since they're unable to be together thanks to life's never-ending complications. Sounds a little like Nash's and my predicament ... maybe ... hell ... maybe not ... I dunno. Part of me wants Nash more than I let on. My newly broken heart is a telltale sign. Though, I'm choosing not to dwell on any of it. It'll do me no good.

A few hours ago, the boys picked me up from my house, where I was moping in the darkness of my living room, overthinking the Nash incident. As soon as we left, I texted Trish to let her know what was up. Now, my phone is off, and I'm enjoying the ride. Or trying to. If only the vision of Nash and his retreating back would stop playing on a reel in my head.

God ... I have to stop thinking about him.

"Hey, you fuckers! There better not be any cum stains on my seats tomorrow," Fat Larry teases, as he reverently caresses his steering wheel like it's his most prized possession.

There's a sensual gasp as lips are unsealed. "We'll be careful," Jack replies, breathlessly.

"You'd better be," Fat Larry adds, then reaches across the seat and taps my thigh before settling his slender hand there, just above my knee. "How ya doin'? You haven't said much. Gettin' pumped about the races tomorrow? I've added a few new touches to your bike. I think you'll like 'em."

Nodding through the darkness of the cab, I pat the top of his hand in reassurance. "I'm fine. Just a bit tired." I yawn, gazing out of the obscure passenger side window. "And yes, I'm excited about the races, and the new parts. Thank you for those, by the way. I just hope I can steer clear of Wes this summer."

My crack at sounding cheerful falls a bit short. I'm typically more enthusiastic about these weekends since they're one of the few times I get to let loose without my family worrying about me. If Nash knew about them, I'd be lectured for sure. But tonight just isn't one of those nights I can be happy. I'm bored and sullen—two qualities that definitely don't mix.

"We'll be fine. No worries," Fat Larry comforts, patting my knee again. "I requested a primo spot at the site. We should have some privacy."

That sounds perfect. The more privacy, the better.

Over the past few years, to keep these summer activities under wraps, I've stored my street bike with Fat Larry. Honestly, that's the safest place for my bike anyhow, since he's a mechanic and the one who transports our unofficial team to and from these events.

Hitched onto the flatbed of Fat Larry's *Chevy 3500* dually truck is a toy camper. It's one of the coolest damn things I've ever seen. Until I'd met him, I had no idea those kinds of trailers existed. It's part camper, part hotel. The front half has a queen suite that Jack and Tony use a leather, four-person sofa in the living room. There is also a dining booth that folds into a full sized bed that has a pull down from the ceiling to make it into a full sized bunk. It's huge. There's also a luxury bath with a stand-up shower, and a kitchen with all stainless-steel appliances, including a full-sized refrigerator. In the rear half of the camper, there's a garage of sorts with diamond plate flooring, a ramp, fold down bench and built-in tool boxes. It's spacious enough to house our four bikes and a few other odds and ends. It sure as hell beats tent camping when we're away.

Another song starts, and my head lulls to the side, my forehead resting on the cool windowpane. Fat Larry squeezes my leg. "You're not only tired, but you're also stressed," he comments, nailing my problem right on the head.

I shrug, even though he can't see it. "I'm a little stressed."

"This wouldn't have anything to do with Nash, does it? Or maybe Trish?" he asks.

I guess I should mention that just because Nash and my family know nothing about Fat Larry, Tony, and Jack, these men *do* know about them. It's impossible not to talk about my family when I'm away. So I've confided in these three guys more times than I can count. And yes, that includes the sordid details of my monthly fuck fests, and the strange relationship Nash and I've always had. I think Fat Larry is secretly wishing I would date my step-brother. I, on the other hand, would just be happy to have him back in my life. Dating him has never crossed my mind, anyhow. Dating is for people you just met. People you are getting to know. Nash and I have known each other for over twenty years, so there's not much else I haven't learned about him one way or another.

A moan emanates from the back, and I stifle a giggle, forgetting my own thoughts for a moment.

"I haven't fucked anyone in over six months, and here you two assholes are moaning in my truck? Come on; give a guy a break," Fat Larry reprimands half seriously.

Smiling, I grab his hand and fold my fingers through his. "Let them have their fun," I torment, skating around his previous questions.

"Fun? They're going to stain the upholstery. And we'll be smelling cum soon enough."

He's right. It happens every time we get together. And it might bother some people, but it doesn't me. I'm pretty laid back when it comes to sex. It's a normal bodily function that needs tending to. I just happen to enjoy it kinkier than some.

Another moan reverberates, followed by loud, sloppy kissing. Out of the corner of my eye, I catch Fat Larry, who really isn't fat at all, remove his hand from the wheel for a moment to run his palm down the muscled front of his chest, and end on his crotch where he adjusts a prominent bulge. Maybe he'll be lucky to find himself a quick lay at one of our races. Looks like he needs it. Not that I blame him. I couldn't go six months without some dick. At least these events are stocked full of just about any type of man or woman you could desire. They're not like the stereotypical Harley riders. You know the ones I'm talking about—men dressed in leather, wearing bandanas, and covered in tattoos. No, street bike racers are an eclectic bunch. From known thugs to the rich assholes with so much money they don't know what to do with. All the way down to the average rider, like me. Or that's what I'd consider myself. Although, there aren't many women who ride in the circuit we run. They're typically used for arm candy, wearing their tight, barely-there clothes. If you've ever watched *The Fast and the Furious,* you'd understand what I'm talking about. That's exactly how we roll. Except we race bikes on long winding roads, in the backwoods of some state where the cops can be easily paid off. A man named Rubio heads it up. Though you rarely see him at any race. It's his minions that run the show, gathering bets, buy-ins, and designating our tracks.

Keeping my fingers folded in Fat Larry's, I stare aimlessly out of the foggy window. I wipe it with my palm, twice, which does little good. The noises in the rear multiply and the scent of sex permeates the air as the telltale sound of a grumbled climax reaches our ears over the music. A few more hours and we'll be pulling into our backwoods campsite. Until then, I need to catch some shuteye. I've got a big day tomorrow.

Night.

Chapter Six

Wearing black pajamas, my hair pulled into a knot on the top of my head, I step out of the camper and into the cool summer morning. The scent of breakfast cooking over a campfire draws me like a moth to a flame. My mouth begins to water. Grass squishes between my toes as I rub the sleep from my eyes, rounding the rear of the trailer where our bikes rest in the lawn. The smoky smell lures me closer, and just as I catch sight of my trio, I halt in my tracks, trying my best to back away quickly and quietly. The guys aren't alone.

"Gwen." Jack notices my retreating form before I make it a safe distance. At his call, I freeze, not wanting to be rude.

"Yes?" I play coy.

He gestures with his hand toward the open fire, where puffs of smoke are billowing into the early morning sky. "I made you some biscuits and bacon. So why don't ya come over and eat? Don't worry about getting dressed, sweetie." Damn Jack and his miniature, twink, dark-haired adorableness. It's going to be the end of me.

Frankly, I couldn't give a rat's ass if I ate in my PJs. These men are like family, and they wouldn't care. The problem isn't them. It's Wes. The man who's busy chatting with Tony near that giant maple tree, a few yards away. Wes, the man who has been the bane of my racing existence since I first started. He's a womanizing, chauvinistic, A-hole. Which is further presented by the gaggle of brain-fried, bottled-blondes standing five feet behind him, like they have nothing better to do at 8 a.m. on a Saturday morning. Hell, they're already wearing full glamour makeup, hooker heels, daisy duke shorts, and crop tops in multiple colors that enhance their massive, surgically enhanced boobs. Boobs that I'm sure jackass Wes paid for with a bit of his 110.7 million dollars. I'll say it once, and I'll say it a thousand more times—that man is a total rich, handsome, dirt-baggy, tool.

Over the past years, I've come to realize that one of Wes's many joys in life is tormenting me. You see, I'm not his type. Not with my college educated brain, natural brunette hair, and average breasts. Add me being his competition to the mix, and he's downright despicable.

And why in the hell is he speaking to Tony, anyhow? My guys know how I feel about him, and they don't like him any more than I do.

"Gwen. Food." Fat Larry snaps his fingers, and my brain clicks into gear, moving my feet forward.

I take a load off on one of the lawn chairs, and Jack sets a plate full of yumminess in my lap. That's one of the perks of having a chef on board. Jack owns his own bistro about two hours north of me, and Tony works as a mechanic with Fat Larry. I know it's a lot to keep up with, but I figured you might wanna know.

Helping myself to the delicious food, I eat in silence as I listen to Fat Larry and Jack run over today's itinerary. Just as I'm about finished, somebody whistles loudly, like they're calling a dog.

They might as well be saying, '*Here, puppy, puppy.*'

Refusing to glance up, I stare at my plate and continue enjoying my meal. Because, unlike Wes's four stick models, I like to savor what I'm eating. Not throw it up later. And yes, I realize I sound like a judgmental bitch right now. Oh well. He gets way under my skin, even when I know he shouldn't.

The pompous whistle slices through the air once more, and I grumble under my breath as my hackles rise.

"I think Wes wants your attention," Jack whispers, nudging my knee with his hand.

Swallowing down my food, my eyes still glued to my white plate, I reply, "I know, but I'm not acknowledging the dickwad."

Both Fat Larry and Jack chuckle.

"Atta girl," Fat Larry praises, and I grin my momentary triumph.

"You-who, Gwen," Wes torments in his condescending tone.

I will not let him get to me. I will not show my contempt. The asshole doesn't deserve a reaction. He deserves nothing.

"Gwen." His voice is nearer now, full of hard edges.

Wes is used to getting what he wants. I know that much. Between his fortune, seedy connections, and model good looks, I'm sure being ignored rarely happens. However, I get a dose of sheer pleasure from dropping him down a peg or two.

"Gwen." He's downright pissed.

Good. His presence is ruining an otherwise beautiful morning, so why shouldn't his morning be tarnished as well? It'll do him some good. Perhaps, humble an otherwise arrogant man.

Shuffling feet grow closer.

"You best stop right there," Fat Larry warns, shooting his thin, six-six frame up from his chair, ready to kick some ass. "The lady obviously doesn't wish to speak to you."

Wes unleashes an enraged scoff. "Well, if the *lady* wishes to act like a *lady*, she wouldn't ignore a gentleman's call."

See what I mean? Total asshat.

Now I'm the one left scoffing under my breath.

"You better watch it, buddy," Fat Larry warns, and I've suddenly had enough of this charade.

Setting my plate on the grass, I stand and glare at Wes. "You rang, Your Highness?" I mock curtsy, rolling my eyes with my lips pressed into a thin line.

Happy to have garnered my attention, Wes flashes me a full set of those pearly whites as his baby blue eyes try to lock with mine, and he puffs up his chest. What does he expect to get from his stupid display of dominance? Why's he acting like a peacock trying to fan his proverbial feathers? Does he think it's going to make me swoon? Want to throw myself at his feet, begging him to give me just one chance? *Oh, please, Wes, pound me with your gigantic cock. Make me scream.*

Bahahaha! As if!

A ball of nausea rolls into my throat at the mere thought.

Yuck!

Wes's minions fall in line behind their master like a wall of silicone.

"You called?" I huff, trying to get this meet and greet over with.

His gaze travels my pajama-clad body up and down before resettling on my face. He grins. "I just wanted to wish you good luck at today's races."

"Sure you did."

Wes frowns at my tone and brushes his hands over his white t-shirt as if I'd just frazzled him. "Contrary to your belief, Gwen, I find your quality of racing to be exemplary." His words are surprisingly genuine, or they seem to be, but I don't buy it for a second.

"Gee, thanks. I *so* needed your approval, Oh Wise One," I deadpan, crossing my arms protectively over my chest as my blood rushes—hopped up on adrenaline.

My trio chuckles and Fat Larry finally sits back down, knowing I can handle myself. You don't have a biker for a brother and not know how to handle your own. Nash and the Crimson Outlaws taught me well.

Feet apart, standing tall, I brace myself, fully expecting Wes to come at me with some of his dickishness. Unexpectedly, though, he whips his head back at my words as if I'd just slapped him. Then he turns and saunters away, giving me a perfect view of his equally perfect ass in those tight jeans. Shit! Now I'm the one who feels like a complete jerk. Maybe he wasn't trying to torment me this time. Or perhaps he was just trying to throw me off my game so I don't race as well today. I know he hates to lose.

Still puzzled by his sudden appearance and departure, I drop back into my chair with an exhausted sigh. It's too dang early to deal with this crap.

"That was strange," Jack notes.

"Yeah. Tell me about it," I agree.

"What did he want, anyhow?" Fat Larry asks, then takes a long drink of his morning coffee that Jack brewed over the fire.

Sitting across the pit from me, Tony scratches his long, graying beard. "He wanted to see which of us was racing in the Devil's Corkscrew tonight."

"Is he?" I raise a curious brow to Tony, and he nods, still itching that beard. Maybe he needs to condition it.

"That's the biggest paying race of the weekend. I know he's running in it. I'm sure he's just scared of us and wanting to scope out the competition. There are thirty-six other racers here today, and most of them only participate in the short heats. They don't want to risk their bikes, reputations, or money on something so dangerous."

That makes sense. My bike cost me almost thirty grand, not including the parts that Fat Larry has graciously installed for free.

"Plus, the buy-in is killer. We're talking five large," Tony adds.

Now, that has my attention.

Sitting forward, I rest my elbows on my knees. "Do you think I should do it?"

My guys all look at each other as if they're searching for the right answer. Fat Larry is the first to break the silence, as he contemplatively rubs his prickly jaw. "I don't know, Gwen. You're a damn good rider. But we're talking night time, no street lights, unknown rocks, and gravel, and that's without the curvy downhill roads to deal with. Roads with zero guard railings. People die racing these things. It's not safe."

NOWHERE

The more he explains it, the more eager I become over the prospect of showing Wes up in one of the most dangerous races I've ever participated in. Sure, I've done the downhill roads with no guard rails before. That's nothing new to me. But *nighttime* is the catch. It's supposed to be cloudy tonight, so that means it'll be near pitch black. Ooooo buddy that sounds like a lot of fun. Kicking up gravel in Wes's face. Giving him the finger as he eats my dust, and I bring home the bacon. I could use the extra money to add a porch onto the back of my little house. My teachers pay doesn't allow for those extras. And Nash, before our falling out, offered to help install one, but I felt too guilty to ask him to do any more than he already does ... *did*.

Damn it. I really have to stop thinking about him. This is my time away to have fun. I don't need to focus on what is, could have been, or whatever else. I can't deal with Nash right now, anyhow. He's not here, and I can't fix our problems in one day. Those will just have to wait.

I stand up from my chair to give myself the boost of confidence I need. "I'm gonna race against Wes in the Devil's Corkscrew, and I'm gonna kick his ass."

The men look at each other again, smiles spreading wide on their faces. "If that's what you wanna do, Gwen, we've got your back." Tony lifts his chin in respect.

"Yeah. Kick his ass." Jack winks, and then stands from his chair, waving for Tony to join him. "Come on. I need your dick shoved in my ass for good luck." He grins devilishly, and that's all it takes for Tony to jump out of his seat, grab his petite lover by the waist, hoist him over his shoulder, and slap his ass all the way into the camper, which will soon be emitting vulgar noises of ecstasy.

"I guess we'll be out here for a while," I comment, retaking my chair.

There is no way I am going to go anywhere near that camper when those men are screwing. Once, last year, I'd dared to go inside and found myself face to face with Jack riding Tony, while Tony fucked himself on a suction cup dildo on the kitchen's tiled floor. I'll never look at that spot the same again.

Fat Larry refills his white mug and takes a deep breath with his head tipped toward the sky. "Today is going to be a good day," he sighs, peacefully.

Following by example, I stare at the clouds and smile. Yes. Today is going to be a good day. I won't let anything else get me down. Today is the day I put Wes, the womanizer, in his place, as I forget Nash and the way he treated me. It's time to put my skills to use. I'm ready to take on the world. Hell, what do I have to lose?

Chapter Seven

With my booted feet planted firmly on the pavement as I straddle my purple bike, my gaze drops to the chalked starting line that commences our five mile downhill race. That simple line represents much more than just a race. It's a new beginning for me. A fresh start. A way to prove myself worthy, which is something I'm desperate to hold on to. I want to be worthy of something … anything.

The rest of today has already been a beautiful day of never-ending adventures; one of which I smoked Wes in. He didn't stand a chance on that last straightaway. Nobody did. Not with the new sick mods Fat Larry installed on my bike. They all ate my dust, just as they're about to do again, tonight. Maybe my confidence is running on a cataclysmic high. But after two first place wins and a third place finish, I'm riding high on life. High on the road. The wind pounding against my skin at high speeds. The addictive rush. I'm more than ready to put Wes's money where his stupid mouth is.

Fat Larry sidles up to my bike, my helmet in one hand. Stretching my arms high, I crack my neck side to side, loosening up my muscles for the unpredictable terrain we're about to encounter.

"Tony's taken care of your buy-in. Word is, if you hit top three, you'll get your money back. Any higher and you'll be rolling outta here richer." Fat Larry's free hand reaches out to massage my shoulder over my skintight leather jacket. "Don't stress, Gwen. You got this in the bag."

Casting my sights toward the dark road ahead, I visualize my impending journey and stiffly nod, twice. "Yes. I have it in the bag." At least, I think I do—or hope.

I send a short prayer to the almighty above to keep me safe, then turn my head to the side to view my competitors. Three spots down, Wes is straddling his sleek, black bike. A scantily clad blonde is draped partway over his lap, giving him a *'good luck'* tonguing. You can practically hear her greedy moans from here. Ick! To his opposite side, another blonde stands in wait for a turn. This has been his ritual all day. The same four blondes, the same kisses from each of them. At that one race that I kicked his ass on, everyone got a flash of some boobs when he began tweaking the tallest blonde's nipples as one of the others fingered her on the starting line. It was vomit worthy ... even though I consider myself open minded. Perhaps my real issue isn't him or the women; it's the lewd displays, and the fact that all of those women resemble Kelly, Nash's lover—the bitch that broke us apart. Hell, for all I know, those four blondes are great gals. I just don't care to find out.

Fat Larry taps my shoulder, severing my thoughts. "Don't let him get to you," he urges.

I shrug my feelings off. "I won't."

"He's only one of eight racers you need to beat. Focus on the road. On the finish line. Nothing else. Clear your mind."

He's right.

I take a deep, cleansing breath and continue to visualize my path to sweet victory.

The man heading up the race takes front and center in his baggy pants and baggy shirt. Lifting his hands to gain everyone's attention, he then proceeds to explain the rules. No sabotage. No weapons. No veering off the route … blah, blah, blah. It's the same rules, different race. I've heard them a hundred times before.

Once he's finished, he leaves the spotlight and the woman who will drop the flag takes her place. Fat Larry kisses my temple and wishes me "good luck" before passing me my helmet and rejoining the trio. Over my shoulder, I spot Tony and Jack, holding hands and smiling at me with glowing pride. They both offer me a thumbs up, making me laugh like an idiot, as I shake my head. Those men, I love them all.

When I turn my gaze back around, I take one final gander at the lineup. All of them are men. All ruthless riders. All hungry for the win. Hmmm … but who I don't see is Wes. Where did he go? Do you see him? Someone else has taken his spot. I shift my eyes backward to see if he bowed out, but he's not with the spectators. Where in the hell would he go?

"Miss me?" a cocky voice singsongs from my left, and I sigh, rolling my eyes before turning my sights upon my nemesis.

"Why'd you move? You were perfectly fine all the way over there." I jerk my chin to Wes's previous spot, praying he'd have stayed put.

Winking at me with that cocksure grin in place, he slides his palms worshipfully over his handlebars. "I thought you might want to wager something more than money for this race. Seeing as though you want to kick my ass." His smug tone never waivers. This man really is full of himself.

Honing my sass, I lift my shoulders and drop them in an exaggerated shrug. "What of it? The glory is worth it for me. To know I can wipe the pavement with your rep, for being bested by a chick…" I pause. "A brunette one, to boot," I tack on, because it's a low blow, and it's fun to hit him where it hurts. Or maybe where it hurts me, since I'm not a voluptuous blonde. Shit, I don't know.

"How about we make it more interesting? Say … you beat me, and I'll give you a quarter of a million dollars … *cash*." He perks a brow, and my mouth nearly drops open at the prospect of that kind of money. Except I check myself and attempt to appear disinterested. I can't let him know I'd love to take the gamble. However, with a bet this astronomical, there has to be a catch. There always is.

Licking my dry lips, I look straight ahead as I deliver my level reply. "On the off chance that you would … you know…" Damn, I can't even say the words.

"Beat you?" There's a smile in his voice, and I loathe it, almost as much as I loathe him.

Flicking my hand out, I toss that absurd notion into the wind. "Sure … that. You know, *hypothetically*."

He chuckles at my words. It's smooth and sensual. I hate it. "If I am to … as you say it … *kick your ass*. Then I would expect you to live with me for a month."

Swiftly, I open my mouth to protest. Then snap it closed as he continues.

"Now, before you overthink what my bet entails, let me set your mind at ease … I wouldn't force sex upon you unless you asked. I wouldn't cause you any bodily harm, in any way. However, should I win, you would attend events with me. You would be—"

"Your arm candy," I gripe.

"No. I have plenty of that."

Of course, he does.

He keeps on. "You would accompany me to events, and willingly do the things that I ask. I know you're a school teacher and don't work in the summers, Gwen. So what I'm proposing wouldn't be a problem for you. I also know your daughter, Patricia, is no longer living with you and now has a life of her own. So this wouldn't be affecting anyone but you, for one month … Thirty days of living under the same roof with me—*should* I win. If not, you take the quarter of a million in cash and buy whatever your heart desires. I'm a fair man, Gwen. And I know what I am suggesting is a reasonable wager."

This has to be the dumbest fucking thing I've ever heard! Why would I do that?! No way! Wait … why does it matter, anyhow? I'm going to win. I'm going to get the money … hmm … decisions … decisions. But first…

"How do you know so much about me? And why make this bet? It seems … *risky*." I snap to face him so he knows I mean business.

Those serious baby blue eyes of his melt into mine. "Gwen, seriously? I know everything about everyone I race against. Especially the women. Do you think my bet was something I just tossed out on a whim? No. I'm a businessman. I make rational decisions that are in my best interest. A quarter of a million dollars to a woman who *kicks my ass*." Pausing a beat, he grins like he thinks that's an illogical outcome. "As I was saying … that kind of money I could make in a day. But it could also do some good in your life. So I find it fair."

Why am I even considering this? I don't know, but it sounds too good to be true. That's a lot of money that I could pay Trish's college with and pay off my house. Here I thought I might have enough money saved to put on a deck. That kind of money could change my life.

Fuck it! You only live once … Right?

"On one condition," I explain.

"Name it."

God, he knows he has me hook, line, and sinker. I can already see the gleam in his eyes. Too bad I'm gonna wipe the pavement with him.

"If I win, you make it three hundred thousand dollars."

"I'll make it half a million if that'll make you feel better."

Holy fuck!

This time I nod, dumbfounded, and he smiles hugely, showing off those pearly whites. "What? Did you think there wouldn't be negotiations? A half a million was going to be my first offer, but I figured I'd see if you'd work harder for it."

Of course, he did. Asshole…

"O … kay. But, should I, you know…"

"Lose."

That word feels horrible battling in my brain—*Lose.* It shouldn't even be a part of the English language.

Painfully, I nod. "Yeah, that. If I do … I agree to your terms … *but* … if money isn't an object for you and you're taking away thirty days of my life, I think you should pay for one year of tuition for Trish, anyhow. You know … out of the kindness of your heart." It's hard, but I resist rolling my eyes on that last part.

"I'll pay for two. Out of the kindness of my heart." He winks, extending his hand to take mine.

Talk about changing my life.

I can't believe I'm about to do this…

Reaching out my hand, I slide my gloved fingers into his huge palm, and we shake. It's firm, warm, and lingers a bit longer than I'd like.

"Deal," I blurt in confirmation, yanking out of his grasp.

"Deal." He smiles. It's smarmy, yet, somewhat attractive. That doesn't make much sense, but it is what it is. "And may the best racer win," he finishes.

Yes. They shall.

See you at the finish line … *sucker.*

Chapter Eight

No! No! Hell no! This cannot be happening!

Why did I agree to that bet?

I fucking had him by the balls. I had *everyone* by the balls. The road was unyielding with its deathly sharp curves and potholes. It tested both my mind and body in ways I didn't know was possible. Wes, another racer, and I tore from the pack within the first half mile. Then after the third blind corner, I took the inside track and shot ahead, setting myself apart from the rest. The triumph steadily clouded my mind as I kept pushing, never letting up. I was sure I had the last quarter mile in the bag since I could no longer hear the racers approaching. Driving my *Ducati* the final neck, I happily tested what I could do—my limits. Until everything unexpectedly changed when Wes gunned past me, seemingly out of nowhere, his bike roaring toward the finish line in a blur of NOS.

Screaming into the night, I revved harder, dropping my chest to fight the wind at speeds no one should have driven on that road at any time of the day. Inch by inch, I grew close enough that Wes's brilliant blue taillights were mocking me. Then, suddenly, we were there—*the end*. It snuck up on us around the last curve, and he was the first to cross the chalk line. People cheered, and I cried. His blondes threw themselves at him in a fit of excitement. And I cried some more, drowning in a dark sea of self-loathing.

Now I'm sitting in the back of Wes's limo, headed to God knows where, with an arrogant SOB and his four groupies who are busy attending his needs in front of my very eyes. If I hadn't been groomed to handle this display of lewdness, I'd be throwing up, or worse, tossing myself out of the moving vehicle. Yet, here I sit, in my jeans and t-shirt, trying to mind my own business as Wes's blondes suck his dick, nipples, and neck simultaneously.

"Don't look so glum," he attempts to speak to me like he's been doing since we left. However, I'm having none of it. Just because I lost and I'm stuck here, nursing a bruised ego doesn't mean I have to talk to him. That was not part of the arrangement.

Before we had departed, I packed my belongings and stored my bike with my trio. Needless to say, Tony, Fat Larry, and Jack went ballistic, trying to fight for me. Even though I told them the deal I'd made, and that I'd planned to make good on it. Still, they didn't approve, and tiny Jack ended up knocking around a few of Wes's bodyguards. If it weren't for those meatheads, I'm sure things would have gotten a lot uglier.

Just as I'd slipped into the back of Wes's limo, I promised my trio that I'd be safe. Even Wes assured them, too. What little good that did. When I can't even convince myself I'm going to be okay. I don't even know this man. When I'd agreed to our little bet, I didn't honestly think I could lose. So I didn't take the possible consequences into enough consideration if I'd lost. Which I did, and now I'm reaping those consequences in living, moaning color.

Wes keeps on, his voice husky with need. "When we get to my home in the mountains, you're welcome to make a phone call to Patricia to inform her of your impromptu summer vacation. And you can also call your guard dogs so they know you're alright. This way, they won't try to murder me the next chance they get. That Jack is a feisty fellow." He chuckles his last sentence like he's mildly impressed. I subdue the impulse to flip him off.

Good luck with that. Those men will never forgive Wes. And if he considers that possible, he's delusional.

The funny thing is, if he thinks those men are guard dogs, I'd wonder how he'd fair if faced with my actual guard dog … or the one who used to care enough to be.

Ha...

I can remember the very first date I ever had. I was barely nineteen at the time and living with Nash in that apartment above my parent's garage. John was the boy's name. We'd met in my college math class, and after a couple of harmless study sessions in the school's library, he'd asked me out. Needless to say, that went over like a lead brick. When he'd showed up to our apartment door, like a gentleman, carrying a bouquet of daisies, Nash intercepted him. Trish was hitched to Nash's hip as he wore his cut, with no shirt on underneath, and proceeded to grill John about anything and everything he could squeeze in before I went ape-shit.

"How old are you?"

"You do know she's not gonna fuck you, right?"

"You better keep your hands to yourself, or I'll remove them for ya."

"You get that I'm in a motorcycle club … yeah?"

I'm sure there were about fifty other questions he'd asked, but those were a few that I caught. Thankfully, John took Nash's rudeness in stride. Even when he continued to be a jerk as I tried to slide past him to leave on my date. We lapsed into a short argument when he'd refused to budge. Once I was finally permitted to leave, I kissed Trish bye-bye, elbowed Nash in the gut, and bound down the steps, hand-in-hand with John.

Sadly, though, John and any other man I've attempted to date never stuck around long. Part of me knew it was because of Nash and his overprotective ways. While the other part of me realized if they couldn't handle my brother, they wouldn't be able to handle me, my daughter, or my family—which will always consist of Nash and his club brothers.

Fruitlessly, I try to smile at the thought of that big lug, but it leaves a bitter taste in my mouth. The blonde with the soulful brown eyes, who was sucking on Wes's neck, takes the seat across from me and our knees almost touch.

"Hi." She waves meekly as if I might kick her face in for speaking to me. I don't seem like that big of a bitch, do I? God, I hope not.

"Hello." I force a smile.

"So, she can speak," Wes groans, fingers threaded in a headful of hair as he thrusts into a wet, eager mouth that moans around his girth.

For a moment, I sort of envy Wes. He's got four hot women at his beck and call. If roles were reversed and I had four sexy men, I'd revel in the attention, too. Heck, I *have* done that plenty of times, so I can't really judge him without being a hypocrite, can I? Guess not.

Ignoring the show, I turn my sights back to the soulful-eyed blonde. She's genuinely smiling at me, her legs tucked to the side, hands folded in her lap.

"I'm Candi with an 'i.'" She offers her hand, and we do a quick shake. Her palms are so soft.

"It's a pleasure to meet you, Candi with an 'i.' I'm Gwen."

"That's good. I'm glad my girls can play nice," Wes interrupts, and I purposefully roll my eyes. He chuckles, which is odd since he's busy getting a blow job. I can't say I've ever met a man less affected by one. Maybe they're not his thing? Oh, why do I even care? That's right ... I don't.

I mean, he is stupidly good looking in a tall, lean, fitness model kind of way. Even his dirty blond hair is tousled in a perpetually sexy, just-crawled-out-of-bed-after-a-long-night-of-fucking way. And you already know about those ridiculously gorgeous blue eyes. None of that I care about. Nope ... not at all...

If you were to put Nash and Wes side by side, you'd observe little similarities. Where Nash is thickly muscled, Wes is more tone. Where Nash is inked head to toe, I'd be surprised if Wes has marred his body with any ink. One man has black hair while the other is blond. I'd say the only thing they have in common is their height. They're both well over six feet. Yet, if I had to be honest ... I still find them sexy in their own ways. Apparently, I don't have a type if both appeal to me. Even though I'll never admit that tiny factoid to either of them. And neither should you. They don't need their egos inflated any more than they already are. Hey, they're the ones with the bombshell blondes. I don't know about you, but I'm no bombshell. I'm just lowly ole me—nothing special.

"Soooo … Candi with an 'i,' what is it you do for a living?" I ask, trying to make small talk to pass the time. It seems harmless enough. A few feet over, Wes moans. It's deep and sensuous as his breath begins to burst in sharp pants. I don't want to say it, but he's getting close to coming. That's how most men sound when they do.

Candi, paying the rest of the car no mind, smiles kindly at my interaction. "I work for Wesley," she explains.

"As in, this?" I signal to the … um … you know … sexual stuff.

This makes her giggle as she shakes her head. "Heavens, no. I was in a pretty dicey part of the porn industry for quite a few years. Then, I met Wes and he helped me."

"Helped you how?"

Candi runs her fingers through her long locks. A troubled expression passes over her features, departing almost as soon as it arrives. "He got me out of the game. You know, I always wanted to be an actress. So when I met a man who told me I could work my way up to major films, I was stupid enough to believe him. I was young at the time, only eighteen. Long story short, a group of men ended up my pimps and used my body for profit. A few years later, at an event they forced me to attend for the porn industry, I happened to catch Wesley's eye, and he's employed me ever since."

This is quite … um … interesting … I think.

Uncomfortable with what I'm about to say, I shift in my seat. "So he bought you instead?"

"If you mean paid for my freedom, yes." She nods. "He paid for me to get an apartment. Get back on my feet. And he got me a job at one of his companies as a secretary. All of us…" She gestures to the women who are preoccupied. "We were all found by him in some way. So now we work for him."

"And you sleep with him," I blurt, tactlessly.

Candi seems to take my brashness in stride when she fluidly replies, "Yes, we sleep with him because we want to. Not because we have to. We signed our contracts willingly, which spells out every minute detail of our intimacies with Wes. And these same contracts are updated every year, for everyone's benefit."

I can't believe I'm playing into this conversation. It seems so weird that Wes *'saved'* these women, and now has them pleasuring him. It's strange, at best. Fucked up, at worst. If I ever speak to him again, I might have to ask him about this little arrangement he's got going. For now, I'm not going to dig any deeper about these quasi-contracts, because they're none of my business. Wes might have an issue with Candi imparting this information to me, and I don't want to get her into any trouble.

The roar of an orgasm thunders through the cab, and I squeeze my eyes temporarily shut at the sound. It's been over twenty-four hours since I've climaxed, and it's rare for me to wait that long. This asshole is making me more envious by the minute.

Out of the corner of my eye, I catch the woman that was between Wes's legs move to sit beside him. A flash of his deflating cock burns into my retinas before it's tucked into his jeans. I can't believe this. Less than forty-eight hours ago, I was being dissed and dismissed by Nash, and now, here I am sitting in a car full of buxom blondes and a sex machine. Jesus, if you'd have told me this weekend would end this way, I would have sworn you were fucking insane.

Candi transfers onto the seat next to me, and we cruise into further casual conversation about her life working at Wes's company. It turns out that she's twenty-six and has a two year old son. I want to ask if her son is Wes's, but bite my tongue before the question leaks out. It's not like I should care. The more we carry on, the more she divulges, as do some of the other blondes. They all seem like lovely gals, except Amanda, the cocksucker. She screams entitled bitch. You can tell by the way she lays her hand on Wes's thigh like she's staking claim. From time to time, Wes chimes in, too, which falls on my deaf ears. Even if Candi and the rest of the women are painting him out to be a do-gooder, I don't believe it for a second. He can kiss my ass. Then maybe that'd help mend a fraction of my bitterness toward him.

Hours pass, and we stop to grab a bite to eat at Taco Bell since they're open twenty-four hours. With a full belly of wannabe Mexican food and cinnamon twists, my bantering dies down, and I begin to nod off.

***

Jostled out of a dream, I'm partially awakened as my body is weightlessly carted out of the limo by something that smells clean and spicy. The attempt to pry my lids open is difficult, so I don't even try. My head lulls to the side, tucking against something sturdy, yet soft.

"It's okay, Gwen. I've got you. I'm just taking you into your room. No need to wake up," a familiar voice whispers before I'm rocked back into the dreamland. The last thing I remember is a fluffy cloud enveloping me, and a warm softness pressing to my forehead, bidding me a good night.

Chapter Nine

Day 1

A single knock at the door rouses me from my slumber. Expelling a tired groan, I flip onto my back where the plush covers rest at the hollow of my neck. Another knock resounds as bright sunlight cascades into the room from a large set of bay windows. The door soundlessly opens, and a head full of short blonde hair pokes around the corner.

"Good morning, Gwen." She smiles cheerily, although I don't recognize this particular chick. Without pause, she wades in further, leaving my door ajar.

Blearily, I sit up in bed. Resting my back on the white leather headboard that matches the clinical paleness of the room. It's triple the size of my bedroom at home.

The female stops at the foot of the bed. "How'd you sleep?" she asks, cocking her head to the side, dressed in a crisp, black pantsuit. This woman radiates intelligence as she assesses me with her penetrating gaze.

"I slept … fine. And you are?"

Jesus, does Wes ever hire someone less attractive? This blonde doesn't even exude sexuality, and here she is, still young and beautiful.

"I'm Mr. King's assistant, Zoe."

Zoe. Hell, even her name is pretty.

I'm not sure what possesses me to ejaculate words foolishly, but I can't take it back as the word vomit begins to pour. "Are you all blondes? I mean, I've yet to see anyone but blondes in Wes's company. Is he taking some of his business tips from *Christian Grey*'s handbook or something?" I run out of breath, and before I can continue, Zoe flashes me an amused smile.

"Mr. Grey's handbook?" She snickers.

"Well, yes." I shrug. "Or is this more like a *Hitler* thing? You know, blondes being supreme and all. You're not going to lock me in a cellar somewhere and kill me because I'm a brunette, are you?"

Oh God, why can't I shut up? I'm digging myself into a deeper hole, even if I do think my points are marginally valid. Okay. Maybe I should just go back to sleep and forget this ever happened. I'm behaving like a delusional idiot. *Hitler* ... *Christian Grey*? Who comes up with this shit? Me ... apparently.

Undeterred by my idiocy, Zoe shakes her head. "I can assure you, Mr. King just prefers blondes."

"Attractive ones with flawless complexions and no cellulite," I tack on.

Jesus, I really need to shut it. What in the world is my hang up?

Zoe nods. "Yes. Attractive ones. Are you done?"

For a fraction of a second, I want to ask her *'done with what?',* but I zip my lip since I'm certain she's referring to my stupidity. Hell, I just met the woman; yet here I am spouting nonsense, in a strange house, wearing nothing but my t-shirt, bra, and panties. Yeah, I can feel that my legs are bare without having to look. I've been trying to ignore the sensation, so I don't dwell on the fact that someone had to have undressed me without my permission. That's the least of my worries at this point.

Flicking my hand out, I gesture for her to carry on. "You're at Mr. King's mountain estate, where he summers. I will be here to assist you with anything you should need. Lunch was served an hour ago, but I saved you a sandwich. I hope you like turkey."

I nod, afraid that if I speak more drivel will filter out.

"Good." She stands taller, her shoulders pushed back. "Once you're presentable, you're welcome to use the phone in the kitchen to call your daughter and whomever else. However, it would be in everyone's best interest for you to keep your vacation details to yourself."

Again, I nod as she keeps on.

"Mr. King is otherwise engaged at the moment, but he will see you for dinner this evening. It's at seven, sharp. Don't be late."

Zoe pivots on her heel, headed to the door when a yell from the hallway draws our attention.

"She's here! She's here! My teacher!" a boy's voice screeches just before my door is thrown open, and a skinny, brunette teenager bounds into my room without apology.

"You're my teacher!" His eyes zero in on me as he fidgets, flinging his words with his fingers next to his temple.

"Garrett," Zoe reprimands softly, unmistakably annoyed. "I thought Dad said you could meet her tomorrow. He told you that he wanted her to settle in first."

"Don't want to wait. Wanted to meet her now." He bounces on his heels as his hands twitch like he's unable to control his excitement. It's adorable.

I smile.

From the way Garrett sways and his mannerisms, it's easy to see he's autistic. I'm not sure how severe it is, but I've worked with many autistic students in my life. It is not difficult for me to point them out, even if their behaviors are subtle. I guess that's one of the gifts of being a teacher.

"Garrett, you know you're supposed to be getting ready to go to work." Zoe slowly touches his arm, and he jerks it away, glaring at her. Perhaps touching is one of his eccentricities; most autistic people have them.

"I know what I am supposed to be doing, Zoe. I'm not stupid." He slaps the side of his head, driving his point home. Then he looks at his watch. "It's 1:15. I don't have to be at work until 2. I have time to meet my teacher."

Both sets of eyes turn toward me; Zoe's are creased with worry like she's waiting for me to bolt, and Garrett's eyes are full of hope. I choose to overlook Zoe and address Garrett since he's so freaking cute.

"I'm going to be your teacher, you say?" I smile at him as I catch Zoe visibly release a breath, her shoulders relaxing.

Garrett rocks on his heels, as he shifts from eager to shy, now that I'm addressing him. Redness dots his cheeks, and all I want to do is reach out to hug him.

Leaning over, I gently pat a section of the comforter at the end of the bed. "Would you care to sit down, Garrett?" I offer, and he meanders over, taking a seat on the edge, almost falling off. That's more than I'd hoped for.

Standing by the door, Zoe opens her mouth as if she wants to speak. Instead, I wave her off, shooing her from the room to give us some privacy. Her expression pinches for a moment before complying with my silent request. I'm sure if Garrett were uncomfortable, she would have stayed, but we're okay here. He's perfectly fine in my care.

Once the door is closed, I continue to give Garrett time to calm himself as his hands tumble nervously in his lap, and he rocks.

"Dad said you were going to be my teacher this summer. He promised me you'd look like *Lara Croft*," he says.

Covering my mouth, I quash a giggle. *Lara Croft*? So cute.

I hate to say it, but if Wes brought me here to help his son, that's so much better than the dirtier things I thought he might have in store for me. This, I can handle. This, I'd love to handle. I adore teaching. Especially children with a thirst for knowledge, as I feel Garrett has. Which is apparent by his bursting into my room.

Holding my arms outward, I draw his attention to me and away from his hands. "How do I fair? Do I look like *Lara Croft*?" I beam, showing all my teeth, and he laughs a little.

"Yes." He bobs his head. "Dad never breaks a promise. I already knew you'd look like her."

To hear him speak so kindly about his father makes my heart warm. Damn. And here I thought Wes was some fatheaded jerk. Maybe that's the way he wants people to perceive him because it's definitely a different picture than his son and employees are painting for me. The man's a Rubik's Cube with pants.

"So, you don't have a thing for blondes, too?" I crack, and Garrett's baby blue eyes light up just before he breaks into a fit of contagious laughter. Soon, I've got tears streaming down my cheeks, as does he.

"What's so funny in here?" A tickled voice startles us both. We jerk our heads toward the door to see Wes, in a white button-down and black dress slacks, enter without knocking.

"Oh, Dad," Garrett quickly rubs the remaining tears from his eyes as his hands fidget near his face. "She's funny, and she looks like *Lara Croft*. Can we keep her all year?" The edge of longing in Garrett's sweet voice tugs at my heartstrings, and part of me wants to say yes, even though I've just met the kid. There's just something about him that I can't help but love. Call it mother's intuition.

Wes checks his watch. "You have half an hour until work, bud. I think you need to finish getting ready so you can meet with Blake in ten minutes. You don't want to be late, do you?"

That gets Garrett moving as he shoots up from the bed like a rocket, gives me a hurried goodbye, kisses his dad's cheek, and then he's racing out of the room to go to work.

Once he's out of earshot, I give Wes *'the eye'*. You know the one I'm talking about. It's the one that says you'd better spill now, or I'll cut off your balls, boil them, grind them in the blender, and then feed them to you through a straw.

Wes takes my expression seriously when he sits in front of the window on a bench that I just realized is there.

The contrast of his dark pants and all of that white is sorta beautiful.

I raise a quizzical brow, and Wes must grasp it when he's the first to speak. "So now you've met Garrett."

"Your son," I observe.

"Yes. My son."

Tucking the blanket around my waist, I set my hands on my lap. "The one I'm going to be teaching?"

"Uhhh…" He shifts uncomfortably. "Yeah … about that. We were supposed to discuss our arrangement tonight over dinner. It seems Garrett couldn't control himself long enough for me to handle this situation delicately."

Meeting Wes's gaze, I hold my head high to show him that I won't be toyed with. "By situation, do you mean me '*unexpectedly*' losing a race then '*magically*' being brought here to teach your autistic son. A son who knew I was coming, for what appears to be a lot longer than a day."

This whole situation is starting to fall into place. Wes just happening to talk to Tony, being overly nice to me, losing an easy race earlier in the day. Then he threw that exciting bet into my lap last minute, so I didn't take the time to think it through or confer with my trio. It's all a little too fishy. If I had paid closer attention to the circumstances at the time, I'm sure it would have risen some sort of suspicion. But I was too high on my wins, too focused, too stupid. Let's face it; he took advantage of my winner's high before purposefully stealing the most significant victory right out from under me. It's brilliant if you spell it out. At the same time, it's also kind of fucked up. Not that I should be surprised. Maybe Wes *is* the kind of slimeball I figured he was from the get-go.

Tearing me from my tumbling thoughts, Wes's tone grows harsh. "We don't use that word in this house."

Huh?

"Which word?"

"Autistic," he clarifies.

Um … okay…

"Then which word do you use?"

"Uniquely perfect," he enunciates, giving me zero chance to laugh or wonder if he's toying with me.

By the unyielding expression on his face, I can tell he's truthful, and it's one of the most oddly adorable things I've ever heard a man say in my entire life. Doesn't call his son autistic, but says he's uniquely perfect? I couldn't agree more. It's true.

A small sliver of iron bitterness falls from my heart, and a genuine grin quirks from the corner of my mouth. "I like that better."

"So do I." He smiles in return, his posture less tense than before.

Confidently, I get down to brass tacks. "Would you care to elaborate on your little hoax?"

"Hoax?" he plays dumb.

Oh … no … no … no. He doesn't get to act all innocent. No way.

My grin is quickly replaced with tight lips when I ask, "Do I look stupid to you?"

Without pause, Wes shakes his head. Smart man.

I keep on. "You totally rigged the race so you'd win. Loading down with NOS—which is just plain dangerous. You knew you'd smoke me. You'd planned this outcome out to a T, didn't you? And I was the fool to fall for it."

Wes pinches the bridge of his nose for a moment, dipping his head down, staring at his feet. A few beats pass before he glances back up, garnering eye contact. "You're right," he sighs. "I did orchestrate it, but you're no fool. I wouldn't go through this much trouble for a fool."

The strange compliment and confession is both bitter and sweet as I swish it around in my mouth like an expensive wine before swallowing it down. It lands into my stomach like a boulder, leaving me uncertain of how to respond.

Taking a deep breath, I choose to let these emotions go. There is no reason to focus on the past when I can't change it. I need to live in the here and now, and we have to move forward. Staying angry about something isn't going to fix a damn thing. God, I just wish letting it go was easier said than done. I'm still edgy, even if I don't wanna be.

Another deep breath in and slowly out helps center me further. "Okay ... in the respect of full disclosure, I want you to lay your expectations on the table for me. Even if you orchestrated this bet, knowing I'd lose, I'm still honorable enough to push that fact aside and do what I promised. But no bullshit. I don't like to be jerked around." My words come out fiercer than I intended, then again they work just as well.

Wes looks impressed. "Straight and to the point. I like that." He smirks.

Expression stern, I wait for him to deliver me his expectations on a silver platter.

"My son is smart and capable. But his reading and writing skills are not where we want them to be. Garrett desires to become a fully functioning adult so he can go away to college. He's quite independent. However, all of his previous teachers couldn't seem to get him to focus long enough to read more than a paragraph or two. We've gone through five tutors over the course of three years. While some of them could help him in certain areas, he hasn't found a teacher that inspires him enough to work on reading and writing. The most I've ever seen him write in one sitting is a paragraph. He gets frustrated when he can't remember how to spell a word, or his writing isn't legible enough. He's my perfectly imperfect son, who is very motivated to do better with his life. Yet, parts of him are holding him back." Wes finishes on a weighted sigh, rubbing the back of his neck like that just took a lot out of him.

"So that's where I come in," I note.

A soft grin passes his features for a split second. Then it's gone the next. "Correct. That's where you will come in. He's brilliant in math and the arts. But he's not going to become an independent adult without the basics. That's why I'd like for you to tutor Garrett two hours a day, five days a week, while you're here. For the summer, I found him a job at the local library. I figured it'd be a good way for him to gain some experience and more self-confidence. Plus, it's simple work. If this expands into a love for books, then it's an added bonus."

An itty bitty part of me is rejoicing in Wes as a parent, even though I haven't seen him in action. Nonetheless, a proactive parent ranks high in my books. You can't imagine how many students I see fall through the cracks because their parents don't care. They figure once their kids hit high school they're old enough to handle things on their own. That's wrong on so many fronts, because high school is where parents should be pushing their children harder while being more involved. Why? Because it shows their support, since high school isn't always easy, and it also keeps kids from slacking or getting into mischief. Teenagers are notorious for putting themselves in sticky situations, both in life and their school work. I can tell from the get-go which students' parents are active in their lives, and those who aren't. Frankly, I wish more parents were like Wes.

Tossing my thoughts into the wind, I dial back into our conversation. "Is there a reason you didn't address this sooner? You know ... actually talked to me about it?"

"Would you have listened?" he contests.

He's got a point...

"Maybe?" I squeak, lifting my shoulders.

Wes gives me a look that tells me he knows I'm full of it, and he's probably right. "I'd venture to guess, no. It's no secret that I repulse you, Gwen."

I wouldn't quite say *repulse*...

"What do you expect with the way you present yourself?" It's true. He's got millionaire playboy written all over him.

It's the first time I've seen it happen, so I'm not sure how to react when Wes is the one to roll his eyes at me. It's kind of funny, yet kinda not. I ignore it altogether as he responds. "I'm a self-assured, self-made man, Gwen. I make no buts or excuses about it. I know what I like, and what I don't. Who I like and who I don't. And I refuse to spend any of my time doing shit that I don't enjoy."

I can respect that ... I guess.

Not wanting to focus on Wes, since it takes away from the real reason I'm here, I revert back to our previous conversation. The one that will do us some good, and get me away from thinking of Wes in any kind of virtuous light. It's bad enough that his son, and employees are trying to inadvertently sway me. Now he's sort of doing the same. I have to stand strong. Women who find men like him charming will easily fall into the limitless trap of despair and heartbreak. I don't think I could ever fall that deep, but you can never be too careful when it comes to your emotions. Self-preservation is a beautiful thing. Trust me. I've started shifting into that very mode because of Nash. I don't want to have to do that because of Wes, too. That's just too much to handle right now.

"Sooo," I drawl, shifting my panty covered bottom in bed. "Two hours a day of tutoring Garrett, then?"

"That is correct. We have a makeshift classroom that you'll tutor him in during the day, and at night, you'll accompany me."

I don't like the sound of this.

"To where?" I try to remain poker-faced.

"Events. Dinner. A movie night ... you know ... whatever." He waves dismissively like it's not a big deal. Maybe to him, it's not.

"What about Garrett?" I ask, only because I have an inkling that Garrett might be our only buffer. Not that I'd want to use him that way since I already like him. But if we're busy doing adult things then what is Garrett up to anyhow?

Wes grins both wicked, and sweetly at my question. *Crap.* "What about him? Garrett spends most of his nights sucked into the teenage world of video games."

Ah...

"*Lara Croft*?" I probe.

He laughs loudly, and his eyes crinkle. It's oddly comforting, like a freshly baked chocolate chip cookie straight from the oven. *Shit* ... this isn't good.

"Yes. *Lara Croft*," he replies, now chuckling under his breath. "She's his dream girl."

"And you promised him a teacher that looks like her."

"I might have." His charming, flirty smile makes its appearance, and I stamp down the need to cover my eyes and shield myself from it. He really is quite handsome. Too handsome.

"You did," I snicker.

"Okay. I did," he concedes, shaking his head in amusement. "My son is like his father; he pays more attention if he's in the company of beautiful females."

"Except he likes a fictional badass brunette, while you prefer, attractive, twenty-something blondes," I remark calmly.

"And that bothers you, doesn't it?"

My brows furrow. "What does?" I hope he isn't referring to what I think he is.

"Me desiring twenty-something blondes. I can tell it's an issue for you. You've spent a lot of time judging me on that fact. Do you ever see beyond looks? I do."

My temper flares, and I'm ready to tell him off, but he's not finished.

"You focus on these women being blonde, instead of being survivors that I happen to enjoy spending my time with."

Oh please. Insert the biggest eye roll in the history of the world. That's what I'm doing on the inside right now. Not wanting to come across disrespectful by showcasing it outwardly.

"Survivors?"

Wes nods sharply, his blonde waves shifting on his head. Then he stands and moves toward the door. "I have over fifty women that I've employed after meeting them in less than desirable circumstances, Gwen. Are they mostly

bottled blondes? Yes. They are. Are they attractive? Sure."
He shrugs one shoulder. "But some of them were in
domestic abuse relationships, others drug addicts, some in
the porn industry, and that's only to name a few. They are
strong women who I chose to personally help because I
found them sexy. Does that make me an asshole? Perhaps.
But they appreciate what I've done for them. It's a
mutually beneficial relationship. I take them with me to
events to open their worlds to more possibilities. I try to
help them get connections, to better their lives beyond my
reach. Now, I'm sure you're wondering … where does my
fucking them come into play?"

Damn, he's right, I am. Though I refuse to ask,
because he's on a hundred mile an hour tangent to scold
me and put me in my rightful place. And damn if it isn't
working, at least a bit. He's making me sound like a
judgmental bitch, and maybe I am.

He's not done. "I fuck them because I like it, Gwen.
Can you honestly say that if you had thirty men you're
attracted to at your beck and call at all hours of the night,
that you wouldn't rejoice in the fact that you could fuck
them anytime you wanted?" He waits for my reply, but
when I refuse to give him one, he coasts along, undeterred.
Jerk.

"I love tits and ass like the next man. Money doesn't
change that for me. I loved women before I was rich. It
just so happens that with money comes opportunities.
Opportunities that I've used to mutually benefit all parties
involved—including yourself."

"What?!" I shrill.

Where do I come into this all of a sudden? We're
talking about him and his gaggle of buxom blondes. Not
me. I don't fit into that puzzle anywhere. No siree bob.

Wes takes another step toward the door and cuffs his hand around the knob. "Sure, I rigged the race, because I wanted you in my home. I'm not going to deny that. But, I'm sure you'll see that this is just as mutually beneficial. All of your meals for the next thirty days will be covered. Clothes paid for. And your daughter, as of this morning, has two years of college paid in full, books included. I told you before, Gwen, that I'm a fair man. It's not ideal that you're repulsed by me or those in my employ. But maybe you should stop focusing on their looks, and pay more attention to your job."

Talk about a slap in the face. *Jesus!* Harsh, much?

He opens the door, and just as he steps through it, he tosses his final words over his shoulder, eyes resolute. "I'll see you at seven sharp, in the dining room. Zoe will be by later to take you shopping and show you the classroom. Think about what I said, Gwen. If it makes you feel any better, I'm happy you're here." And with that, he's gone, shutting the door in his wake, not giving me a chance to respond. Not that I could, anyhow. I'm kind of struck speechless.

What the fuck was that?

Look, I'm a big enough person to recognize that he might have a point. Then again, I'm out of my element here. Thrust into a month long *'vacation'* that I never actually wanted to begin with; Wes is right, we are both profiting from this. His son is getting a tutor, and my daughter is having some of her college paid for. That's awesome. A fair trade. However, that's not the issue here. It's the unknown that concerns me. *Wes* concerns me. What if he decides he wants to walk on the wild side for a moment and attempt to sleep with a brunette who's in her thirties? I won't be at his beck and call like his actual employees. If they want to do that, fine. They enter into that agreement with full knowledge of what's expected. While I'm here, diving into the black abyss, wondering if I'm going to be eaten by sharks or not. It's scary and thrilling in equal parts.

Well, now that I'm finally alone, I guess I should get outta bed, look around this room a bit more, and clean up. By the looks of this place, I'd bet that there's a massive tub waiting behind that door right over there. You see the one I'm talking about? It's right next to that matte white dresser that has a white porcelain cat adorning its top. I'm pretty sure this sterile room is supposed to seem modern and chic. Yet, it leaves me feeling cold and aloof. Remind me to buy a throw blanket and a couple of accent pillows when I go shopping with Zoe later today. If I'm going to be sleeping in here, my eyes need a bit more color.

But, for now … shoo, will ya? And give me some time to snoop. I don't need any witnesses. I'll see ya later on.

Chapter Ten

Still Day 1

"Come on, Zoe. Do I really need this many outfits?" I groan, shoulders slumped as I pad my way back into the fifth dressing room of the day. This is getting ridiculous. I'm not much of a shopper. That's probably why my mom and daughter end up buying most of my clothes, or I just order them online and hope they'll fit. Wes did say, he likes what he likes, and knows what he doesn't … or something along those lines. Well, I'm the same way. And these dresses—yes, as in plural—are not something I like. Especially not this one.

Stepping in front of the full-length mirror, I cringe. God, look at me. I'm dressed like Wes's women, except I'm not as tall as most of them, or as thin. I'm average, everywhere. A size eight, with C cup breasts. Not Double Ds. My ass is average, stomach mostly flat, and I do have some curves. But I definitely can't pull this off. If I bend over, you would get a full shot of my ass and birth canal. The damn thing hits me mid-thigh. Plus, the neck scoops too low, and there's no back; I couldn't wear a bra if I wanted to. To make matters worse, it's flaming red. I'd stick out like a sore thumb. No way am I buying this. I look stupid.

"Yes. You need clothes, so get the dress," Zoe commands from the opposite side of the door before tossing another garment over the top. "And try this one on, too."

"Fine," I gripe, carefully peeling this dress off to try on another red one that she brought.

Unhappily, we play this little song and dance for another half an hour. The more I try on, the more I detest my body, dresses, and clothes shopping. I should have just stayed at Wes's.

Earlier today, after I'd bathed in a giant tub, which I told you he'd have, Zoe was in my room waiting for me. I'd thrown on some clothes, a little makeup, and then made my phone calls before we headed out. Zoe stood idly by throughout the conversations—monitoring them like a prison guard or something. It was annoying. At least, the phone calls were short and to the point. Trish was more than happy I was going to be gone. Not sure why, but she seemed genuinely pleased to hear it. Though, I can't say the same about Fat Larry, who was both equally relieved to hear from me and pissed off about the situation. We didn't talk long because I couldn't take the complaining anymore. I've made my bed, and now I have to lie in it. I just wish he'd understand that. Unfortunately, he doesn't, and I don't think he ever will.

With an armful of clothes, I make my way out of the dressing room and toss them at Zoe. She catches them, ejecting a loaded, *"uhhh"* from the weight.

"You decide which ones Wes wants me to wear or not. Like I've already told you, I don't like clothes shopping. And I don't see why we can't just buy some jeans, and summer dresses from *Old Navy*. They're a lot cheaper, and I like their clothes," I express, shuffling around Zoe, headed to the front of the store. "I'll be outside," I call over my shoulder and see myself to the bench that's directly across from the entrance.

The first three stores I wasn't such a sourpuss, until I saw the astronomical amount of money that was placed on Wes's credit card. Now I've decided I'd rather live in blissful ignorance. If I don't physically choose the clothes, then my guilt doesn't bother me as much.

Ten minutes later, Zoe is handing over another shopping bag to our driver to store in the limo. Plopping down beside me on the bench, she bumps her shoulder playfully into mine. "You know, I'm kind of glad you don't like shopping," she remarks.

That catches me off guard. "Um ... why?"

Zoe exhales a long breath, relaxing against the seat back. She crosses her lithe legs. "Every time Wesley hires a new *employee,* he sends me to help them shop for a new wardrobe." The way she explains it, she doesn't sound too keen on shopping with these *employees*—a.k.a: hot blondes.

"It seems like you know your way around here. I can see why he would," I praise, trying to suck some of the mounting tension out of the air.

She folds her hands demurely in her lap and nods. "Yeah, I suppose that is the correct assessment. But I have to say you're the first who hasn't cared a bit about what we buy. And more importantly, about what we spend. I'd fair to guess that you're uncomfortable spending the money we have today."

She's right about that.

"I'm not into designer clothes. Some people are, and that's fine. I just prefer my jeans and t-shirts. And I have no desire to be dolled up, poked, or prodded to appear more beautiful for someone that I barely know. I'm plenty comfortable in my own skin. I don't need someone else's approval." *Except Nash's*, I silently tack on.

Her instant response is a light chuckle. "I want to say I feel sorry for Wes since I know he's going to have his hands full with you. But I don't feel sorry for him at all. You're nothing like the rest of the women."

That's quite the compliment.

"You mean these employees that Wes sleeps with? I'm guessing that you're nothing like them either. At least, I don't peg you for a chick who spreads her legs to make her employer happy."

Over the course of the day, I've gotten a read on Zoe. From what I can tell, my assessment is spot on. She doesn't overdo her makeup or wear hooker heels. She's classy, refined, and perhaps a bit too stuffy. But she's not snobbish or rude. I'd say that Wes picked a perfect assistant. I'd hire her, too, if I were him.

Zoe awards me with another chuckle. "It's not for his lack of trying," she snickers, tucking a piece of her hair behind her ear. "I think that Wes has come to realize that I'm not interested. Unlike the others. After working for him for seven years, which is far longer than any other female, he's grown to respect me and my indifference to him."

Yep. I think I'm starting to love this chick. Not love-love, but I feel like we could be friends … maybe. I guess what I'm saying is I get her. She can't be oblivious to Wes's charms, yet she's smart enough to put herself in check. I admire that.

"Well, that's enough about me," she states matter-of-factly as she pushes up from the bench before her eyes cast down upon me. "We should head back. I think we've got plenty to tide you over for the next month. At least six dresses, a few pairs of shoes, accessories, some day clothes, and if there's anything else we may need, we can always come back."

"Sounds good." I stand, then follow her through the oversized mall. I come to a sudden halt as we pass by a small furniture store.

That's right. I almost forgot. My room needs some color.

Zoe is a few feet ahead of me when she finally realizes that I'm no longer behind her. She flips around to catch me staring in the store's window. It's full of cute knickknacks.

"Did we forget something?" Her tone is friendly.

I lift my chin toward the entrance. "No offense, but my room is too white. *I* want to buy some throw pillows, and maybe a blanket to add some color."

With an extra pep in her step, Zoe grins as she enters the store before I do. "I think that's an excellent idea," she says as we wade through the tight aisles jam-packed with artisan furniture. The place is wall-to-wall home accessories, making me want to burst with joy.

Hey, I might loathe clothes shopping, but I never said I hated shopping for home goods. That's one of my favorite things to do. Especially at swap meets and garage sales. One person's trash is another person's treasure, right? Nash calls it junk, but I find them to be tiny prizes that warm my home with memories. It's sort of addictive.

As we make it toward the back, my eyes find just the perfect pillows resting on a black chair. They're orange and teal, so I tuck two of them under my arm and snatch the fluffy orange throw off the back of the same seat. Still not satisfied, I discover a blown glass blue bird and an orange crab on a nearby table. Now that should add some serious color.

"Can I take some of that for you?" a delightful, elderly woman offers, holding out her wrinkly arms.

"It's okay." I smile, not wanting to trouble her. "I've got it."

She takes a step closer. "I insist, dear. I'll set them on the counter for ya."

Not wanting to upset the sweet woman, I concede and hand over my stuff. I thank her, and just as I turn around to find Zoe, she all but smashes into me, not paying attention to where she's going.

My hands grasp her shoulders, halting her.

"Ooops. Sorry." She rights herself by dusting off her arms, then stands tall, her eyes meeting mine. "There's just so much to see in here," she states in awe.

"Yes, there is. I'm buying, so is there anything that might tickle your fancy?" I sweep my hand toward the table I found the bird and crab on. Excitement glitters in her eyes like I've never seen before.

Meekly, her hand touches her mouth, lost in thought. "Um … I probably shouldn't."

"Of course you should." I grab her by the forearm and escort her to the table. Unleashing my inner sales lady, I lift the glass sailboat and showcase it in my hand. "How about this beautiful, blown glass treasure that you can sail the seven seas with?" My attempt to sound like a pirate is pretty lame, but it gets a laugh out of her nonetheless.

"I'm not into sailboats. I think I like this better." She cradles a black, glass skull in her palm.

That's definitely not what I thought she'd pick. It's cool, though.

"That's perfect." I pluck it from her hands before she can put it back. "My treat."

On the way to the counter, I snatch a pair of *Tetris* themed socks off a shelf, and a tin of mints. I pay, and thankfully Zoe doesn't fight me on it.

With my arms loaded down with bags, Zoe and I finally make our way out to the limo where Randy, our driver, takes the goods and opens the rear door.

For some reason, Zoe is smiling brightly the entire ride home, as we chat about the weather, children, and the classroom that she'll be showing me once we return. I'm looking forward to it.

***

"Good evening, madam."

An older man wearing a tux offers his arm as he greets me just outside of the dining room. It's not quite seven, and as instructed, I'm not late. Which is remarkable, since I've spent the past hour with Zoe in the bathroom, struggling to look presentable without overdoing it. I have to hand it to her, she knows her stuff—like ways to braid my hair so it appears fancy, when all it took was five minutes, a few bobby pins, and a shit load of hairspray. I'm dressed in my new black, A-line, knee length dress that Zoe paired with simple black ballet flats. Never thought I'd see the day that I actually knew the names of fancy shoe styles … *bleh*.

"Good evening," I return, half tempted to curtsy.

Instead, I slip my arm through his and allow him to escort me to my chair in the dining room. It's immaculate and tastefully decorated in here, with three cream walls adorned with sconces. The other is a wall of windows that overlook the majestic mountainside. In the middle of the room is a long, ten person, mahogany table. Wes is already seated at the head, his back facing the impending sunset. Boy oh boy, does he look nice tonight, in a white button-down shirt, and his hair in its naturally disheveled state. He hasn't shaven, so there's a slight five-o-clock shadow on his face.

Silently, Wes watches me as I move across the room. The unusual attention makes me uncomfortable.

My escort pulls out a seat for me directly at Wes's left, leaving the rest of the vast table unoccupied. "Thank you," I express sincerely.

Wes smiles at me as he raises a hand in thank you to his employee, who then dismisses himself with a shallow bow before exiting the room.

"So how was your first day?" Wes queries, taking a flawless sip from his wine glass.

I'm so out of my element here.

Folding my hands in my lap, I sit up straight to keep myself from slouching and attempt to play whatever part it is he expects. Even though, I'm not sure what that is right now. "It was agreeable." The hollow words taste like sewage as they leave my tongue.

Wes sets his wine glass back on the table, then fiddles with his shirt collar like he's nervous. "Well, you do look lovely this evening," he compliments, tugging that collar once more before unfastening the two top buttons. Then a third is popped free, exposing a smattering of dark blonde chest hair.

The blush that creeps up my neck, and across my cheeks is impossible to stop. So I wear the crimson with poise, pretending it's not there, and that his compliment and show of chest hair doesn't flutter something strange in the pit of my stomach.

Looking away from him, I reply a whispered, "Thanks."

The bustle from a side door snaps me out of whatever I'm feeling, as two women set fancy plates in front of Wes and me.

"Bon appetite," the one comments in a French accent before departing.

Staring down at my dish, I try not to curl my lip in disgust. This cannot be my dinner. I poke it with one of my forks, not caring if it's the right one or not. There are like six lined beside me. Who even needs six forks?

"Do you not like?" Wes gently touches my arm, and I flinch, pulling away. He *can't* touch me. That's not a good idea. None of this is a good idea. Why did I agree to this in the first place? What was I thinking?

"Please tell me this is not our dinner," I remark, glancing up to meet his eyes, which are closed off as he frowns. That expression doesn't suit him, and I don't like it one bit, so I keep talking. "I'm guessing it's not. But why are you serving me caviar on bread?"

"It's a crostini," Wes corrects. "But I thought you'd like this as an opening course." He nods to my plate, and I resist the urge to roll my eyes. Men are sometimes clueless, aren't they?

Again, I poke the baby eggs with my fork. "Why would you think that? And how many courses are we talking?"

"Five."

"Five courses for just you and me?" I squeak temporarily, then swallow thickly to center myself, which is harder to do since Nash isn't here. "And where is Garrett? Doesn't he eat dinner with you?" Who doesn't have supper with their sixteen year old child? I always ate meals with Trish when she was his age.

"I thought you'd like a night of exquisite food, and some peace and quiet."

"And why would you think that, exactly? Or is that what you wanted, and assumed I would, too?" Yes, it's confirmed; men are clueless.

I can tell Wes is taken aback by my quick retort when his eyes burst wide. Then he recovers quickly, schooling his features once more. "Listen, Gwen," he starts.

Uh oh. He's going all dominant A-hole on me. I can sense it in his tone. This isn't good. My guard goes up, locking into place.

He continues. "I have a plan that I stick to when I hire new women. Zoe assists them in purchasing a new wardrobe. They attend a nice, quiet meal with me over pleasant conversation. And we end the night strolling along the edge of the pond—"

"Then you sleep with them," I tactlessly cut in.

"Now that's uncalled for," he grumbles, and my belly whirls at the sound. These stupid feelings have got to stop. "I thought we had this conversation earlier about you being judgmental."

"I'm not acting judgmental, Wesley, if I'm stating the truth. You wine and dine these women, and then they fuck you. That's how you hook them. Am I right? I mean no offense. I truly don't. I can understand how women would enjoy your company. You're an attractive man. You

135

live in a fancy house. You have a fat bankroll and connections. I'm well aware of these things. But what *you* don't understand is that's *not* me. I didn't meet you, and, no offense, swoon at your feet. If you wish to feed me while I'm stuck here, fine, I'm grateful for that. But I don't need," I shove my plate away, my temperature rising, "three hundred dollar meals … or expensive clothes." I pluck at the fabric of my dress…

"You're not going to buy me. If that's what you think might happen. I'm sorry. It doesn't work that way. I'm thrilled to be here to help Garrett, and had assumed we'd be having a nice meal with him, too." I inhale a deep breath to relax. It does little good. "If you knew me at all, or cared to know me at all, you'd respect the fact that I'm not in my comfort zone here. I don't do fancy houses, or eat baby fishies on bread." I gesture to my plate to drive my point home…

"You said that you know what you like and what you don't like. Well, so do I. I don't like eating meals that could feed an entire family for a month. I like jeans and t-shirts. And I'd be much happier eating a cheeseburger and French fries instead of something pretentious. Especially if I know that you use this tactic on all of your new employees."

Wes's face becomes redder and redder with anger the longer I blather. And just when he goes to open his mouth to respond to my word vomit, I continue with it, not allowing him to speak. I'm not done yet.

"You were right when you said I judged your employees. Frankly, that is something I'm ashamed of. But it's kind of hard to take them, or this situation seriously, when it's so, pardon my French, *fucking weird* to begin with. But, you want to know something?" I don't wait for him to answer the rhetorical question. "I think your assistant, Zoe, is amazing. She helped me today when she bought clothes that I didn't want to buy. All because she knew they'd please you. The even stranger thing is, I don't even know why I care. I shouldn't care about any of this. I should just walk out of his house, return your money, and never look back."

This time, Wes doesn't care if I'm not finished when his arm shoots out, and his hand grasps my forearm, making me forget my words. It's hot and hard against my flesh. I lose my breath. *Oh no.*

"Please don't leave." His words are surprisingly soft and gentle, filled with something I can't put my finger on.

For a couple of agonizing moments, I delight in our small connection. Then I shake out of whatever fog his touch has put me in, and push his paw off. He lets it drop without protest.

"I never said I was leaving," I remind. "I want to stay and help Garrett. But this—" I wave my hand toward the food, and then my dress. "This stuff has to stop. I won't have fancy dinners with you unless it's at some event you need for me to attend. This isn't a social thing, Wes. This is a business transaction. Nothing more, nothing less. And I'd like for you to respect that."

I'm done. I've said my peace. No more Gwen rants.

Wordlessly, Wes shoves his chair back as he rubs the back of his neck. Seconds or minutes, I'm not sure which, tick by at a snail's pace before he breaks the pregnant silence. "Okay," he sighs, his sad eyes cast downward. "I will try to be respectful. But I would like for you to realize this is also different for me as well. I hire people, they obey me, and they wish to make me happy. You do not."

The need to shout, *"You're right. I don't,"* tingles the tip of my tongue. Nevertheless, I keep my trap shut.

He keeps on. "I think it would be in our best interest right now for you to please go back to your room, and put on something you'll be more comfortable in. Then I'd like for you to please meet me back here in half an hour. I promise to fix this."

For about half a second I wonder if I should deny his reasonable request, and pout in my room for the rest of the night. Except, the seriously heart-wrenching look on Wes's face has me caving big time. I don't know if it's those puppy dog eyes or his frown, but he's sorta breaking my heart. If this is a ploy, he's a marvelous actor. If not, I'm done for. He makes me want to wrap my arms around him, and give him a hug. Which isn't good for either of us. Hell. I'm even afraid to smell him, in fear of getting turned on when I do. That sounds screwed up, I know. But it's been nearly two days since I've climaxed, and I desperately need a release—or six.

Heeding Wes's request, I agree to meet him back here in thirty minutes, then leave the dining room without another word. Down hallways, I stroll until I take the final turn to my bedroom, in this house that could comfortably fit a family of twelve with its long corridors, tall ceilings, and larger than life size.

In my room, I change into a pair of my comfortable jeans and one of my Harley t-shirts that Nash bought me on one of his runs. Then I do a once over in the mirror to pass some time before meeting Wes back in the dining room two minutes early. It's quiet in there when I return and find him staring thoughtfully out of the wall of windows just as the sun dips below that final edge of the horizon. It's stunning.

NOWHERE

Not wanting to disturb him, I wait in silence for the last of the day to bleed into night. It's like we're sharing this moment, yet, not. Since I'm not even sure he's aware that I'm standing across the room from him. He looks so peaceful, now dressed in a pair of yellow and black *Batman* pajama bottoms that I find oddly sexy. Especially the way the cotton cups his exquisite ass. He's also barefoot and wearing a cutoff black tee that exposes his toned arms. Jesus. His body is carved with diamond cut precision, and those tanned biceps are simply biteable. Damn it. No, they're not.

"Are you enjoying the show?" he teases with his back to me. I can see his reflection in the window, where our gazes clash. He smiles, and I fidget. *Crap,* I wonder if he noticed me checking out his assets. I sure hope not.

Disregarding his comment, I reply, "I'm here and ready for whatever it is you have planned … *within reason.*" I add the last just to be on the safe side.

"Great." Wes claps once then pivots on his heel and walks straight through the dining room and past me, into the hall. "Follow me," he says, and I comply.

Down the hallway I just came from, we pass room after room, including mine, until we stop in front of a set of white double doors. Wes doesn't hesitate to shove them both open at once. A massive bedroom is sprawled out before my very eyes. The bed itself has to be custom made, since there's no way they make regular mattresses that big. Jet black and stark white encompass the entirety of the space, alongside random pops of color—like the ocean blue throw pillows, or a red box that sits atop the black dresser. Since I've arrived here, I wondered if Wes had a thing for white. I figured he had to since my bedroom is colorless. Now my question has been answered. It's obvious that he has a thing for monochromatic interior design.

Wes wades into his room, and I glue my feet to the floor, refusing to budge. I understand he said he'd fix things, but he never did elaborate on what that meant. Under no circumstances did I consider him asking me to his room. There's no way I'm setting foot in that space. I'll just stand out here in the hallway, and we can carry on a conversation like this.

"Are you coming?" he calls, having disappeared from my line of sight.

"I'll wait out here!" I holler into the vastness, my voice echoing.

"Don't be silly, Gwen. Come inside."

"This is your bedroom. I most certainly won't come inside."

He sighs loudly from somewhere. "My master bedroom has a retreat built back here. It's like a small family room. Why don't you come in and see for yourself? It's harmless. I promise. I didn't think you'd want to sit in my large living room. A cozier setting seems more your speed. Or did I get that wrong?"

No, he definitely didn't get that wrong. Small, simple spaces feel more at home. It probably has to do with the fact that I've always lived in quaint places. Even though my parent's Victorian is decent in size, it's nothing compared to this. And my mother has always filled the place with knickknacks and little things that make it feel homey.

Wes's house feels impersonal. There are very few pictures anywhere. And those that are scattered around are usually made of actual art. However, from where I'm at, I can see a picture of Wes and Garrett standing together on some beach. It's resting on his nightstand. The sight of it is what breaks down my barriers enough that I willingly shuffle my feet inch by inch into the spicy, man-scented room.

Around the corner, I come to a comfy alcove that has a short couch, flat screen TV, coffee table, and chaise lounge. Along the far wall, there's a set of glass doors that open to what appears to be a private patio, complete with fire pit and loungers.

Relaxing on the couch, looking right at home, Wes unobtrusively watches me take in the space. Then he pats the cushion beside him, smiling non-threateningly at me. I take the bait and round the back of the couch to sit. It's awkward at first, but I quickly adjust to our closeness.

Taking a deep breath, I smell the aroma that encapsulates his room more potently as it emanates from him, enticing all of the pleasure centers in my brain. For a split second, I close my eyes to bask in it before stamping down the heat it percolates in my belly. One final moment, and I swallow an impending groan of sexual frustration and dial back my hormones. As predicted, I knew this would happen if I caught his scent. Smell, taste, sight, touch, and hearing—they're magical gifts that we were born with, but when they work against me to make me feel things, they steal a part of my strength—my will. It's not fair.

Unfortunately, men—beautiful, sexy, virile men— are my downfall … my kryptonite. Nash being the most tempting of them all. But right now, he's not here. Wes is. And what he's unknowingly doing to my senses is wreaking havoc over my body. It needs to chill the hell out. I knew I shouldn't have come in here because by doing so I had to let my walls down. And letting them fall is not a good thing. This … this was not a good idea.

A hand startles me as it touches my thigh, stalling my breath. "You okay?" Wes's voice is concerned.

Numbly, I nod without looking at him.

He's still touching me.

"You sure? You're breathing awfully hard. Please don't have a panic attack on me. I promise nothing is going to happen in here. I'm not going to make a move on you. It's just two business associates having a casual meal. I said I'd fix this, Gwen, and I have. Please trust me."

Okay. Alright. I can pretend that his pajama pants aren't turning me on. And that this isn't weird. Or that me being in his bedroom isn't both a turn on and off. I'm a sexual woman. I have been for as long as I can remember. No matter how many times I tell myself otherwise, it's true. If it weren't, I wouldn't be wet right now from thinking about his bed that's a few feet away. Or his hand that's on my leg, and what those fingers could do to me. Sweet Jesus, like I told ya, I'm ten ways of fucked up.

Leaning back into the couch, I ignore my naughty thoughts and focus on something else. "I'm fine. No problems. So what's up with the pajama pants?"

Wes removes his hand from my thigh to pat his own. "*Batman* not casual enough for ya? I think I've got some *Underdog* ones in my closet," he jokes, and that's all it takes for every single strand of tension to leave me, melting into a puddle on the floor. Thank heavens.

Chuckling, I turn just enough that I can sort of face him so we can talk. It's nice, even if his proximity is a bit too close for my liking. "I just never pegged ya for a cartoon pajama pants guy."

"What kind of pajamas did you think I wore?"

Evasively, I shrug. "I dunno. I have to admit you're more complex than I first thought. So I would have initially said nude. Now, I'm not so sure. But I can say *Batman* wouldn't have been any of my guesses." This time, I grin, because I can't help it. The way he's looking at me, all open and relaxed, is pleasant. Much better than a stuffy five-course dinner.

"I do sleep nude. These are just my throw on lounge clothes. I'm not much of a robe guy. My son has told me since he was little that my suit and ties were boring. So for every Christmas, and my birthday, he buys me a pair of printed pajama pants. At first, I thought they were stupid. Now, they're a tradition that I've grown to love."

Awe! That's so damn cute.

For the next half an hour, Wes and I carry on about Garrett and his quirks. From video games to hating to read, all the way to his distaste for anything green … including green jelly beans and green chewing gum. It gives me a chance to get to know Garrett a little better, and by association, Wes, too. His face lights up when he talks about his son. The love he feels is so palpable that it seems to float into the air, and capture me as well. I find myself laughing at his stories of *Underdog* pajama bottoms and Garrett's strange obsession for milk. It's warm and comforting. Before we know it, a woman pushing a hotel tray quietly enters his room and places two plates of disassembled cheeseburgers and fries in front of us, along with an array of condiments.

"I didn't know what you liked on your burger, so I told her to bring everything we had," Wes comments while assembling his burger. He's so close that our knees are a hairsbreadth apart. Except this time, I don't freak. I let it be, and create my own stacked masterpiece.

143

Just as I whisper my thank you, he lifts the ketchup bottle. "Do you want some?"

I nod.

Instead of handing it over, he squirts the ketchup into the corner of my plate. The sweetness of the gesture hits my heart a little too hard. I don't think anyone but Nash has ever done anything remotely that nice for me before. After he's done dispersing the red yumminess on my plate, he does the same to his. Then, we dig in. The burger is juicy perfection as I take bite after bite, holding back the orgasm sounds I want to unleash. It's *that* fucking good. Wes has some talented chefs on his hands. I guess that's one of the perks of being rich.

Once we're finished, I lean back on the couch and curl my legs onto the cushions to get more comfortable. Reaching over, Wes slips my shoes from my feet and tosses the black throw off the back of the couch over my legs. I'm kind of in shock at yet another domesticated gesture, so my words evade me as he begins to speak.

"Now that you're fed and relaxed, why don't you tell me more about yourself?" He, too, gets more comfortable as he hikes one leg up, so we're facing one another. His bare foot touches mine, and I'm okay with that, so I don't move.

Not a fan of talking about myself, I change topics. "Why don't you tell me more about your businesses? I've heard about your employees. Yet, you've never said what it is you do."

In hindsight, I probably should have *Googled* Wesley King before coming here, even though I'm not sure when I would have had the time. My phone didn't have range in the mountains on our way here. And afterward, he confiscated it. It was part of the deal, so I let it go without a fight. I don't use it much anyhow.

Wes appears stunned by my question when his brows jump and forehead crinkles. Maybe it's because I'm asking about him and not talking about myself. Or perhaps it's because he assumed I already knew what he did. Not sure which.

When he doesn't reply right away, I add, "If this is something I shouldn't ask, tell me."

Rapidly, Wes shakes his head. "No, no. That's perfectly fine, Gwen. I guess most women know about me, and what I do. I take it that you don't?"

When I, too, shake my head, he keeps on. "I've dipped my toes in an abundance of lucrative businesses over the years. But for the past six to seven, I've spent most of my time building partnerships with about forty different strip club owners, acting as their silent partner. I not only get a cut of their profits, but I also place my own contracted strippers in these joints to increase quality and clientele. They want to boost profits and to do that they need talent. I provide that."

Now I know why I didn't *Google* him. If I'd have known he owned a bunch of strip clubs, I would have never agreed to the bet in the first place. When they were talking legit businesses, I guessed modeling agencies or something. Not nudie joints. Although, I'm not sure why I'm surprised. I shouldn't be. Those blondes *do* look like strippers. Not that stripping is a bad thing. It pays the bills. Like I've already said about Kelly, who works in a strip club, you can't be in that business forever. Looks fade. Then what are ya gonna do?

"So the blondes sign contracts to strip in these clubs, and to be at your beck and call? Are these the only type of enterprises you're a part of? Or are there more?" I'm not being a bitch, or rude. I genuinely want to know. No judgment here.

"I mostly dabble in the strip club industry with a few side businesses as well. What I failed to mention earlier, is that after I hire these women and we have our private dinner, I then send them to be trained. Following six weeks of classes, if they turn out to be lucrative for a club, I send them to one. Which is where they dance until their contract is up and they don't wish to renew, or I pull them to work somewhere else," Wes explains.

This is interesting. Being a school teacher, I'm sure you'd think I'd be bored. Yet, I find myself intrigued by self-made business owners. Nash has run his bar for many years, as well as my mother running her shop. There's a serious appeal to it. If I had enough guts, I'd start my own business. Then again, I don't have a clue what I'd start. I'm not good at much else other than being a teacher and racing. Unless you consider having tried hundreds of sex toys to be an expertise. Then I guess I could go into the sex toy industry. Which is something I'd never do.

Wes and I chat about his businesses in more detail—the inner workings, if you will. The payments and all kinds of fascinating elements that some people never think about. I find myself truly in awe of him, and his ability to make so much money in the industry. As time wears on, I start to think about his other side businesses, and about Kelly, who, thanks to her looks, would fall into Wes's *type*. So when I bring this up to him, I don't even think twice.

"My brother, Nash, happens to be dating a blonde just like the women you associate with. She also works as a waitress in the strip club that's in the town where my parents live."

"Your brother who owns *Nowhere*, right?"

Holy fuck! How'd he know that?

Wes raises his hand to stop me before I go on a tirade, wondering how in the hell he knows about Nash! The hairs on my arm stand on end, and I sit up straight, my eyes burrowing into his, seeking answers.

"Now, before you get all bent outta shape, I wouldn't have strategically hired you if I didn't know who your family is. Yes, I'm well aware of your brother being in the Crimson Outlaws motorcycle club. I know about your mom and step-dad, too," he explains calmly.

"Then you know about Kelly, as well … Nash's girlfriend."

Wes nods, rubbing the back of his neck. This is his tell. I've already picked up on it. Whenever he's uncomfortable, he rubs there. It's sexy in a way since it gives me a fantastic view of his bicep contracting. Mmmm.

His voice draws me from ogling his arm like a hungry wildebeest. "She's … now don't get mad—"

Uh oh. When someone tells you that, it's not a good sign.

"I won't," I lie.

Wes frowns like he doesn't buy it, but continues regardless. "Kelly is one of my employees," he speaks carefully.

I grind my molars.

You've gotta be kidding me. Why don't I know this? Nash has been dating the chick for years. Wouldn't I have known she works for some millionaire playboy? Nash would surely mention that to me. Unless, he was afraid of how I'd react. It's no secret that I haven't exactly loved all of his womenfolk. Most of them I found barely tolerable.

"Seriously?" I remark, keeping my tone neutral.

More neck rubbing ensues, and he starts to fidget. It must be terrible. I *almost* feel sorry for him. *Almost* want to reach out and hug him to calm his nerves, since I can tell they're going haywire. *Almost...*

"I met Kelly about four years ago. Hold on, let me back up for a minute," he says. "I'm not sure how well you know Kelly—"

"Not very well. Apparently."

"I figured. Kelly is one of those I found in an abusive relationship. A real dirtbag who knocked her around when he got drunk. So I cleaned her up and offered her a job. She was working as a waitress at some biker rallies for me since she could never make it as a dancer. It kept her busy. Then she met your brother at an event and asked to be transferred. I gave her the okay, and that's how she ended up at the club in Chartlotteton."

An obvious question pops into my head, and I'm powerless to use restraint. "Have you slept with her?"

If looks could talk, Wes's would say, *'Duh. I sleep with everyone I can'*. So when he confirms my assumption two seconds later, it doesn't come as much of a shock. "Of course I have."

"When was the last time?" I can't help it. When I'm on a roll, I'm on a roll. Bear with me. You know you'd ask him this, too.

Fuck, more neck rubbing, and this time, Wes glances away from me to stare at the wall. If he tells me what I think he might, I'm killing Kelly as soon as I get home. It's one thing to piss me off and butt your nose into my business when you shouldn't. It's one thing to convince the one man who means the world to me that we're too codependent. But it's another to cheat on my family. My brother. The best man I know. The serial monogamist. I can already sense my mood shifting, and it's not a good sign. My hands twitch in my lap.

"Well?" I prompt impatiently when Wes keeps staring and rubbing.

"It was … maybe … six months ago?" His words come out staggered—edgy.

Oh hell no. One second, I'm seated, and the next, I'm launching myself at Wes, slapping him across the face. The sting in my palm means nothing to me as I go to swing with the other. On guard this time, Wes protects himself from another attack and grabs my hand, twisting it behind my back. Then the other goes there as he seizes it, too. Secured by brute strength, Wes's chest is now molded against me. I can feel his heartbeat pounding through my breasts, or perhaps that's mine. I can't be sure. Collectively, our lungs pump air in and out at a rapid pace. Locking eyes, I glare at him while grumbling unhappily in my throat.

I can't believe this fucker slept with a claimed woman six months ago! Who does that shit? And what kind of whore cheats on Nash? That's even more disturbing. I guess Wes doesn't really owe anything to Nash. Except man code should suggest some sort of decorum about fucking an already claimed chick, shouldn't it? I mean, whatever happened to bros before hoes? Does that not extend to men you don't know? Assisting a woman in cheating on her man is screwed up, but not as bad as the dumb bitch for doing it to begin with. Hell, I shouldn't be mad at Wes. I know this. Though, I can't seem to calm myself enough *not* to try and defend

Nash's honor. If Kelly were here, I'd be the first to knock her block off. Yeah, yeah, yeah, I know. You're probably thinking about me kissing Nash and all. So fucking what? That's different.

Wes is the first to burst this sweltering bubble of fury and aggression as his blue eyes go attractively soft. A small part of me wants to lean further into him at the knee buckling sight. It's a good thing I'm sitting down, even though I'm still pissed at him.

"Listen, Gwen, I know you're angry with me for this. But I don't actively seek out my employees with boyfriends to fuck them. That's not my thing. However, if they're throwing themselves at me, I'm not going to tell them no. I'm a man with only so much restraint. If she didn't have any, then why should I?"

I don't know. He's got a valid point, and I hate that.

Wes's words steal all of the wind out of my sails, making me suddenly tired. Today has been a long day, full of a bunch of shit. Between Garrett, Zoe, Wes, and his sex appeal that seems to cloud the entire room, I'm nearly tapped out.

The hands securing mine loosen some but don't let go. Being this close to Wes has his scent capturing my attention again. This time, I'm struck defenseless when the needy whore who lives deep inside my soul decides I need a little more of … *something.*

Instinctively, I find my nose inching closer to the sexy curve of his neck. Wes grumbles lustfully in his throat as I rub my face there, reveling in the intoxicating spices.

"Your smell is incredible," I babble stupidly, taking in another long, luxuriating breath. My pussy takes notice of our proximity and its lack of play time when it throbs involuntarily.

Even if this is *oh so wrong,* I can't seem to give a damn right now as I continuously nuzzle my nose against Wes. The feeling of his flesh on mine, the way his body twitches when I touch it, and his hands as they tighten to tug me a bit closer, force me to bite back a moan.

A predatory rumble battles in his chest. "You're making my dick hard, Gwen. You either stop this now, or I'm taking you to bed and eating your pussy 'til the sun comes up." The darkness in his tone both excites and makes me shiver all at the same time. Even my pussy loves the idea as it gets wetter and my nipples harden, eager to be toyed with.

My nuzzling persists as I bite my lip, wanting to taste his skin. Is it salty? Sugary? Mmmmm … I wonder…

"Gwen, I'm serious," he's pained. "I … fuck … Gwen … Stop."

Abruptly, everything is over. Wes is releasing me and yanking himself to stand as he pants for breath. The stout tent in his bottoms forces me to stare, and I wantonly lick my lips.

Shit, this isn't right. That dirty woman in me is taking over. This can't be happening now. This isn't me. He's a male slut. I … I … what was I thinking?

Without saying a word, I spring up from the couch and dash from the room. Guilt floods my system as my bare feet pound the hardwood and tile floors all the way to my bedroom. I vaguely hear Wes hollering for me to stop, but I don't listen.

In the safety of my room, I slam my door shut and throw my body against it, sliding down to the floor in shame. Dropping my head as tears of humiliation threaten to slip free, I slide my fingers through my hair. Damn it, I smelled him and let him touch me. Why did I do such a thing? It had to have been those cute pants, and all of that sensory overload. He fed me that yummy food and was honest when he spoke. Everything turned me on. Hell. I'm *still* turned on.

More guilt slices me like a knife as I wallow a bit longer, trying not to cry. I have to keep everything professional between us. No more attraction to Wes. His charms cannot work on me or the whore that's burrowed herself into my soul...

Steeling my emotions, I push up from the floor with renewed strength. First, I've got to fuck my pussy into oblivion with my vibrator. Then I need to get some rest. It's going to be a busy day tomorrow. Hopefully, Wes will forget this ever happened. I know I'm going to try.

Wish us whatever luck you've got.

Goodnight.

Chapter Eleven

Day Two

Leisurely pacing the long dock barefoot, I listen to Garrett read to me as he sits on the edge with his feet swishing in the water. Afraid of drowning, Zoe is sunbathing on a nearby lounger that's sinking into the white sand beach.

"*'Got to go, Bob. Nice hang'*," Garrett recites *Deadpool*. "*'S'Cool the horse tranquilizer is kicking in'.*" He chuckles under his breath, and I catch him shaking his head in amusement as he continues down the comic book page. " *'When he passes out, please put one of those Dog Cones around his neck'.*" Garrett snickers again, wind bustling through his hair. "*'You paid cash. So sure…'*"

No sooner than my eyes fluttered open this morning, did I have an excited sixteen year old welcoming himself into my room. It was a good thing I wore pajamas to bed.

"Time to learn, Ms. Gwen. Time to learn!" Garrett shouted, eagerly flinging his words next to his temple using his fingers. Which looks a lot like he's trying to cast a spell into the air as he concentrates on what he wants to say.

Flipping onto my back, I groaned, teasingly. "Come, on, Garrett; just another five minutes."

Garrett was having none of that when he yanked my covers off the bed and dropped them into a pile on the floor. "No, Ms. Gwen. I have to work today at the library. I need to learn now," he explained. And with that, I poured out of bed, scurried into the bathroom, tossed on a pair of shorts and a blue tee before tying my hair up into a ponytail before starting my day.

"Breakfast first, Ms. Gwen," Garrett said as he escorted me to the kitchen where he ate a bowl of *Lucky Charms* sans the green clovers that are magically delicious. He'd picked them out beforehand, as I ate a bagel on the stool beside him.

Afterward, we headed to the classroom, which isn't anything more than a white room with four walls, one window, a dry erase board, and two desks—one for him and one for me. It's blah, and not conducive for learning. So I decided we were going to have class outside today on the deck. It's beautiful out here at a balmy sixty-five degrees without a cloud in the sky.

We've been outside for a few hours, moving from one comic book to the next. At first, I'd tried to peak Garrett's interest with a *Harry Potter* novel. Nope. Didn't work. Then, I tried another tactic. I sent Zoe out to collect some comic books at this shop in town that we'd passed yesterday. Once she returned, I promised Garrett that if he read five of them to me nonstop, I'd give him a prize. Those *Tetris* socks I purchased yesterday are for him. I was just going to give them as a gift, but why do that when they can be earned? The motivation seems to be working. He's almost finished with comic number four. Apparently, his past teachers were idiots, because it took me less than a day to have him reading aloud. And not only that; he does it quite well. There's something about the way he holds the pages of the book that keep him from having to twitch or throw his hands as he talks. It's a damn good feeling to know he's moving in the right direction. At the end of the week, we'll shift into writing. But for now, we're gonna have fun doing this.

Leaving Garrett to read more *Deadpool*, I walk off the dock and over to Zoe, who's chilling in a sundress. "Are you getting any color?" I ask just as the back door opens and a shirtless Wes saunters out in a pair of running shorts.

My mouth literally hangs open at the sight. Holy fuck! Look at those abs! Nash has abs; they're thick and yummy as they ripple. But Wes's abs are like a fucking washboard of eight. Yes, *eight*. Who has eight ridges? Evidently, him! Sweet Jesus! And I was so very wrong. He does have tattoos. One on his pec, and something across his stomach. Umm … www-wo-wow.

I swallow to keep from drooling down my chin.

"You might wanna close your mouth and stop staring," Zoe suggests while giggling, and I comply, looking away from all that maleness. I haven't seen or spoken to Wes since last night when I ran from his room. Is that why he's out here? To show me what I'm missing. Because if it is, consider me schooled. His body be bangin'.

"Wesley," a high-pitched chicky voice calls, and I turn my attentions briefly back to him as two blondes in 'Band-Aid bikinis' exit the house.

"Don't let them bother you." Zoe touches my arm, stealing my attention.

"What? Why would they bother me?" I lie through my teeth.

I can't help it; they do irritate me. Especially after what I found out about Kelly last night. That little fact I still haven't decided what I'm gonna do about yet. Nash deserves to know. And my fist is very excited about the prospect of becoming intimate with her stupid fucking face. Yep, I'm not bitter about it at all … *Nope.*

Zoe eyes me like she knows I'm full of myself. "It does bother you. You were basically melting into a puddle of goo before those women came out. Now you're sneering."

I am? Crap … *I am.* With effort, I school my features.

"Hey, bud." I watch Wes stride across the dock and sit beside his son. "What'cha readin'?"

Garrett and Wes carry on for a bit as the blondes stand in wait at the edge of the dock like good little puppies.

To keep my sanity, I tug the towel off the back of Zoe's chair and lay it in the sand before plopping down on it. "I don't know why they bother me, but they do. You don't, of course. I like you."

Zoe pats my shoulder in sympathy. "You like Wes. It's okay. He's a good looking guy."

What?!

I glare at her as she grins. "I do not like Wes. I happen to have feelings for someone else from back home."

Sure, he's hot and loves his son, which is attractive, but I barely know the guy. And I definitely don't like him in any significant way. I don't do insta-love shit. That's all fairytales, and I live in the real world.

The backdoor opens again, and one of Wes's chefs comes ambling down the steps carrying two wicker picnic baskets.

I incline my head toward the woman. "What's she doin'?"

Wes stands from the deck, pulling Garrett along with him. They look so damn cute together, father and son.

Zoe shrugs. "I dunno. We usually have lunch in the kitchen. And Wesley eats in his office."

Wes and Garrett grab the baskets from the woman, then their gazes cut to us. "Ms. Gwen and Zoe, come and eat with us!" Garrett waves us over.

For a moment, I glance to Zoe, and she looks back at me as we share a look of disbelief. Then we both walk over to the group.

"A picnic?" Zoe asks Wes, taking the words right out of my mouth.

Wes shrugs coolly, tagging one of the hot blondes around the neck and yanking her close. Bile rises in my throat. "Since Tonya and Terri were already here, I thought we should share a meal together. And because Gwen decided to teach Garrett outside, I figured we should have a picnic outdoors. Does that answer your question, *Zoe*?" Wes says her name, yet his eyes linger on me, as if he's not speaking to anyone else.

It becomes stranger as Wes's gaze dips to my breasts, legs, and then back up again, leaving a trail of goosebumps in his wake. I visibly shiver, and Wes takes notices as he grins like a cocky bastard. *Jerk.*

"Come on, you guys!" Garrett calls from across the pond. Shit. I didn't even realize he'd moved.

Wordlessly, we follow Garrett until he picks the perfect patch of grass for us to eat on, next to a row of trees. Then the guys pull two blankets out of the baskets and stretch them over the land. Zoe, Garrett, and I take one while Wes and his babes use the other.

My mothering instincts kick into full drive as soon as we're seated. I dive into the baskets to dish out the food until everyone is settled and happily eating. Then I purposely sit with my back to Wes and his chicks, so I don't have to see them. I've already caught him running his hand up one of their legs. It's better this way. Especially since he's still shirtless, and I can't control my eyes. Those abs are ridiculous. It can't be held against me that I want to lick them from top to bottom, swirling my tongue along those tight ridges. It's a natural reaction. You wanna do it, too. Don't deny it.

"So how are you liking the house, Ms. Gwen?" Garrett is the first to speak as a dash of mayonnaise cakes his cheek. I rub it away with a napkin, and he grins hugely at me, his mouth still full of food. He's so freaking cute. Before pulling away, I ruffle his wild hair, and he laughs a little as his body twitches. Beside him, Zoe smiles at us.

Not sure of how I should respond, so I play it simple. "It's pleasant."

"I saw that you added a crab, and some pillows to your room," he notes, and I nod, taking a bite of my turkey sandwich.

I swallow down my food. "Yup. Zoe helped me shop for it yesterday."

"How do you know Gwen has new stuff in her room, bud?" Wes inquires sternly, and I visibly watch Garrett clam up, his eyes shifting weirdly and his hands twitching so badly that he drops his carrots. I pick them right off the blanket, grab Garrett's shaky hands, and give him back his food without letting go. I meet Garrett's blue eyes that are bouncing every which way.

"Garrett," I coo, and his eyes finally stop twirling as they settle on mine. "Your dad is just asking a question. It's okay."

Everyone is unusually quiet while Garrett and I get his reaction under control. Slowly, his body calms, and he stops twitching. Kindly, I grin at him to convey that everything's going to be alright. It must work because it doesn't take but a few minutes to get him back to his level of normal. Once I release him, he takes a bite of carrot.

Wes clears his throat. "Gwen, I—"

"This morning I … I went into Ms. Gwen's room to wake her up. I saw her crab and pillows," Garrett flings his words next to his temple using his fingers, as he looks at his dad. Then his gaze shifts to me. "They're very pretty, Ms. Gwen. I like the blue and orange. Blue's my favorite color. I'm glad you didn't pick green."

A giggle slips from my belly. "Is this because you don't like to eat green things? So you don't like the color either?"

Garrett blinks rapidly for a few moments, looking deep in thought. He chews his lip. "I … No, Ms. Gwen. I don't mind the color green. But green isn't your color. You're too pretty."

"Garrett," Wes warns lightly.

"What, Dad? She is very pretty. I've always loved *Lara Croft*, but you're even prettier than she is. Gwen kind of looks like Mom, doesn't she, Dad?"

Garrett's words are innocent enough. However, the eerie silence that descends upon the group tells me that mentioning Garrett's mother is a bit of a sore subject. Although, Garrett doesn't seem to notice the uncomfortable mood when he merely takes another bite of carrot then keeps talking.

"My mom was real pretty, Ms. Gwen. She left when I was six, so I don't remember her. But Dad has pictures of us. And some of them that he showed me are of them when they got married. My mom wore a beautiful dress. Too bad Dad doesn't still have it. I'm sure it'd fit you."

"Garrett, that's enough!" Wes snaps like a twig, shooting up from his blanket and moving across the yard to pace. Garrett looks at me like he doesn't know what's going on.

I'm not sure what to say, so when Zoe comes to the rescue, I'm relieved. "Hey, Garrett. I think it's time we get you cleaned up for work."

Doubting her, Garrett frowns then checks his watch. "It's only one, Zoe."

"Yes, but I have to get Ms. Gwen's gift for you from her bedroom before you go to work. I think you'll want to wear it," Zoe says, glancing at me to back her story.

"Oh, right. Yes. Garrett, go with Zoe and get your prize." I grip his hands, holding them tight as I beam at him, showing my teeth in an attempt to be more convincing. "You did a great job today, reading to me. We'll read some more tomorrow."

"Outside?" He sounds hopeful.

"Outside," I agree.

"More comics?"

I nod. "More comics."

"*Deadpool* ones?" He smiles brightly, showing off that crooked bottom tooth. I noticed it earlier today, and I've decided it makes him even more adorable. It's all Garrett.

"Is that your favorite out of the ones we read today?"

Garrett bobs his head. "Yes. He's funny."

"Then more *Deadpool*, it is." I squeeze his hands once more before letting them go.

Zoe chaperones him back to the house, throwing the blondes an evil eye before giving me a knowing wink. Shaking my head, I grin, and give her a little wave as I mouth, *'thank you'*.

Over in the side yard, close to the mountain's ledge, Wes still paces, rubbing the back of his neck. The blondes who I've never met before stay seated on the blanket, too busy talking to care that their boss is in serious turmoil right now. Standing up, I move toward him and stop a few feet away.

"Penny for your thoughts?" I mutter, squishing my toes in the soft grass.

Wes doesn't break his broad gait back and forth as he speaks. "I can't believe he brought her up. And that I was such a dick to him. I'm gonna have to apologize later. I shouldn't have snapped. He's such a good kid." He shakes his head in disbelief, visibly distraught. I ache for Wes. I know dealing with this can't be easy. Being a single mom wasn't easy for me. I can't imagine being a single dad to an autistic son.

"I'm sure he's okay, Wes. Don't worry," I soothe, trying to cleanse some of the guilt from the air. You can't always beat yourself up. It's tough being a parent.

A few beats of silence ensue before I softly ask, "Is Garrett not allowed to talk about his mom?" I hope that's not the truth. No parent should force their child not to talk about their mom. That's wrong. Even if she did leave. My birth dad died when I was little. I don't remember him, but

Mom and Dad have always encouraged Nash and me to talk about our biological parents, should we want to. I haven't done it in years, but when we were kids we did.

Halting, Wes closes his eyes and takes an audible breath before blowing out a long sigh. "I've had plenty of teachers for Garrett. None of them who could make him read. None of them he talked with personally or raided their bedroom in the morning. He's never like that. He usually understands boundaries. The very first tutor I hired for him was a nice blonde woman, and Garrett hated her. He refused to do his work or talk to his counselor about why he disliked her so much. And to this day, I still don't know why."

I get it. Garrett being friendly and sharing with me is a tremendous gift. It makes me feel a little fluttery inside. I like it … *a lot*. He's a great kid.

When Wes doesn't carry on, I tread lightly and ask, "Why'd his mom leave?"

"Because he's autis—*uniquely perfect*. She didn't want to deal with it. It became too much for her." He snorts, staring off into the distance. The bright sun glimmers off the golden flecks in his hair and the stubble on his face. He still hasn't shaven. Wes is a beautiful man. I wish I had a camera right now to capture him like this. Distraught or not, he's a chiseled masterpiece.

"Did she think it was easy on me?" he snips. "Garrett didn't talk until he was four. He wasn't potty trained until he was six. It wasn't easy then, and it was even harder after Angelica left. Garrett started acting out, not understanding why his mom disappeared in the middle of the night. We'd had another fight about him. About how tired she was. How tired we both were. The next morning, I woke up hearing Garrett scream in the kitchen. She'd left a note along with signed divorce papers on the shelf by the front door. And we haven't seen her since."

Every word that imparts Wes's lips breaks my heart more and more. I don't think twice when I close the distance between us and pull him into a much-needed hug. Wes is taken aback at first when he stands stock-still as I embrace his middle. Then he wraps his arms around my shoulders and lays his head against mine, expelling a calmed sigh. It isn't lost on me that my cheek is resting on his toned pec, the tattooed one. Or that his body is warm, soft, and smells like heaven. I throw all of those observations to the back of my mind and just *be*. He needs this. Hell, after hearing his story, I need this, too.

"Your ex was a fool to leave you both. Garrett's a great kid," I divulge, *and you're a great dad*, I internally add, unable to say the rest. It's not the time. It feels too personal.

Wes's broad palms flatten on the middle of my back, holding me closer. I have to force myself to keep breathing. Sweet Jesus, he's too damn much. And it has nothing to do with his looks. It's him. Every time I turn around, there's another facet of Wesley King that keeps me on my toes.

"Thank you for all of this, Gwen. I mean it. And about last night—" he begins.

"Water under the bridge."

"You're sure?"

I can hear the echo of his words in his chest as he speaks them. It's terribly intimate. Though I can't seem to tear myself away. This, right here, feels wonderful. It's been forever since anyone has hugged me just to hug me without an agenda. Or perhaps it merely feels that way. Nash and I together, hugging, laughing, being family, seems so distant. Like another life when I'm standing here with Wes.

Nodding, my cheek shifts along his smooth pec. "I'm sure."

"I hope you know what you're doing here is invaluable to me, Gwen. You're a special person."

Nope. No. I can't hear that. That's too much emotion. Savoring one final moment of our touch, I pull away and take a few steps back to give us some distance.

Using my thumb, I point toward the house. "I think I should head in. Make sure Garrett got his socks."

"His socks?" Wes rubs his pec, the same one my cheek was just resting on. It's distracting. I wonder what he's thinking. No … No, I don't.

Head tipped down, I kick the grass with my heel to focus on something else. "Yes. I told him if he read the comics that I'd give him a prize. I bought him a pair of *Tetris* socks yesterday. Don't worry, I spent my own money on them." *Woo.* That came out smoother than I thought it might. I'm getting flustered. Why won't he put a shirt on?

"Gwen, I don't care if it was your money or mine. I'm sure he'll love them."

"Yep. Me, too." I speak fast so I can get out of here, and away from him. Those eyes are searing through me. I can't take another second of it. Waving a brief goodbye, I jog around the pond and into the house in search of Garrett.

He's in his room getting ready when I arrive.

As suspected, he's beaming when he shows me his socks. "They're awesome!" he praises, lifting his pant leg to show me.

"Perfect fit," I grin as Garrett walks across the room toward me and surprises me when he wraps me in a too-hard hug. I pat his back and kiss his cheek like I do Trish. It feels natural.

He's the first to pull away. "I've got to go to work, Ms. Gwen. I hope Dad was okay when you talked to him outside. He doesn't like it when I share about my mother. I think it bothers him that she left us because I'm like this." He knocks the side of his head, twitching.

"There's nothing wrong with you, Garrett. You were made the way you are for a reason. Just as your dad was made the way he is for a reason. Your mother leaving has nothing to do with that." I hope he realizes this and doesn't blame himself. It's not right to feel guilt over someone else's bad choices. He can't help the way he is any more than the sun can help the way it shines.

"You like my dad, don't you?" He sounds hopeful. Too hopeful. I don't want him getting any weird ideas. This is temporary. Then I'm going home to spend time with my family again. I miss Trish like crazy.

"Your dad's a good man. Now it's time you get to work." I grab the crinkled collar of his shirt to flatten it before sending him on his way with another peck on the cheek. "Have a nice day, Garrett."

"You, too, Ms. Gwen. I'm glad you're here," he states on his way out the door.

"Me, too."

Now it's time for me to take a long bath since I didn't get a chance to this morning. Lots of hot water, here I come.

Chapter Twelve

Day 7

"Okay. Let's go over my duties again."

I glance to Wes, who's seated in the limo with two of his blondes beside him. Each of his hands are resting on their exposed thighs as another one of his blondes sits across from me. It's Candi. We've been chatting it up for the past twenty minutes, so I can cool my jets. I'm not looking forward to tonight. Not at all.

The bitchy blonde from earlier this week—I think her name is Amanda? She reaches down to cup Wes's junk over his slacks. With considerable effort, I ignore her to comprehend his explanation. "We're going to go into the back of the strip club. I will escort all of us to a private room where three men will be seated. You, Gwen, will serve their drinks throughout the night, while the rest of the ladies give them lap dances and whatever else they desire."

"And why will I be delivering them drinks all night?"

I know we've discussed this twice already. I just can't seem to grasp any of it. When Wes said that I'd be attending functions with him, I didn't think he meant waitressing at a strip club for a private party. And I sure as hell didn't expect to be wearing tight leather daisy duke shorts and an equally tight leather, backless top. I've got so much cleavage going on that it looks like two mountains have sprouted out of the top of my shirt. If that's even what you can call this leather contraption.

Wes eyes me sternly. "You lost a bet, Gwen. Remember?"

Somberly, I nod.

Oh, right. *A bet.* Sometimes you forget about that little thing when your week has been like mine. And by that, I mean *great*. It's been simply amazing. I've enjoyed every minute up 'til this point. This entire week I've tutored Garrett outside. Well, aside from Thursday since it rained, and we watched *The Avengers* in the living room instead. I lied and said it was comic book research. Either way, we had a blast eating popcorn and laughing at *The Hulk*. The nicest part of this week has been Garrett's significant improvement in his reading, and we've just begun writing. That'll be more difficult, but I think we'll do just fine. Wes has been eating lunch with us every day. Zoe's been my sidekick around every corner. It's been a seemingly perfect week. Like I said … until now.

When I'd woken this morning, Wes told me we were going out tonight. So I spent the day sunbathing on the beach with Zoe and Garrett. It was pleasant, and I even got half of my *JR Ward* book finished. Then … the bomb dropped. I'd showered, shaved, and all of that girly stuff after all of us had eaten a late dinner in the dining room. Zoe, in the midst of me putting my face on, laid my outfit on the white marble vanity in my bathroom. I nearly fainted at the damn sight.

"Just put them on, Gwen. You'll look hot," Zoe cooed as I sneered, shoving them to the floor.

"No way," I argued, and lost minutes later when Zoe practically begged me to take one for the team. Like always, I caved. Only because I adore that woman.

Honestly, the only time I've worn anything remotely similar to these clothes is when I go to my monthly fuck fests at *Nowhere*. Any other time, I wouldn't be caught dead in this shit. Even then, I only wear them because they give me a false sense of confidence to follow through with my needs. It somehow awakens my inner whore long enough to allow me to fuck a roomful of men without imploding from suffocating shame.

Now, here we are, seated in the back of Wes's limo, and I'm miserable. What a way to let a single part of a day ruin what turned out to be a perfect week. I could almost slap him for it.

Refusing to glance toward Wes as Amanda unbuttons his pants and goes to town between his thighs, I stare at the opposite side of the limo and talk to Candi instead. She babbles about her son and the apartment they live in. I pretend to listen, although it's difficult with the loud slurping and hushed moans flooding the air as the windows steam. Just when I think Wes is a good guy, a nice guy, a guy I might want to get to know, a blowjob goes and wrecks that image for me.

Truth be told, Wes and I have grown closer this week. We've talked a lot, even about stupid stuff like who our favorite actor is. I said Johnny Depp, while he argued Robert De Niro. I've even learned how he takes his coffee, that he loves everything bagels for breakfast, and has a scar on his right arm from playing hockey when he was a kid. Aside from Nash, I've never spoken to another man like I have Wes. First of all, Nash would have never allowed it. And the men I've hidden from him bored me to death within the matter of a few dates. Wes is different, though. He's unique, and as I've said before, keeps me on my toes. I like that. It's kind of endearing.

My belly concurs when it flips as we park behind a brick building in a dimly lit alley.

Wes taps Amanda's head that's busy working in his lap. "Time's up." His voice is husky, and I squirm at the erotic lilt. God, I bet he sounds even better after he's fucked. "We've gotta go inside. I can't leave my clients waiting."

Amanda tilts her head back, staring at Wes's face. "I'm not done," she whines, wiping her mouth.

Oh, please.

Internally, I roll my eyes.

"Sorry, babe," he taps her chin with one hand as he folds his still erect member back into his pants. "I'll let ya finish me off later."

She grabs the tops of his thighs. "I'll do the even dirtier stuff to you later if you give me a chance." Her tone oozes smutty sexuality. It makes me wanna gag.

The door opens. "Sir and ladies, they're ready for you inside."

"Thanks, Randy," Candi says as she slips out of the limo first.

I'm hot on her tail, not wanting to be left behind to hear more about these dirty deeds that Amanda's going to perform on Wes later tonight. I wonder if he sleeps with them in his house, or takes them elsewhere? I've yet to hear anything coming from his room, and Garrett's never mentioned noises either. Hmmm…

In the skeevy alley, Candi and I wait for Wes and the rest of the chicks to pile out of the limo. Entering the establishment from a metal back door, the music pounds off the walls as we make our way down two corridors until we come to a black shellacked door with a number one on it. Oozing confidence, Wes invites himself inside with one blonde tucked under each arm. Following his lead, Candi and I enter by ourselves. It's kind of insulting to go in alone, but I brush it off and play my part.

Exhaling, I step across the room's threshold, and the door magically shuts behind me. I jump as I quickly shove away the urge to try and see if it opens again. I don't want to be locked in here. Not like this.

Daringly, I turn my attention to the room and scan its contents with a clinical regard. The walls are draped in lush blood red fabric that skims the black lacquer floor. It appears to glisten as muted can lights illuminate us from above. In the corner, there's a small bar and a male barkeep, outfitted in a tux standing astutely behind it. In the middle of the room sits three men on plush black armless chairs. Across from them, Wes takes his own seat. Between them is nothing but an oval coffee table that's set with a decorative bowl of condoms, coasters, and two shiny guns.

For a moment, I stand and watch them shake hands until a sense of recollection prickles the back of my neck. Those men, or that one, looks familiar. They're all wearing cuts. The one with the ponytail—he's … oh shit! That's the guy who stabbed the prisoner in Nash's cellar! What are the Sacred Sinners doing here? Is this about that shipment or something they were trying to get information about? Fuck, I shouldn't be here. What if that man recognizes me? What if he thinks I'm a rat or something? It's not like I don't already stand out. I'm wearing all black and have brown hair. The rest of the women are in bright colors to match their blonde locks. This isn't good. This isn't good at all. Nash and Wes are both going to kill me.

Candi, touching my arm, rips me from my awkward stare down. "The bar's over there." She gestures kindly. "The men are waiting on their beers. You need to serve them."

Fuck. Okay. I can do this. I can play this cool and pretend I don't recognize them. In all honesty, I only know the one. The one with the name Steel on his vest. Taking a deep breath, I say thanks before forcing my feet to move and my face to remain impassive. At the bar, I gather their drinks on a silver tray and deliver them quietly to the group, including Wes.

A big burly man with a long beard eyes me suggestively as I hand him his bottle of Bud. "How are ya, sexy lady?" He smacks my ass playfully, and I almost want to laugh. He's got a fun vibe coming from him.

Smiling tightly, I bow my head out of respect. "I'm fine, sir."

The big guy barks a huge laugh, holding his pudgy gut. "Sir? Who the fuck are ya callin' sir?"

My face blanches, sweat dampening my brow. I don't want to draw attention to myself. And I don't want to offend him either. That wasn't the plan. I need to travel under the radar, and this big guy isn't allowing me to do that. *Damn it.* Has that Steel guy already recognized me?

Still smiling, I try to maneuver around him. But he doesn't let me pass as he grabs my hips, forcing me to sit in his lap. A hard cock immediately pokes me in the ass as his arms fuse around me, palms landing awfully close to my tits. I freeze, unsure of what to do. He smells heavily like marijuana and peppermint. It's not an altogether bad scent. Just not appealing, either. And I'm not a fan of dicks prodding my behind without my permission. At this second, I want to scold him, but think better of it, since I don't need to make this worse.

"You gonna call me sir, *now*?" he whispers hotly in my ear, and I shake my head, eyes blown wide. Across the way, Wes is glaring at us through tiny eye slits as he clenches his jaw, muscles stiff. What? I didn't ask the man to play. He's not my type anyhow.

"Blimp!" The attractive bald man beside us slaps the big guy in the back of the head. "Pussies after business. Now let the girl up. You're scarin' her, and pissin' *The Boss* off."

The Boss?

Expelling a cursed grumble, Blimp kisses the side of my head and pinches my ass before he plants me firmly on my feet. "I'll see you afterward, sexy." He rumbles his intent, and I scurry off to the other side of the room. Woo, thank the Lord for the bald, sex god.

Over the next hour, I sit at the bar, watching the men carry on. I deliver drinks when needed, but most of the time, I just observe. Observe Wes glancing my way every minute or two, sometimes offering me a small smile that I'm happy to return. Observe the blondes in their element as they provide a triple strip show in the corner as side entertainment. The men seem to stop talking here and there just to watch the women touch each other. Yes, I said that—*touch each other*. They're sucking each other's nipples, and Amanda's now getting on her knees to lick

Candi's smooth pussy. Throwing her head back, Candi grabs Amanda's hair and moans, grinding her juices on her colleague's lips. If I were a lesbian or a man, I would totally get off on this. They're hot. I have to give them that. However, aside from my general appreciation for their dedication to Wes, I'm bored. Female on female action does nothing for me. Yet, it doesn't disgust me, either. I'm indifferent.

The bald man, who I've learned is Gunz, raises his hand for another beer. Quickly, the barkeep gives me one, and I saunter over there in my modest heels to deliver his bottle, sans tray. That thing was pointless anyhow.

"Thanks, babe," he praises as I hear Blimp say, "Forty cases should do it. Make sure there are extra mags in the crates. Big *expects* extra mags."

"Not a problem, boys. Not a problem at all," Wes responds coolly, leaning back in his chair like he doesn't have a care in the world. "Hey, Kitten," he calls, so I take the hint and return to the bar, but stop short when he commands. "*Gwen*, please come here."

Backtracking, I turn to face Wes. He pats his lap. "Why don't you come and play for a while, *Kitten?* I think these gentlemen would like some pussy, and I'd like some, too. So come and sit, will ya?" His facial expression says I better not argue, while his eyes remain soft like they're begging me to not make a scene.

A few feet away, that Blimp guy grumbles his dislike and things start to click into place. Wes doesn't want me to have to deal with that other man. Neither do I. My belly whirls and heart hammers as I make haste climbing into Wes's lap, straddling him like the stripper I'm pretending to be.

Out of nowhere, he produces a tiny remote and flicks on some sensual rock music. On cue, the girls stop licking one another and find their way to the men. Each of them fully nude begin rubbing their tits in the guys' faces. Eagerly, they palm the women's asses, going to town on their bodies while I return attention to Wes.

Playing the part, I grind my covered pussy against his dick. Leaning forward, my breasts flatten to his chest, and I grab the back of the chair. Dipping my head, I brush my lips along his earlobe. "Thank you for saving me from him," I whisper, purposely fanning my breath over his skin.

Ignoring my words, Wes palms my ass, too. A flutter of something kindles between the apex of my thighs, and I bite back a moan. Damn. I love a man in charge. And I love the way his hands splay over my cheeks perfectly. It's so fucking hot. To the music, I swivel my hips and allow myself to let go as I channel my inner stripper.

"Careful, Gwen," Wes warns half-heartedly as his fingers dig into my butt, igniting a hungry heat to rush through my veins. My nipples harden.

"Careful about what, Wesley?" I nip his earlobe between my teeth, tugging it a bit.

Wes's fingers grip my ass harder as he groans, powerfully rocking me over his growing thickness. The devil inside of me rises to the surface, and this time, I embrace her with open arms. If he wants an actress, he's going to get one hell of an actress. Flipping off the moral center of my brain, I go on feel and fuck everything else.

His hand slides up my spine and possessively cuffs around the back of my neck. Wes pulls me backward, so I'm forced to see him face to face. His pupils are blown, swallowing the icy blue whole. Lips slightly parted. Chest rising and falling like he's unable to catch his breath. It's so hot. Add his dirty blond hair lying haphazardly on his head, and I'm nearly panting alongside him. It's been too damn long since a man has touched me. And I don't know if there's ever been a time anyone's touched me like this. God, why does he feel so right?

"Why are you acting this way?" That sexually pained voice delivers its intended blow, hitting me in both my heart and between my legs.

I swallow thickly. "You wanted me here for this." Swaying my hips, I confirm my explanation.

Wes's face screws into a scowl as the sound of a man in the midst of an orgasm reaches my ears. I almost forgot we weren't alone.

"I didn't ask you here for this," he clarifies.

The boldest part of me springs forth, and I grab Wes's erection over his pants. He moans on contact, throwing his head back, eyes fluttering shut. "If you didn't want me here for this, then why am I dressed this way? And why are you hard?" I ask seductively, not sure if I want to know the answer but ask it anyhow.

Swiftly removing his hand from my ass, he uses it to peel my fingers off his junk and secures it behind my back just like the other night. Then he takes a breath of relief, body visibly unwinding. "You're here as my guest. Not as my whore, or my employee. You're here so I can watch you."

Even in a room full of people, Wes securing me like this, as his eyes delve into mine, feels like we're the only two people on the planet. My heart offers a fierce beat in agreement. "I don't understand," I comment, licking my lips. Why would he bring me here in the first place if not to act like the rest of the women?

Wes pulls me in closer, so our bodies mold together. My lips float an inch above his. I can smell the tang of beer on his breath, and his unique man scent that drives me wild. Every single day for the past week, that scent has shadowed me. It's been screwing with my equilibrium. So much so that I found myself leaning closer to him yesterday so that I could get a better whiff. It's divine.

"You're my son's tutor. You're not meant to take your clothes off. Even if I wouldn't mind seein' what ya look like under all of that sexy leather." His smirking lips ghost over mine and my heart swells, feeling like it might explode from my chest. "You're *my* Gwen. Not anything else. You're here to accompany me. I expect nothing more." His tone is edgy—no nonsense, leaving any trace of his excitement in the dust.

"Then why—"

"Why tonight? Why have you in my lap?" he interrupts, and I nod, taking in his temperate expression. "I needed you in *my* lap and not in someone else's. These aren't the nicest men, Kitten. They're just another side to my businesses. The darker side. And the last thing I need is you getting caught up with them. You're not gonna end up another notch in someone's bedpost. And I don't wanna have to break an agreement with this club *if* they piss me off. I think Gunz understands that. He's a sensible man."

A piece of me wants to tell Wes that I know who they are. But an even larger piece is screaming for me to keep my mouth shut like Nash always taught. I embrace the latter.

"I think I understand."

"So then sit here with me and pretend we're having a nice time. Then we can leave whenever they're ready. This meeting has been a long time in the making. You don't wanna know the lengths I've had to go to get in bed with a club this big." Wes speaks low enough that only I can hear. A beat later, he unbinds my arm, and I wrap them both around his neck, playing with his nape. Smiling devastatingly, he keeps talking. "You look smokin' hot tonight. I'm not surprised that one of these men saw past my blondes to want a piece of you." Wes's palms resettle on my bottom. He kisses my chin, catching me off guard.

I jerk in his arms, startled by both his touch and compliment. A sentimental warmth buzzes in my chest.

"Sorry," he snickers. "I've wanted to do that all day."

"Kiss my chin?" Skeptically perking my brow, I regard him like he's nuts.

"Yes." He kisses it again. This time, I don't jump, and that unwanted heat just seems to grow. "You have the most adorable chin."

Next, the internal butterflies take flight. *Damn it.*

"Are you sure you're the same man who just made a gun deal with a big biker club?" I tease, letting him *know* that I'm in the *know*.

He doesn't seem to mind when he replies, "I've got many sides, Kitten. Many sides."

"I'm beginning to grasp that." I twirl wisps of his hair between my fingers.

He sighs. "That feels nice."

"So guns, huh?" I probe. As much as it should bother me that Wes sells, distributes, or whatever it is pertaining to guns, it's not really a shocker. I grew up around Nash, so there's not much I haven't heard about.

Ya gotta make a living somehow. To be blunt, the strip clubs rub me more wrong than running guns does. Morality and legality say I shouldn't feel that way, yet I do nonetheless.

Wes nuzzles his nose to my chin. "I gotta make a livin', Kitten. The strip clubs are legit cash. The guns are my play money. What most people don't know about me is I'm the progeny of an outlaw biker and a stripper. It seems as though fate has dealt his hand and now I'm in both industries."

Damn, that's quite the parental concoction. No wonder he's not a typical boring Joe Schmo.

Seriously looking at Wes, I keep my gaze glued to his. "Where are your parents?"

"Not living in a lovely home in Charlotteton like yours," he evades.

I frown. In most cases, Wes is an open book. Why's he avoiding this? I get that our location isn't ideal for casual conversation, but this isn't him.

"Yes, my parents are in a nice home. But that doesn't answer my question."

Wes squeezes my ass cheeks in warning. "There are some things better left unsaid."

Hmmm ... that doesn't explain a thing.

To avoid an argument, I choose to let it go ... sorta. "Okay. So you won't tell me about your parents, but you'll talk about your ex-wife. How about we talk more about her instead? Or how about your choice of businesses?"

Just as the words fall from my lips, another climax erupts, and I foolishly turn my head to see that Gunz fella tag teaming with Blimp. Gunz is pounding the cocksucker Amanda in the ass while Blimp is feeding her his cock from a chair. For a moment, I soak up the scene. Sensing my inner whore struggling to resurface, I unconsciously start to grind my pussy against Wes yet again. *Fuck.* That's hot. What makes matters even more thrilling is that Amanda doesn't seem to be enjoying herself in the least. Her noiseless, rigid frame is evidence enough. If I liked her, I might feel sorry for the relentless ass pounding. However, I don't, so this is a bonus. Call me a sadistic bitch if you want.

Out of the corner of my eye, I catch Steel sucking Candi's taut nipples while fingering her. Though, strangely enough, he's not allowing her to touch him. It doesn't matter, anyhow, since she's obviously floating in that bliss filled euphoria that claims you after you've had an earth shattering climax or two. And from the looks of it, she's headed into another one as we speak. Candi's head thrashes back as she screams into the air. Body violently shuddering in Steel's arms, he holds her tighter as his fingers continue to plunge in and out of her pink depths.

A potent wave of envy washes over me as my clit throbs from neglect. Seeking friction, I hump Wes harder, my eyes fixed on the gloriously filthy porn scene unfolding before my very eyes. Moans and groans impart from the men and women as they submit to basic instincts. Spontaneously, I cup my breast and rub my nipple through the top. The familiar sizzle of wanton desire heats me from within. The palms on my ass tighten to bruising levels, flooding molten lust through every cell of my body. I begin to pant. Sweat dampens my palms. A nose nuzzles my exposed neck, and the distinct scent of Wes dominates my nostrils.

Fuck. He's touching me and smells so damn good. I've gotta… Shit. I *need* to get off. His smell … his touch

… him… It's killing me … slowly. I can't stave this need any longer.

Fuck it.

Intense, body quaking pleasure builds between my thighs as my clit swells, seeking more attention. More of anything. Seizing the back of Wes's neck, I force his lips to my flesh. He doesn't disappoint when his thick tongue laves my skin from ear to collarbone then back again. My fingers slip into the base of his hair and grip it tightly, not wanting him to stop.

Yes. More.

"If you need to come, Kitten, I'm not gonna st— *nuhh*," Wes grunts as my pussy gains purchase on his stout thickness.

Hijacking control, he centers me there with his hands and begins a frantic rhythm of fucking me with our clothes on. Over and over, his dick achingly collides with my clit so that I'm forced to give in to this invading hunger. Basking in the onslaught of paradise, I moan freely as lips seal themselves to my neck, sucking in tandem with the brutal thrusts.

"Oh, fuck!" I squeal, slithering closer to the brink of no return.

"Yes, Kitten." Wes's husky tone vibrates against my skin, mingling with the steam of his heavy breaths. He's driving me insane. My mind whirls. "If you need it, take it, Kitten. Take whatever you want. Use my cock to come. Come on, Kitten. Use me to come. Let go … just let—"

With one final thrust, the spark ignites, and I lose myself in explosive white-hot ecstasy. Tremor after tremor rockets through me as I wail my release, riding him rougher to prolong my orgasm. My eyes roll into the back of my skull, and toes curl in my heels as my climax flows onward, down into a river of white water rapids. Another small wave crests then crashes. Running out of gas, my legs quickly turn to noodles, unable to propel my hips any longer. My trembling body slumps forward, arms loosely draping over Wes's shoulders.

Somehow knowing what I need, Wes braces both hands on my ass to help me fuck him. Repeatedly, I'm guided from one shattering moment to the next as my swimming head rests in the crook of his neck. After number ten—or is it twenty?—my brain fogs. And my inner slut revels in the glory of weightless euphoria.

Magically reading me once more, Wes ceases his ministrations. Thank God. I … I can't take any more. My pussy is happily sated. I'm as light as a feather. I … this feels … beautiful … magnificent … *incredible*. If I could speak, I'd tell Wes that. I'd also say thank you. It's been weeks since I've come this much. Hell, I've never come like this. Not over my clothes. Not by one man. Not in front of others who never touched me. Not … not so completely. Oh … Fuck. What does that mean?

Ignoring all wayward thoughts, I float peacefully inside my head. Movement and chatter registers, but I can't make out any specifics. It feels so distant. Then my body is suddenly in flight. Yet, I still can't seem to pry my eyes open. It's too much work.

"Wrap your legs around my waist, Kitten," Wes whispers to my ear, and I comply. It takes me three weak tries before I finally lock my ankles around his hips, my high heels clattering to the floor in the process. More movement and talking ensues. Then a blast of cold air hits my frame, making me shiver.

"Just a few more seconds," Wes comments. He's right, 'cause no sooner do those words filter through my muddled brain before I'm enveloped in heat once again when his body dips and a car door closes.

Wes unlocks my legs from around him so that my knees can settle on the supple leather of a seat. Too tired to pay attention to much else, I drift in and out of consciousness as a warm, caring hand caresses my back and people chat. Lips pepper kisses along my face from time to time and a ball of happiness builds in my chest so tangible that I could almost cry.

The last thing I remember is a familiar cloud welcoming me home, and the press of soft lips touching my forehead.

"Goodnight, Kitten."

Goodnight, delicious smelling Wes. Thank you for bringing me back to heaven.

Chapter Thirteen

Day 8

It's 11 a.m., and I'm seated at the kitchen island alone, munching on a bagel with cream cheese. Three hours ago, I awoke to a playback of last night's festivities frolicking on a turn style in my head in vivid, humiliating color. For 2.3 seconds, I'd sworn it was a nightmare. Then the soreness radiating from my pussy twinged, knocking that fragment of hope loose. Dwelling, like I'm good at, I laid in bed berating myself for hours, confused as to why I let it happen. Any of it. The touching. The tongue. The ass grabbing. The whole gambit. And what torments me even more is the fact that I loved every single millisecond of it. Every one of those hot as hell, melt my panties touches. Every enticing smell. Every fevered noise. Every blinding climax.

Once I'd finally rolled out of bed, my legs were sore from exertion. One look in the damn bathroom mirror offered more evidence of last night's mischief when the dark purple hickey on my neck mocked my disheveled reflection. For a few moments, I stood there staring wide-eyed at myself, at my seemingly satisfied eyes, rosy cheeks, and just fucked hair. I don't know if I've ever looked better, and that's the problem. A problem I've been dissecting since I've waited for the coast to clear so I could eat. Thankfully, Wes, Garrett, and Zoe have left me alone this morning. I definitely need it.

Inhaling my final bite, I slide off the stool and carry my plate to the sink. Running it under the water, I rinse the crumbs down the drain to waste some time. I don't want to do the walk of shame back to my room. I'm more likely to run into someone on the way.

I set the rinsed dish on the counter for later.

"I wondered when you'd finally leave your room," Wes's voice startles me, and I accidentally bump the plate, screeching its damp base over the marble. I cringe at the sound.

Keeping my back to Wes, afraid of facing him, I hide the crimson that's begun to dot my cheeks as a memory of last night assaults my mind. I turn rigid, hands lying flat on the counter, eyes staring aimlessly at the subway tile backsplash. "I slept in late," I lie.

The slap of bare feet on the tiled floor rings in my ears just before a set of firm hands drop on my shoulders. A chest covers my back from behind. Fuck, he's already too close, and touching me when he shouldn't. Those hands turn into magical creatures when they start to massage like little tentacles of bliss. "You're tense, Kitten. You need to relax."

I blow out a breath I didn't realize I was holding. "It's kind of hard to do when you're touching me."

He doesn't stop. "Is this because of last night?"

"No," I blurt a little too quickly. Shit, I need to learn to lie better.

"Uh huh. You're thinking about last night, aren't ya?" I'm not sure if he's more amused by this or indifferent.

"No." I sound more confident. Good.

"You're a terrible liar."

"Well, you're a terrible masseur," I lie some more.

Apparently, that's what I'm going to be doing all day. Lying to him. Lying to myself. Hey, if it gets me through the next twenty-four hours without a meltdown, then fantastic. Generally, when I'm feeling like this—like I might lose it—I talk to Nash. He's a great sounding board. But now ... now I'm on my own. It's not as easy as it sounds. And I sure as hell can't confide in Wes. Not when he's the one fucking with my head. With ... *everything*. It doesn't make any sense.

"That, I might be, but you need something to relax." He's still as calm as ever. It's annoying.

"Then maybe you should stop touching me."

He must not think that's a good suggestion, because he doesn't back the hell away. What is it with him and invading my personal space? "I have a better idea. How about you go sit down on the stool." Using my shoulders as a steering wheel, he navigates me to said stool and puts me on it. I don't argue, because the sooner he leaves me, the better. His proximity is already driving me batty. Let's not forget my pussy. She seems to enjoy this attention. Her stupid clit is already starting to throb. What a slut. *Fuck you, traitor down under*.

Wes casually kisses the back of my head, like it's the most natural thing in the world. Well, it's not. He needs to stop with these damn touches. "That's better. Don't move." He affectionately squeezes my shoulders once before letting go. Then he moves across the kitchen with masculine grace. I wish he weren't so sexy.

Lifting the old rotary phone off the counter, he yanks its cord far enough that it reaches the island. He sets the cream dinosaur smack dab in front of me. "It's Sunday. You should call your daughter or your parents. I don't care which. Maybe it'll make you feel better. Then you, Garrett, and I are going to visit town."

"To do what?" I finally look at his face. It's disgustingly beautiful. I hate it.

Why did I have to *come* on his lap? *Why?*

Wes shakes his stupidly sexy head. "Nope. Not gonna tell you a thing. Just talk to your family and meet Garrett and me out by the pond in one hour."

"What do I wear?" Damn it. Why am I asking this? Do I really need permission or suggestions on what I like? After Zoe duped me into wearing that leather ensemble last night, I've decided I won't be falling for that tactic again. No way.

I wave off my words before he can answer. "Never mind. I'll wear whatever I want."

Raising my head in defiance, I wait for him to correct me. He doesn't. With a final goodbye, Wes smirks before departing the kitchen. Sadly, my eyes watch that magnificent tight ass go. I can't fucking help it. It's a great ass.

Swallowing down all of my frazzled nerves, and some other feelings I'm just not willing to think about, I dial Trish's phone. She picks up on the third ring.

"This is Trish."

"It's Mom."

"Hey! Mom!" she squeals, and I smile hugely at the sound of her voice. I've missed her so much.

"How—" The words die on my lips as an abrupt argument ensues in the background of Trish's call. There's static for a moment as I hear someone cuss, and then the phone is clear again.

"Where the fuck are you? It's Sunday, Gwen. It's family day. You haven't been here for two weeks. That's unacceptable. You better be here next weekend, or so help me!" Nash unleashes his fury and my smile fades, drooping into a frown, then to an angry grimace. This is not how I expected our next conversation to go.

"Stop yelling at her!" Trish defends in the distance. "Now give me back my phone!"

"No!" he growls in return. "I'll give it back when I'm damn ready."

"Nash, if you expect to have any sort of conversation with me, I suggest you pull your head out of your ass and stop talking to Trish that way. It's unacceptable," I scold, holding my ground without blowing the hell up.

There's no acknowledgment that Nash heard me. But when he tells Trish he's sorry for yelling and that he's taking the phone outside, I know that he got my message loud and clear. *Good.*

Movement registers through the phone, as does Nash's heavy breathing, and a squeaky door that shuts.

"Okay. I shouldn't have lost my shit. I'm straight. Now tell me what the fuck is goin' on and where the hell are you? Trish told me you were takin' some vacation, except your cell is off and this line is untraceable."

"You tried to track me?"

For a second, the sense of warmth and home that I always feel when Nash is around returns with a vengeance, making my insides cartwheel. Then the bitterness of our last encounter bulldozes every bit of it, leaving me numb. Which is a hell of a lot better than pain.

"You're family, Gwen. Of course, I did."

Gwen ... not Gwennie ... not Gwennie-bee. Things really have changed. *Nash* has changed.

The sourness of my new reality hits tenfold. We're never going to be Nash and Gwen against the world ever again, are we? We're never going to... *Fuck.* I can't think of any of that now. It's over. This is over. He made that bed, and now we're both lying in it. What a cruel bastard.

Tapping my nail on the counter, I muster the courage to keep talking. Even though I'd rather hang up. "I called to speak to Trish, Nathaniel. I didn't call to talk to you. If I'd wanted to talk to you, I would have called your cell number."

"What is with this *Nathaniel* bullshit?"

"It's your name."

"*Right,*" he seethes. "But I'm Nash to you."

"No. You're Nathaniel now. Nash is used for family who doesn't piss my daughter or me off. It's used when I'm respected and loved. Not when I'm scolded for living my fucking life."

Oh, this isn't good, I'm starting to lose my cool. If I blow and release all of these emotions that I've kept bottled up for weeks, it's going to go Hiroshima up in here. That cannot happen. Not with the promising afternoon waiting for me after I get off this phone. I can't go atomic. I've gotta keep a tight leash on my anger. Sooner or later, I'll get my chance to let loose. Today just isn't the day.

"You're fuckin' with me, right?" He's furious.

Shaking my head even though he can't see me, I sigh, my temper deflating. "Not a bit. I only called to tell

Trish that I'm doing fine. That I'm havin' the time of my life. And that the weather here is pleasant and the water's warm. One of these days, I hope to bring her here."

Everything that comes out is true. Even that last part. I think Trish would love it here. Zoe would be her new best friend since they both love fashion so much. Don't let Zoe fool ya. She may not like to shop with Wesley's blondes, but she does an excellent job of shopping on her lonesome. I've yet to see her in anything less than spectacular. She's made for designer duds.

"Where are you?"

"On vacation."

"I get that, smart ass. But where?" There's the hint of a smile in his voice. I'll take that over anger any day of the week.

I glance at the oversized clock on the wall. Forty-five minutes until I get a reprieve. "If I'd wanted to tell someone, I would have. You've made it abundantly clear you wanted space. A nice vacation gives us both that. It was unexpected. But I'm safe, and I'm happy." *Albeit, a bit confused.* "It shouldn't matter about anything else. I'm sorry that I'm missing Sundays, but I'll be back before ya know it."

The thought of that should excite me. Yet, all I can seem to muster is dread. Molasses thick dread. Coming face to face with Nash again, after he coldcocked me with melancholy, isn't on my to-do list. At first, I thought Wes's phony bet was a prison sentence. Now, it's my escape from reality. I don't know if I'll ever want to leave if that means going home to this man on the phone … the one who stomped on my heart, shattering it into a million pieces.

"When you get home, Gwen, we'll talk about that."

"There's nothing to discuss, Nathaniel. We're brother and sister—nothing more. We'll see each other on Sundays and live separate lives. It'll be fine."

Nash groans in defeat. "I never said I wanted that."

"You're right. You didn't say *anything* at all. You walked away. Which is exactly what I'm going to do. I have nothing left to say to you." Hesitating for a beat, I float the phone away from my ear, ready to slam it on its base.

A wave of worry washes over me, scared that he might let me go again without a word. At the prospect, my heart kicks my ribs as I squirm on the stool. What if he does let go without fighting to clear the air? Does that mean we're officially through? Through with what … I dunno. But it's something.

"Gwen." If I didn't know any better, I'd say that sounded a lot like pleading. "I'm not gonna do this over the phone."

"Then don't," I clip.

"Fuck! You're gonna hang up on me, aren't ya?"

He's a fast learner.

"Yup."

"Please don't." Gut-wrenching sadness pours out. It shouldn't bother me, yet, it does. I hate to hear him like this.

"Give me one good reason why I shouldn't."

"I'm sorry," he mumbles so lowly that I barely hear it.

Taking a page from Wes's book of anxiety, I rub the back of my neck to center myself. "That's not a reason," I remark.

Nash sighs. "Listen, it's not the time to talk about this over the phone while I'm sittin' on Mom and Dad's porch. Okay? I'm dealin' with some shit. I shoulda told ya about it earlier. A lot earlier … *years earlier*," he emphasizes, pausing to let the words settle. What does that even mean? "Kelly helped me understand some of it."

Of course, she did. Cheating, lying, irresponsible fucking Kelly.

"Then maybe you should give her a juicy kiss for helpin' ya." Yup. I'm bitter as hell. So what?

To distract from the expanding pain in my chest, I tap my nail harder on the marble.

"I know you don't like her, Gwen." He's not happy about this. I can tell.

"Whatever gave you that idea? Of course, I don't like her. She's a manipulative bitch who butts her nose into our family's business. I tried to like her. But then you picked her over me. So what does that really say?" That I'm pathetic for even mentioning it aloud. Crap. I should have just kept my mouth shut. The word vomit has a tendency to sneak up on me at the most inopportune times.

"I'd never do that." He's fierce.

"You have, and you did. This is done, Nathaniel. I am done having this conversation. You're obviously not going to spill whatever it is you need to tell me. So you're just wasting my time with idle chat that'll eventually get ugly. Let's do each other a favor, and hang up now before I say something I'll regret later. Tell Trish, Mom, and Dad that I love them. I'll see you when I see you."

Just as I move to hang up without Nash's reply, I stop when he yells, "Wait!" So I do. "You can't hang up yet, Gwennie. I love you so fuckin' much. So very much. Even if you're pissed that I fucked a lot of shit up. I still love you. And I know as much as you might hate my ass right now, you love me, too. And I'll be damned if I hang up without lettin' ya know. Yeah. We'll talk all this out whenever ya get home from wherever the fuck place you're at. But ya need to know that you and Trish have always been my world. Period. It's not the club. Not *Nowhere*. Nothin' else fuckin' matters if I don't have my two best girls. Ya got that?"

Oh, my... *Shit.* Tears well in my eyes and my bottom lip quivers. He can't do this. He can't go from pissing me off to... *this*. This is my Nash climbing out from under the blanket of assholishness. The man I love. My home. My rock. My center. My ... *everything*. Or what used to be my everything, until now. Until ... *here* ... Wes ... Kelly ...Garrett ... *The Bet*. Life is so fucking fucked up.

I suck in a ragged breath, tone meek. "I, uh, okay. Yes. I do love you, too."

"See. There's my Gwennie-bee. Just be safe for me. Can ya do that? It's bad enough I dunno where ya are. If anythin' happened to you..." he trails off.

"I know, and I promise to be safe."

"Lunch!" my mom hollers in the background.

"Fuck! I gotta eat then hit up *Nowhere*. We've got church tonight. We'll talk whenever ya get home. Don't forget I love you."

"I won't."

I couldn't if I wanted to. These damn warm and fuzzies are killing me. *Nash loves me* ... Damn.

"Later."

"Bye."

I hang up, and my mind spins. What the hell just happened? Did Nash and I do what we always do? Fight then love?

Climbing off the stool, I pad my way back to my room, lost in thoughts of two very different men who've just turned my world upside down.

Chapter Fourteen

Still Day 8

"Come with me, Ms. Gwen. You have to see this." Flapping his hands, Garrett's big, excited eyes flash to the large display of *Deadpool* in the local comic book store's front window. It's complete with a cardboard cutout of the man himself.

Smiling back at Garrett, I follow right on his tail. He picks up a stack of comics and sifts through them, careful not to damage the pages.

"Look at these. They're awesome!" He's speaking more to himself than me. It's so damn cute.

A palm settles in the middle of my back, followed by half of a man pressing himself there. His other hand slips around my waist, and my heart flutters. "Someone has turned my son into a comic book nerd." Wes chuckles, kissing the back of my head.

"Says the man with the *Batman* pajamas," I kid, oddly savoring the heat of his palms. Which is a drastic contrast on how I thought I'd be feeling.

After I'd freshened up in my room before our outing today, I had some time to think and was finally able to gain a bit of clarity in my life. Nash is hundreds of miles away, yet, seemingly not, since he owns a piece of my heart. So, at times, he's right here, whispering in my ear, telling me what to do. As much as I hate to say this, I have to let that go. I can't feel trapped by a man who's not even mine. Not when I have one right here, giving me affection and his undivided attention.

Why's Wes doing it? Why is he openly touching my hip when his son is here? I don't have the answers for that. All I know is that my body likes it, my mind loves it, and I have to stop fighting my attraction, even if part of me welcomes that this is temporary. That I might get hurt in the end. That he could be playing me for a fool. If that's the case, then I'll have to deal when the time comes. I can't live in the, *what ifs,* and I sure as fuck can't be drowning in this guilt any longer. The whore that resides within me craves Wes. There's no doubt about it. So why should I cage her if that's what she desires? Why should I cage myself, if that's what I also enjoy? It doesn't make any sense. Not when I'm a single, grown, adult woman with a sexy, albeit confusing, playboy here to keep me company, if only for a little while. In the wise words of *REO Speedwagon* … *'I can't fight this feeling anymore. I've forgotten what I started fighting for. It's time to bring this ship into the shore and throw away the oars, forever…'* Or something along those lines.

Good-naturedly, Wes squeezes my hip. "Hey! You like The Bat."

"I dunno. I'm thinkin' this *Deadpool* guy might be better suited for me. Garrett seems to love him. And there's just something about a man in a red suit with a cocky mouth that gets me all tingly." Grinning like a dork, I faux shiver to solidify my point.

Warm lips brush the outer shell of my ear as that hand on my hip grips tighter, sending a blast of cosmic heat between my thighs. Oooo ... I like when Wes plays like this. "Don't abandon The Bat for some mutant in red. Bruce Wayne has it all, Kitten. Money, women, a secret identity, and an addiction to a certain feline." He purrs to my ear. Goosebumps break out, flooding down my frame. I shiver for real this time. Fuck, he's already started foreplay in the middle of a comic store, and I *like it*. Sweet Jesus, I'm sick.

Thankfully, Garrett goes and bursts our hot little bubble when he lifts a fat stack of comics in the air. "Dad, Ms. Gwen, can I get these?"

"Yes." I nod at the same time Wes says, "Are ya sure you don't wanna try some *Batman* ones, bud?"

Without warning, Garrett busts up laughing. "Dad, I'm not into *Batman*. We've gone over that. I like *Lara Croft*, and now *Deadpool*." Fidgeting, he hugs his stack of comics to his chest, so he doesn't drop them. "*Batman*'s all yours." Garrett's eyes shift to me, gleaming with mischief. "Has Dad shown you his bat cave?"

Glancing over my shoulder at Wes, he gripes. "Bud, that's a secret."

"Not anymore." He beams, all teeth and adorableness. "You should see it, Ms. Gwen. Dad has this secret door in his office that opens into a room that he calls his *bat cave*. It's awesome!"

Perking my brow, trying not to laugh at Wes's caught-red-handed expression, I ask, "So what's in this bat cave, Wesley?"

Wes doesn't get a chance to answer when Garrett happily fills in the blanks. "He grew up watching *Batman and Robin*. You know, that old show?" I nod. "Well, he's been collecting *Batman* stuff for years. And he even has comic books from *before I was born*." Garrett's eyes flash wide at the thought. As if sixteen years is really that old. Silly boy.

"Enough about that, Bud," Wes stammers uncomfortably. "Let's get you those merc with a mouth comics and get outta here." Wes doesn't say another word as he leads the way to the register and pays for his son's reading material.

Returning his hand to the small of my back, Wes escorts me from the store. Our driver is standing outside of the limo as we step onto the pavement. "Bud, give Randy the comics so we can go grab some ice-cream at *Sally's*."

Garrett does just that, and we walk down the street, window shopping all the way to *Sally's*. Inside the quaint shop, Garrett finds us a booth, as Wes and I take to the counter. This place is cute. Not as nice as *Whisky's Corrupt Confections* in my town, but it's got a nostalgic red and white fifties vibe going on. Wes orders a white mint chocolate chip milkshake for Garrett, a peanut butter sundae for himself, and then he sideways glances at me, waiting for me to decide. The handwritten menu scrawled on the wall is enormous. It's too hard to pick just one. I love banana splits, just as much as I love a cookie dough flurry, or chocolate dipped cone. Hmmm … what to choose … what to choose… *Uh. I can't.*

"You pick," I command too sharply.

Wes drapes his arm casually over my shoulders, locking me closer to his side. "Come on, Kitten. You should pick." Coolly, like the *Fonz* himself, he points to the board. "I don't even know what ya like."

The aging, white-haired woman behind the counter gives us a sweet smile, as she spends a little too much time ogling Wes's hotness. With considerable effort, I attempt to pay no mind to her roaming eyes that are eating him alive. How can he not realize this? Does he not comprehend how sexy he is? Wait, of course, he does. He's Wes. Knowing him, he's probably got a stiffy right now from all the attention.

Call me territorial, or cray-cray, or something less pleasing, but my vindictive self, curls further into Wes so I can place my hand right on top of his t-shirt clad abs. They bunch under my palm, and I feel him quiver. Locking my other arm around his lower back, I hook my thumb into his side belt loop. My head leans onto his pec. *Yep, lady, take that.*

I hear his throat work. "Kitten?" His tone is hoarse.

Oh … right.

"I like banana splits with no strawberry or pineapple toppings. Only hot fudge. But I also love cookie dough flurries with extra cookie dough. Or those cones—you know the vanilla ice cream dipped in chocolate ones. They're messy but soooo good." My mouth waters at the thought.

"You heard the lady," he notes.

"Wait, what?" I cry.

No way!

"Sir, you want all of that including your other orders?" The woman bats her eyelashes at Wes.

"Yes," he affirms.

"No. No, he doesn't. He's mistaken." I speak quickly, my pitch higher than normal. Then I gape at him as he glances down at me. "I can't eat all of that, Wes. That's too much. Please, it's a waste. Just pick one of those."

"Nope. You can't decide so you should try 'em all. It's just ice-cream, Kitten. It's not a big deal."

It's a *huge* deal.

"Do you want me to get fat?" I croak.

Wes's corner lip quirks into a snicker, and he shakes his head. "Fat or not, you'll still be beautiful." He lifts his eyes from me to the ogling woman. My belly does a flop. Sometimes, he's too damn sweet. "We'll take them all," he finishes. And just like that, it's done. I can't win, anyhow, so when Wes guides me back to the corner booth where Garrett's seated. I slip in first, and he drops in beside me, throwing his arm over the back.

Throughout our ice-cream lunch, Garrett animatedly speaks about his new comics and some level he's made it to on his game. Wes carries on with him like he knows exactly what his son's talking about. I do not. So I spend my time gorging on delicious ice-cream and listening to two of the most amazing guys I've ever met.

Throwing a twenty on the table, Wes gracefully stands from the booth and offers me his hand. I take it, and he yanks me to my feet directly at his side. That soothing palm finds its place in the middle of my back all over again as we exit the joint.

"Where to now, Dad?" Garrett tosses his words next to his temple like he's casting another spell as we stop on the sidewalk. Twitching, he starts to sway.

A fat man passes us and downright stares at Garrett. It pisses me off. I glare at the jerk as I wrap Garrett into a hug to shield him from the asshole. He's taken aback for a split second before he returns the gesture.

"If you're excited to read your comics, we can go home now," I offer, stepping out of our hug to see Wes

watching us in a strange way. I try not to notice, and keep
my attention fixed on Garrett instead.

"No way, Ms. Gwen. Can we go to the park?"

"Sure we can, Bud. Anything you want."

At the park a couple blocks over, Garrett plays with
the other kids. Kids that are much younger than him, but
that he seems to relate better with. They're busy playing
tag.

The nicest thing about younger children is they care
even less about your differences as long as you're fun and
friendly.

Squealing, he escapes a little blonde girl trying to
tag his back. She misses him by an inch, and he laughs, his
red face glowing with exhilaration. It fills me with joy to
see him like this. He's an amazing kid. A kid who's
changed me forever. Being a teacher, you meet children,
hundreds of them throughout your career. Then there's that
special few that stick like glue, taking up space in your
heart. Garrett is one of those kids. He's special. Not
because he's autistic. It's his zest for life, big heart, and
willingness to overcome his obstacles that make me love
him. He's truly one of a kind.

On the bench seated beside me, Wes pats my knee,
letting his hand settle there.

"You're awfully touchy-feely," I observe kindly,
resting my smaller hand atop his huge one. Wes flips his
palm over and folds his fingers through mine. I let him. It
feels weird, yet nice. I couldn't tell you the last time I've
held someone's hand. Those fluttery feelings return.

"There's just something about you, Kitten. I can't
help myself."

Not wanting to, I blush at his compliment. Giddiness
I've never felt before fills me to the brim.

"Thank you," I mutter, rotating my head away so he doesn't see my heated cheeks, which'll just embarrass me more. "You're not one to shy away from complimenting a woman, are ya?" The question is rhetorical.

"The truth is the truth. No use in hiding it. So how'd the family chat go this morning?"

"It was alright." Frowning, I shrug. "Nash stole the phone from Trish, so we talked."

"You don't sound very happy about that."

I stare off into the distance, thinking of the best way to explain Nash and me without actually having to explain. "Nash and I have a complicated relationship." That's vague enough.

"Define complicated."

Shit. He's not going to let this go. I can tell by Wes's interested tenor and body language. He's still holding my hand, with our shoulders and legs touching. Guess I should just get this over with. Rip off the Band-Aid.

"You promise not to judge?" Fuck, this is hard. I've never had to discuss this with someone before. Ever.

An offended sound battles in Wes's throat. "Seriously, Kitten? Have you not seen the way I live?"

Touché.

Taking a deep breath, my chest expanding, I wrap my mind around any strand of confidence I have and travel forth into the scary unknown. Let's hope I don't get eaten alive. "Ummm … let's just say … Nash and I … uh … We've always had a *unique* kind of relationship. Since childhood, we've never had that I hate my step-brother, I hate my step-sister rivalry. To make a twenty-plus year story short and sweet, let's just say Nash has always been my rock. At fifteen, something happened to me and he stood by my side. And through my birth of Trish. And raising her. Even when he joined the club." There. That's answering a question without giving too much detail. I'm not interested in delving into my past unless I have to. It opens horrific wounds that I'd rather leave alone. The past is the past for a reason, and I like to keep it that way.

"But now things are different between you two?" Damn, Wes sounds very interested in this, and in me. It's weird. Good weird, I suppose. Yet weird nonetheless.

"I guess so." Lifting my shoulders, I drop them in a hefty shrug. "On Sundays, we've always had family luncheons at our parents. But about a month ago, something happened at one that basically tore us apart. And I'm not sure why. The day before the race, I went to see him, to talk things through, and he basically kicked me out after he had said we were too 'codependent'." I air quote with my free hand.

"Ahhhh ... So there's more than brother sister love here?"

Hopefully, he's not angry with what I'm about to admit. "Yes ... um ... I have this need. It's more of a split personality thing—"

"What?" Wes interjects.

Humorlessly, I laugh with my face twisted every which way. Then I chew my lip. "I'm not crazy. At least, not any more than a typical female is. I just have this part of me that likes ... dirty things. Naughty, filthy, very bad things." God, was that so hard to admit? My heart's about to erupt from my chest. It's beating wildly. And my hands are sweating.

Gnawing my bottom lip, I await his reply. He doesn't make me wait long. "You're kinky is what you're sayin'?"

How does he make it sound so easy? So normal? It's not.

"More or less," I clam up, shoulders stiffening.

"You can tell—"

"Dad, Ms. Gwen, can I go play over there and swing?!" Garrett hollers from across the way, severing Wes's words. He points to a different playset a few yards away.

Using his free hand, Wes waves him forth. "Yeah, Bud. Go on."

"Be careful," I add.

"Okay!" Cracking a giant grin, Garrett skips with a group of his new friends over to the play area. With innocent gusto, they attack the swings first.

Wes squeezes my hand, reestablishing our private bubble. "As I was saying, you can tell me, Kitten. Just spit it out."

"I-like-group-sex-with-men," I blurt so fast that the words basically merge. Then I take a deep breath, feeling a hundred pounds lighter for confessing it aloud. I've never done that before. Not to anyone. Not even Nash. Not like that, anyhow. Relaxing into the bench, I tip my head to lay on Wes's shoulder. It's cozy here with him like this. Our bench is tucked under a bank of trees. A gentle breeze skitters through the air, carrying the scent of fresh cut grass. It's peaceful.

"Are you safe when you do this?" There's zero judgment in his tone. If it were any other man, I'm sure they'd cringe at what I just confessed. But not Wes. He's calm, and I'm kinda shocked, kinda not. He is the open-minded type—obviously. I guess I just assumed he'd be more bothered or something.

My cheek rubs into his shoulder as I nod. "Yes. They're Nash's club brothers. He's there the entire time."

"Watching you?" Again, no jealousy, no judgment.

"No. He kisses me, and sometimes he holds me. He's like my anchor. I don't think I could do all of that without him. I … it feels wrong," I whisper.

"Yes, but you love it. So you feel guilty for feeling that way."

How could he know that?

"Are you a mind reader?" I quip, breaking into a smile. Man, there is something about divulging your secrets that make the world less dark. People should do it more often.

Wes chuckles. It's deep and yummy. "No, Kitten. But I get it. You're a classy woman. A school teacher, no less. So you don't know how to process this level of desire. It eats at you, doesn't it?"

"Yes," I breathe.

How did he know that, too?

"And if you go without it, you crave it to the point of constant arousal?"

"Yes."

"Is that what you meant by split personalities? One part of you wants it, while the other's telling you it's wrong?" Wes tests.

He's freaking me out here. It's like he's living in my damn head. "Yes. That's exactly it. How did you know?"

Wes moves our folded fingers into his lap, laying them on his thigh. Instinctively, I curl my legs onto the bench, shuffling my body so it's cuddling closer to him. My knees rest partway on his thigh, right next to our joined hands. "I can just tell, Kitten. Last night, at first you wanted to touch me, then you didn't. You stopped. But then you started watching those men play with the blondes, and it gave you a push. Your resolve folded once you touched your nipple. I could feel the change. It was sexy as fuck."

Bashfully, I murmur, "It was?"

"Yes."

"But I rode you just to get off. And then I…" Damn it, I didn't even help him finish. "I'm such a bitch. Didn't even think about your needs after I took care of mine."

"Don't worry about that." He brushes his thumb over the back of my hand.

"Don't? You were turned on, too."

"Yes. I was. It was one of the hottest things I've ever witnessed, let alone felt. So yeah, I was hard as fuck. But you needed it more. Your body was desperate. The way you rode my dick like that… It was…" He trails off, lost in thought, as he stares straight ahead, his eyes glazed over. Wes is so damn handsome with all of those hard lines, his supple lips, shapely nose, and those eyes. They're one of his best features. Because, unlike his dirty blond hair, his eyelashes are thick, long, and black. They're utterly stunning.

Like a cat seeking forgiveness, I nuzzle my cheek against his shoulder, still ashamed about how I left things last night. I was so out of it; I didn't even think to help him finish. "I'm sorry."

"Don't be. It was taken care of after I carried you to bed."

"How?" Oh, my shit. I can't believe I'm asking him this. Call me crazy, but I'm nosy. I wanna know.

His thumb stops stroking my hand. "How, what?"

"How'd you finish?"

I want to ask if he tugged it in the shower, or maybe in bed. Perhaps he watched porn? Or did he go off memory? Oooo … It's so bad, but I love when a guy jacks himself. There's something so sexy about it. A few months back, I asked Toa to masturbate in front of me while Price and another one of the brothers double teamed my ass and pussy. It was out of this world hot. I came like a freight train.

I grin. *Ah … Good times. Good times.*

Shifting on the bench, Wes begins to rub the back of his neck. Uh oh, something tells me I'm not gonna like what he has to say. *Fuck.*

I brace.

"Amanda came over, and we went into my sex suite by the garage. She did all of those dirty things she promised, and then some."

What? I can't believe it. Why her? Why last night? Why … why … what the hell? And in a sex suite? Since when does Wes have a sex suite? How come nobody told me about this place? What the ever loving fuck?

A big fat ball of jealousy lodges in my throat as my stomach lurches, wanting to puke at the thought of him with her. Why does it bother me so much? I don't get it. I've never gotten like this … *jealous.* There's no other name for it. Since when did I start caring for Wes enough to even feel jealous to begin with? How could I have let this happen? This isn't good. Kelly … I've always had a few ounces of jealousy when it pertains to her, or anyone Nash is with. I've accepted that. But not Wes, too. What is wrong with me? *Damn it.*

"You fucked Amanda after all of that happened?" The phase *'how could you?'* tosses around in my brain like a salad, but I keep it to myself. It's too possessive. Too much of something that I shouldn't be feeling to begin with.

More neck rubbing continues. "No. I didn't … um … *fuck* her." Nervously, his voice waivers.

"Then what the hell are you talking about?"

"She fucked me," he blurts.

Huh? Like she rode him?

"What?" I nearly shout.

"Fucked me. She. Fucked. Me. You're not the only one with kinks, Kitten. On, you know, special occasions, I like to be pegged. And last night, after all that friction, my dick was too sore to stroke. So … yeah…"

Hold on … huh?

"What the hell is pegged?"

"Fucked in the ass by a strap-on. The male g-spot is a powerful thing. Only stupid men don't take advantage of its perks." He sounds like an infomercial.

"So Amanda came over, put on a strap-on, and then fucked you while Garrett and I were asleep in the same house?" My anger and jealousy are going head-to-head at this point. I can't tell which is winning out.

Wes's voice cracks a "Yes."

"I can't … I can't believe it!"

"Calm down, Kitten. We're outside," Wes tries to reason. Yet, all I can feel is my adrenaline surging, as my mind conjures some dirty little scene where Wes is on a white bed, resting on all fours while Amanda pumps a blue dildo in and out of his sexy ass. Why it's blue, and he's on all fours, I don't know, but that's how I see it.

Blinking rapidly, I scrub that disturbing image from my brain. "No. I can't calm down. I can't believe you did that."

"Hey." He's defensive. "It's perfectly normal for a guy to like his prostate played with."

"That's not what I meant. I don't give a shit if you like a dildo up your ass or not. I like anal sex, too. So why shouldn't you? And I'm the chick who just told you she likes to be gang banged by a bunch of bikers. I'm the last person to judge you on whatever kink you've got goin' on."

Gently, he resumes stroking the back of my hand with his thumb. "Then what's the problem?"

I can't withhold the truth when I shout, "Amanda!"

"What about her?"

"Why didn't you use Candi? She's at least nice. Amanda wants to have your babies. She's possessive. And, I don't like her. Hell, if you needed a dildo fuck, you coulda woke me up. I'm sure I could pound an ass damn well." My eyes shoot wide when I realize I just said that last part aloud. A level of mortification I've never felt before settles with the lump of jealousy in my throat. "Oh, my god. I can't believe I said that. I'm soooo sorry. It's none of my business." I speak fast, trying to pull away from Wes. However, he's having none of it when he grabs my knees to keep me curled next to him.

Refusing to let go, Wes laughs. "It's fine, Kitten. And thanks for the offer. It's nice to know that if I need a good *pounding* that you're up for the job."

Somebody kill me now.

Overcome by embarrassment, I bury my reddened face in his shoulder. "I lied. I'd be a terrible ass pounder. I've never even touched a prostate in my life. I wouldn't know the first thing about them. I'd be like a dead fish, lying there with a fake cock strapped to me. You'd have to do all the work." Jesus! Why can't I shut up? This word vomit has got to stop. Duct tape would come in handy right about now. Hell, I'd use it on myself.

"Calm yourself. I was kidding."

Thank the Lord.

Blowing a relieved breath, I try to heed his words and calm myself. "Oh. Okay. Great. But I'm serious about Amanda." I'd much rather focus on her, instead of the fact that I just offered to fuck Wes's ass with a strap-on. Shit, I still can't believe I said that.

"That you don't like her," he remarks.

"Not just that. But that rest about her, too. She's bad news. And not the good kind of bad, either. Bad, bad."

"Duly noted. Thanks for looking out for me."

Great. Now he's amused.

Tugging my hand from his, I cross my arms over my chest. Then I turn even more so that my legs drape over Wes's and we're talking face to face. I look him straight in the eye. "I'm being serious."

"So am I." He taps the end of my nose like I'm adorable. I want to bite his finger off. "It's cute that you care as much as ya do. But Amanda never has, and will never be anything more than a contracted employee."

Challenging him, I raise a brow. "Does she know that?"

"Yeah. Why?"

In the distance, my eyes lock on their target that's about fifty yards away and headed toward us. "Because here she comes along with Candi and two other blondes. How did they know we were here, anyway?" Derision drips like honey from my lips. Internally sneering, I take in their barely-there clothes as they stroll through the grass. Why they thought it was acceptable to dress like that and come to a public park where children play is beyond me.

Amanda's jugs are heaving out of her top. Any minute now, there'll be a nip slip.

Wes follows my line of sight, then checks his watch. "Shit. I was supposed to meet with them in my office today at four to discuss an outing they'll be attending with me on Wednesday. It's almost five now. I guess time kinda flew by." He tips his head in my direction, giving me one of those charming smiles. It's amazing how warm and gooey that face makes me feel when it's like that. He's the devil. Evil and sweet in equal measure. No wonder Amanda is addicted to him. If I'm not careful, I'm bound to become addicted as well.

"Am I going to this outing on Wednesday, too?" I ask.

"I planned on it. If you're up for it."

I nod in agreement.

Leading the pack of she-wolves, Amanda stops directly in front of us, along with the three others crowding her back. "Zoe told us you were in town. So we thought we'd drop by since you missed our meeting."

Her bottom lip pokes out like she's sad about that. Then she sways her hips seductively as she steps closer, and squeezes her tiny ass between Wes's hip and the bench's arm. It's a tight fit, so her body is literally sucking his. Although he doesn't seem to mind when she lays her cutesy head on his shoulder and her hand on his inner thigh, way too close to his junk.

What a fucking bitch. If this isn't her staking claim, I dunno what is. It doesn't help that she's ignoring me completely, acting as if I'm not even here. That I'm somehow beneath her. Obviously, Wes is clueless. This bitch may as well tattoo her name to his dick with how possessive she's being. Why doesn't she just piss on him, too, while she's at it? Uh!!

Amanda whispers into Wes's ear about something, and he chuckles his sexy, amused chuckle. That's it. I've had enough of this. Peeling my legs out of Wes's grasp, I slide off the bench to stand. "I'm going to go check on Garrett," I comment, which is pointless because it falls on deaf ears since Wes is too taken by whatever Amanda's saying to pay any attention to me. The corner of her eye glimmers victoriously in my direction as she smirks. Of course, this bitch knows what she's doing, or her hand wouldn't be moving closer to his dick as we speak. Hell, I wouldn't put it past her to give him a blowjob right here, right now. She's a piece of work.

Pivoting on my heel, I fling my ponytail behind my back with attitude and set off toward Garrett, who's pushing that same little blonde on the swings. "Higher, Garrett. Higher," she cries happily as he whips her harder. Sweat drips down the sides of his face, but he doesn't seem to mind. Not if the giant smile he's wearing is any indication.

I approach them, standing at the bar on the edge of the swing set. "Hey, Garrett. How are you doing?"

"Great, Ms. Gwen. I'm tryin' to get Sammy really high."

"Is this your daddy's girlfriend?" the girl squeals, pumping her little legs.

"No." Garrett's smile dissolves for an instant before it's back again. "My Dad has lots of girlfriends. Ms. Gwen is more special than they are. She's my teacher and my friend." With jerking arms, he does his best to push Sammy again. Then cuts his gaze to me. "Right, Ms. Gwen?"

Appeased by his admission, I grin softly in return. "Of course, Garrett. We're friends, and I'm your teacher."

His gaze drifts over my shoulder to the bench Wes, and I were seated on. "The blondes showed up, did-didn't they?" He doesn't sound happy about this, as his shoulder twitches.

Indifferently, I shrug, pretending to downplay their arrival. Even if it does irk the crap outta me. One day, one fucking day, I wanted to spend with Garrett and Wes alone, without the blondes tagging along. And do I get that? Nope. Of course, I don't. They've been at the house constantly. Touching Wes, constantly. It's starting to grate on my nerves. And this time, it's not just this rare jealousy rearing its ugly head. It's the whole dynamic. How does this affect Garrett? What is this teaching him? The boy has lived long enough without a mother. And aside from Zoe, he's never had a motherly figure in his life. It's sad.

Tamping down my climbing irritation, I plaster a smile on my face for Garrett's benefit. That's what mothers do. They fake it until they make it. Trust me. I've got plenty of practice with Trish. *"Where's my daddy? Why doesn't he want to see me?"* She used to ask me that question all the time. *"He's not that kind of daddy, Bug. I'm here for ya, though. I'll be whatever ya need me to be."* Nash would reassure her. Over the years, those questions floated away, because Nash was there to love Trish as she needed. He put her hair in pigtails. He gave her butterfly kisses at night when I had to work. Went to her volleyball games when I couldn't.

Sadly, Garrett's never had that. It's no secret he admires his father, and that Wes loves his son. It shines through whenever they're around each other. They have a bond. I'm just disappointed that Garrett was never able to

NOWHERE

have that kind of relationship with his mother. And with
Wes's gaggle of blondes continuously parading around,
he's never going to get that. I wonder if Wes even dated
after his wife left?

"Ms. Gwen," Garrett calls, tearing me from my
musings.

"Huh?"

"The blondes are here, aren't they?" he reiterates,
flinging his words as he steps away from pushing Sammy.

He's getting worked up. His mannerisms are sharper
now, which only happens when he's upset. Last week,
when he couldn't read a word, he'd started these jerky
movements. Then they stopped as soon as I helped him
figure the words out and then gave him a big hug. Some
autistic children don't like to be touched. However, Garrett
doesn't seem to mind it. At least not from me. I'm not sure
about anyone else.

"They are here." My sickly sweet smile remains in
place.

Pushing Sammy once more, Garrett runs his hands
through his disheveled hair then steps away from the
swing set entirely. I follow on his tail as he heads toward
the parking lot.

"What are you doing?" I ask.

"Leaving." He strides faster, his long legs eating up
the distance, feet kicking up grass. I have to triple my
speed to keep up with him. My legs aren't nearly as long
as his; not when he's close to six feet tall.

Falling in step beside him and getting some serious
cardio at the same time, I touch his shoulder. "What's
wrong? Are you okay? You didn't even say goodbye to
Sammy."

Garrett shrugs my hand off and doesn't speak another word until we're at the limo. Randy is magically standing by the door. Garrett climbs in first, and I'm quick on his heels.

Inside, he twitches and rocks in his seat, mumbling under his breath. His dancing eyes are unable to lock on any one fixture.

"Garrett, what's wrong?" My concern is growing by the second.

"Nothing," he lies.

Reaching across the seat, I take one of his hands into mine and hold it. He allows this. "What's wrong?" I'm firmer, channeling my inner Wes.

Garrett jerks with zero control. "He-he wasn't supposed to have them here today. He promised. I asked to get comics. I-I asked." His free hand goes crazy, tossing his words into the air, nearly hitting the ceiling. "I asked that you come, but not his-his women. He-he said tha-that they wouldn't come. That-that'd you." He tries to point to me, but his hand's flopping too much to aim true. "That you and us would have fun today. No-no one else would come. Why-why did he lie? He-he promised. He-he never breaks promises. He's a goo-good dad. But you're up-upset, too, that they're here. I-I don't like them."

"Calm down, sweetheart." Slipping closer, I pull him into my arms. He comes willingly and lays his head on my chest as his arms lock around my middle. Caressing his back in soothing strokes, I kiss the top of his hair. "It's okay. Dad didn't mean it. I promise. They showed up unannounced. He didn't break his word. He didn't lie. Now, I need you to take a deep breath."

Garrett doesn't respond, but I hear him inhale a deep lungful of air before blowing it out. A wave of calm finally settles over him. Slowly, he begins to stop twitching. The back door opens, and Wes pokes his head inside to see us embracing. An indistinguishable expression washes over his features.

"What's going on in here?" He's unhappy.

"You li—" Garrett starts, but I cut him off to stave off an argument.

"Garrett said you promised him no blondes today, so he got upset and came back to the limo to wait for you. But he was still distressed. So we're trying to calm ourselves, aren't we, Garrett?" He nods into my breasts as I continue to soothe him, refusing to let go until all of his tremors are gone.

Wes's eyes widen as he, too, takes a seat and Randy shuts his door. Just as I figured, Wes begins to rub the back of his neck while his gaze settles upon us. "I'm sorry, Bud. I didn't know they were coming here. I was supposed to have a meeting with them. I missed it on accident. Gwen and I got to talking and…"

"And he lost track of time. The girls came by so your dad didn't have to take you away from playing with Sammy," I add for Wes, downplaying the whole thing. It's true. He didn't know. Although he could have sent them back to the house. He does have that authority. And he could have also told Amanda to fuck off. But, he didn't. He spent however long over there eating up her attention. *Bleck!*

On the rest of the drive home, no one speaks. Garrett returns to his seat after his tremors have ended, and I stare out of the side window. Upon arrival, we each exit the limo without a word. However, as I proceed to go inside, Wes grabs hold of my forearm to stop me. His big hand is hot and heavy, grounding me.

"Come in and watch a movie with us. We can eat dinner in the living room," he requests, stepping close enough that our toes touch. The urge to lean into him and sniff his chest, his neck, his yumminess, rides me hard, but I throttle that desire and take a hefty step backward, to give us some distance. Even if it's only a mere foot.

Tilting my head back, I meet his gaze. "We who?"

Before Wes can reply, a fancy silver sports car pulls in behind the limo and the blondes start piling out. There's my answer. Wes, me, Garrett, *and* the blondes for dinner and a movie. Nope. No thanks.

"I'd rather not." Tugging out of his grasp, I pivot on my heels and leisurely strut to the door, so he doesn't realize how pissy I am.

"Please, Kitten. Come and eat with us … *Garrett* will want you there." He calls to my back.

My hand hovers over the door knob. That's completely unfair, using Garrett to get what he wants. If Garrett hadn't already escaped into the house with his comics, I would ask his opinion. Though, I already know what he'd say. He'd want me to spend time with them. To endure watching a movie with a gaggle of blondes hanging all over Wes. My stomach drops at the thought. After today and the way he touched me, the way we talked, the intimacies we shared, I … I can't witness that. It'll be just as bad as watching Nash shove his tongue down Kelly's throat. At least I've never seen Nash get a blow job from any of his ladies. I'm pretty sure that'd kill me. Why do I have to like unavailable men? I'm an idiot.

Straightening my spine, my head held high, I cast my eyes at the white door ahead of me and accept my fate of taking one for the team—for Garrett. "Fine. I'll join you there in twenty minutes," I bite off, casually yank the door open, and strut the rest of the way to my room. It's going to be a long ass night, and I'll be damned if I do it being uncomfortable. It's time to freshen up and change clothes.

Chapter Fifteen

Day 11

"Put on the red dress," she said. "Wear a black thong," she said. "Don't worry about your shoes," she said. "Leave your hair down and curl it," she said. Well, fuck Zoe and all that she said! I should have never trusted her when she coerced me into wearing this skimpy thing. I told myself after the leather contraption that I'd never take her advice again. Apparently, I've gone soft because here I am doing it once more, standing at the larger than life entrance of a B.D.S.Fucking.M club, wearing a dress that could fit a toddler. To top it all off, did I mention the B.D.S.Fucking.M club? Yup, I'm here with Wes and a bevy of his blondes. However, they're already inside and have been for the past twenty minutes while I stand on the front porch of this mansion looking like a moron. Did I mention that this mansion has been converted into a BDSM club? I'm pretty sure I did, twice. I just want to make sure you're grasping the severity of this situation. This club is for naughty people. People like … *me*. It's like standing in front of the cookie jar, and telling yourself you're on a diet—tempting and scary as hell. I've always kept a tight leash on my inner sex-fiend. Yet, here I am in this dress, wearing flats, with my long brown hair draped down my back. And, I'm not wearing a bra. Why? Because this dress isn't conducive for one. It's like a Band-Aid; it covers all of the critical areas but leaves the rest bare.

Leaning my shoulder against the wall, I tap away on Randy's phone. I'm texting Zoe to give her a piece of my mind. We've been duking it out since I refused to leave the limo. However, thus far, the negotiator has talked me out of the car and onto the porch. She's got mad skills. *Kevin Spacey*'s got nothin' on her.

Z: *Just go inside. Aren't you the least bit curious?*
Me: *No!*

Z: *Stop being a big baby. There's nothing to be scared of. Wes is there to talk with Geo. They're friends and business partners. He would never let anything happen to you that you don't want.*

That's the point! *That you don't want.* What if I don't know what I want? What if I want a lot? Or what if I don't want anything? How will I know? The group sex at *Nowhere* came out when I was drunk. I can't get drunk tonight. I have to stay sober so my mind doesn't play tricks on me. This is fucking with my head.

Hell, it's bad enough that I've had to keep everything else in check this week. Let's add my rampant libido to the list. On Sunday, we'd watched a movie after a cheeseburger dinner that the blondes refused to eat. Can't say I paid much attention to the flick because Amanda was all over Wes, straddling his waist throughout the entire thing. Afterward, Garrett left. I'd walked him to his room, and when I reluctantly returned, the living room was like a scene out of a porno. Wes was eating Amanda's pussy while Candi rode him. The other two were busy playing with each other, and Wes's nipples. It was obvious that I was not needed. So I went to my safe space, where I may or may not have cried myself to sleep.

Honestly, I'm just sick and tired of being surrounded by these women. These hot, sexually untethered women. It's wearing on my mind, heart, self-confidence, and just about everything else. The only thing I'm loving, even more, is Garrett. His writing progress this week has been slow but steady. We've played some fun, educational games. Read more comics. Sunbathed by the pond with Zoe. He's made me laugh numerous times just by being himself. That part of my life is amazing. Then Wes comes galloping into the picture and obliterates all of that with his sexiness, occasional sweetness, and his collection of blonde hotties. If one's going, another is coming. It's an open door policy where Wes and his house is concerned. Those stolen moments we share are what is driving me the most insane. Kisses to the back of my head. A hand around the waist in the morning over breakfast. A forehead peck when Garrett and I are outside working on our tans. It's those moments that I wrap up into a little present and save for later. For the moments when blonde mayhem wreaks havoc over every part of my day. From their skimpy, bikini-clad bodies traipsing around the house to their never-ending Wes groping. It's right there in your face all the time. At first, it angered me. Now I'm frustrated and a tiny bit jealous. I wish I didn't like him at all, but I do. There's just something special about him.

Me: *I don't know.*

Z: *I do. Wes has had his blondes around more in the past week than I've seen them in months. There's got to be a reason for that. You need to go in there, enjoy yourself, and fuck what anyone else thinks. What if you find your dream man waiting in the darkened corner with a paddle? Do you want to piss off fate by not going in? Obviously, you were supposed to be there, looking as hot as you do, or you wouldn't be there to begin with. Just suck it up, sister, and get your fine ass some love taps.*

Me: *That's easy for you to say. Have you ever been paddled before?*

Z: *Ask Randy. He'll tell you what I like.*

Oh, I suppose I forgot to mention that Zoe and Randy are sort of a thing. According to her, Wes knows but refuses to acknowledge it. So they continue with their jobs as scheduled, but spend their evenings in Zoe's bed. They make a cute couple. He's tall, dark, built, and handsome. While she's petite and blonde, with a great personality. I'm happy for them. Truly.

Me*: I'm not going to ask your man what you like in bed.*

Z: *If you can't ask someone what they like, how are you going to walk into that club?*

I sigh.

Me: *Stop being a pain. I thought you were my friend. Have my back, chickie.*

Z: *I am on your side. That's why I want you to go in there, strut that hot ass, and get your kink on.*

Me: *Whatever happened to the sensible Zoe that I thought I was friends with? Are you secretly a domme?*

I grin, knowing that she's no such thing. At least she's helping buy me some time.

Z: *See! You already know the lingo. Get to moving! It's a beautiful place. I've been there a few times with Wes to talk with Geo. Just go inside. There will be a guard that'll take your shoes. Then he'll have you sign a form and give you bracelets. Be honest on the form; you'll thank me for it later.*

Me: *I'm not going in.*

Z: *Yes. You are. Do it for me, so Randy can call on his break. If you don't go inside, Randy won't get a break because he'll be busy playing babysitter.*

Me: *Gee thanks. Guilt me into it, why don't ya?*

Z: *Is it working?*

It is. The pain in my ass is such a good negotiator. She's peaking my interest when I don't want it peaked. Earlier when I'd refused to come inside, Wes barely batted an eyelash at my obstinacy. It's like he couldn't care less if I'm here. That's partially my problem. I'm a little hurt by the brush off. Not that I need him to beg me. I'm not a child, and I can make my own choices. But it's nice to be wanted sometimes. Evidently, today isn't one of those days. He's barely looked, or spoken to me all night. On the ride over, he played with the blondes and got another blowjob, while I sat in utter boredom the entire journey. On a positive note, or perhaps not so positive, depending on how ya look at it, I think I'm becoming immune to his sexual proclivities. Same shit, different day.

Turning my head, I smile at Randy, then hand him back his phone. "Your girlfriend can be a real ballbuster."

He barks a short laugh. "Yeah. Tell me about it. She's a handful. So what's it gonna be? Are you going indoors, or back into the limo?"

Swapping my gaze from the limo out front to the large double doors, I steel myself before replying. "I'm going to go inside. But if I need to come back, will you be here?"

Randy nods. "Yes. I'll be out here all night, talking to Zoe and playing on my phone."

With a parting wave, I see myself indoors, and just like Zoe explained, there's a massive man seated at a desk in the foyer. He's wearing a fancy tux. As I approach, he flashes me a wide grin and sets a paper and pen on the desktop.

"Are these for me?" I pick them up.

Nodding, the man remarks. "I was wondering when you'd get the courage to come inside."

Winking playfully in my direction, he rounds the desk and kneels at my feet. Gently snatching one foot at a time, he doesn't ask permission when he slips my shoes off like Prince Charming. Then, he tucks my flats under his arm and retakes his seat behind the opulent desk, which matches the rest of the lavish surroundings. It's rather beautiful in here with marble floors, cathedral ceilings, chandeliers, and a golden, ivory, red scheme that feels oddly romantic.

Unable to bend over in fear of flashing my assets, I hold the paper in my hand and try to write that way. It doesn't come without difficulty, but I manage. It's a simple form. Name, birth date, address, phone number. Then toward the middle, the questions get more personal: sexual orientation, last menstrual period, allergic to latex, ever been to a BDSM club before, and my personal favorite: dominant, submissive, or switch. Then there's a box to check off things that you're comfortable with. This is probably the most difficult one to mark. Why? Because it's not so much the things I'm comfortable or uncomfortable with. It's what I'm okay with or not okay with doing here. That's the issue. The options range from light spanking to wax play, piss play, all the way down to double penetration and blindfolding. It's a broad spectrum. Then at the very bottom, there's a place to sign after reading their rules and a line to note any hard limits. My only hard limits are scat or blood play, so I mark those. Even though I'm sure those are normal. As for pain limitations, I can take that quite well. I'm not opposed to a good spanking. Although it's been awhile since I've been exposed to that.

Once I've completed the form and handed it over to the big guy, he opens a drawer and produces a set of white cuffs. He places colorful rubber bands on them and explains what they signify. Which means little to me, because I have no plans of doing anything while in here. Concluding our chat, he slips the cuffs on my wrists and latches them into place before calling someone to escort Mr. King's guest to the main floor.

A shirtless man, who could easily be Toa's estranged brother, quickly sees me through the halls, down a flight of stairs, and into the lower level of the house where music pulses and the scent of sex and leather hangs in the air. Dim wall sconces replace ceiling lights. The floor is now a dark travertine. Wordlessly, the brute of a man walks me past a bar filled with half naked bodies, and into a room littered with leather couches and chairs arranged into conversation nooks. In the furthest corner, there's a velvet rope separating the space. Wes and his blondes are lounging on couches behind it.

Taking a step in their direction, I'm stopped when an exotic man with light green eyes, and toffee skin, softly, yet, authoritatively grabs my forearm. "I've never seen you here before."

His timbre voice fires a shockwave of desire straight to my toes. Squeezing my thighs together, I take in his massive form. He's built. Big arms, thick abs, a tapered waist, hugged by a pair of made-for-him jeans. He, too, is barefoot. Damn, and even his feet are sexy. Maybe coming in here wasn't such a bad idea after all. Remind me to thank Zoe later, if I'm surrounded by hot men all night. This one is stunning.

Unsure of standard *switch* protocol, I meet his gaze with an air of confidence. Where that came from I'm not sure, but I'm going with it. "This is my first time … *here*." Sensuality charges my words as his hand travels to my cuffed wrists and stops there.

"You're not claimed," he observes, checking my bands.

"No. I'm here with some friends."

Wrapping his hand around my wrist, he tugs me closer, until my chest is smashed to his abs. Woo, he's tall. I have to tip my head way back to save eye contact. "I'm Master Luca, and you're a pretty little thing." He curls his arm around my waist and splays his hand along the curve just above my butt. A knowing tingle sparks inside my panties. "What's your name?"

"Her name is *mine*. Now back the fuck off!" a familiar voice booms at my rear, sending a shocking tremor down my spine. *Wes.*

Undeterred, Master Luca holds me firmly in place like the strong dom he is. I can feel the heat radiating off his body as it seeps through the thin fabric of my dress. His manly scent is a rich blend of sandalwood and leather. My brain swirls as I melt deeper into his arms. He's exquisite.

"Ahhh … Master Wesley. I should have known she was with you. Although, she's not your usual company. A brunette?" The dom's eyebrow and lip quirk simultaneously.

"Let her go, Luca," Wes growls.

The lip quirk curls into a breathtaking smile. All white teeth, all gorgeous, contrasting with his darker skin. "Now why would I do that? The female apparently likes me, and she's not claimed. Her bands tell me enough." His head inclines in Wesley's direction. "You've got yourself four willing females. I have not taken anyone tonight, so I am within my rights to play with this woman."

"Gwen," I intercede so he can call me by name. Why I'm not pulling away from him? I don't know for sure. Wes's tone isn't friendly. Then again, Master Luca's right. Wes has four willing females, and I'm tired of competing for scraps. If that's what you'd call it in the first place.

Master Luca's eyes drop to mine once more. "Gwen. That's a lovely name."

"Thank you." I grin bashfully.

He brushes his fingertips over my cheek. "Would you like to sit and talk for a while, Gwen? Then after you're comfortable, perhaps we can have some fun? I'm a respectable man. I won't push ... *too far*. I'll play nice." He sounds like he means it, and for whatever reason, I trust his word. He has an honest face. My gut also concurs when it dances at the prospect of spending some one-on-one time with this handsome master.

"She's not spending any fuckin' time with you, Master Luca. She's *not* a masochist," Wes answers, yet Master Luca isn't looking anywhere but me for permission.

"Gwen?"

The hand on my back presses harder, so I'm forced to slip my feet between Master Luca's. A thick erection crushes to my belly. *That* wasn't there before. Redness speckles my cheeks, knowing that I've excited him. I bite the side of my lip. If I had any thoughts of saying no to begin with, those doubts have vanished into thin air. I love the way he feels, smells, and that he genuinely wants to spend time with me. I couldn't tell you the last time any man has made me feel this way—wanted. Wanted without the lingering thoughts of who's to come afterward. Kelly? Amanda? Candi? Wes and Nash are always too caught up in their women. I deserve more than to be second rate. I deserve *this*. It's time to dip my hand into that cookie jar.

"I'd love to."

Wes curses under his breath. "Kitten, I will not permit this."

"She's not asking for your approval, Master Wes. Now please leave us. You know interfering is forbidden without consent."

"Fuck!" Wes explodes. Then all is right in the world again as I hear him storm off. Angering him shouldn't please me as much as it does. It serves him right for dragging me along, then ignoring me.

Master Luca guides me over to the private couch where we can be alone. He sits first before pulling me crossways onto his lap. "So it's your first time here. Have you played in a club like this before?" As he talks, he softly brushes his knuckles over my skin—everywhere. Across my exposed legs, up my neck, cheeks, around my ears, down my arms, and into the top of my cleavage. Goosebumps sprout, trailing his touch, and I lose my breath. He grins. "You're responsive and quite beautiful. I can see why Master Wesley is so protective of you."

"I..." Swallowing thickly, I clear my throat. "I've never played in a club before. I've dated a few men who've spanked me, and I've liked it. But this wasn't my idea. I'm working for Wesley this summer. Tonight, he decided his employees were going to accompany him to this place." Just as I finish, a woman tied to a giant X screams her pleasure when a man snaps her bare breasts with a bull whip. It's awe-inspiring, in its own way. I'm intrigued.

Distracted by the scene, Master Luca takes the opportunity to tug my dress to the side, exposing my breast. He begins to knead it with his palm. It feels so damn good that I don't care he didn't ask permission. Sighing, I lean further into him instead, my thong soaked in arousal. "Your breasts are perfect. I'd very much like to strip you out of this dress and have you sit on my lap. Will you permit me to do that?"

Aren't Master's supposed to be bossy and domineering? Not sweet like this.

"Are you always this nice?" I tease.

"No." He chuckles. It's deep and sensuous. *Damn.* I grow wetter at the sound. "Most of the women here are regulars and know what I expect. You're different. Which is one of the reasons I'm so attracted to you."

Dipping his head, he draws my nipple into his mouth, and that's all she wrote. Every cell in my body runs on instinct and instinct alone. I submit to this ravenous hunger and straddle his lap with my dress still in place. His rock hard body feels amazing between my thighs. Greedily feeding himself my nipple, he nibbles and sucks it in hard, toe curling pulls as he slips his hand into my dress to fondle the other. Moans of raw ecstasy flutter from my lips. I grab his shoulders for leverage to grind my pussy over his erection. One urgent thrust and Master Luca seizes my hips, forcing me to stop. Sucking my nipple, groaning sensually in his throat, he laves it with his tongue once more before drawing away.

His fiery eyes meet my lidded ones. "You're not in control, my dear. I am. It's time to take this—" Off comes my dress with one swoop, and then we're off the couch, moving. Master Luca carries me across the floor, my legs wrapped around his waist. He stops at the far wall. A set of long chains dangle from the ceiling, and he grabs two of them, clicking them onto my cuffs before I get a moment to process what the hell is going on. Carefully, he peels my legs from around him and sets me on the floor. Bending at the waist, he clicks two sets of padded shackles around my ankles. They're attached to chains coming out of the floor.

What the fuck is happening?

Taking a step back, he admires my form with feral intent, then slaps a lever on the wall. Up, up, up, my arms retract until I'm standing bared to the room, stretched wide, arms immovable, legs locked in place, like a prisoner prepared for slaughter … like the man in the cellar. My exposed breasts hang just slightly, my nipples rigid from both the chill in the air and this strange excitement. My heart batters my rib cage.

Facing outward, I get a full view of the entire great room. People don't seem to bat an eyelash in our direction as they mill about touching and talking with one another. Not sure why that surprises me, but it does. A woman less than ten feet away is restrained much like I am. Red welts dot her frame as her Master thumps her flesh with a flogger. Dazed, her head drops back, staring at the ceiling. Air pumps from her lungs in a maddened beat. I can see it from the rapid rise and fall of her chest. Sweat glistens her flesh in the pale light. It's beautiful. *She's* beautiful. Lush. Excited. I can almost taste her need from here. The flogger swings, hitting her inner thigh, and she wails, yanking on the restraints. They jingle harshly, sending a shiver up my spine. Her Master runs his fingers gently over his handiwork, then kneels to kiss that spot. She thrashes, begging for more. He slips a finger between her thighs. I can't see, but I can guess that he's fingering her by the way she sobs.

I ... Jesus. I'm so turned on from just watching with envy. This ache in the pit of my soul opens like the petals of a flower. I shouldn't want that. But I do. I want relief ... release ... anything.

Tapping my cheek, Master Luca claims my attention before he unzips his jeans, lowering them part way, giving me the shameless view of his dick. Jesus F'in Christ, he's huge! His heavy erection bobs between his legs, with a pearl of pre-cum on the crown. A set of hefty balls hang between his thighs. *Fuck.* How does that even fit into a woman? It's *that* enormous. At least eleven inches, and so damn thick I don't think I could fit my hand around it. Taking a step toward me, a dominant aura surrounds him. He's in his element. This is his domain. I'm the sheep, and he is the Shepherd ... or perhaps the wolf, and I his prey. He's incredible.

Running his knuckle across the apple of my cheek, he grins. Then kisses my jaw, skimming his lips higher to the shell of my ear. "Tell me your safe word," he whispers there, his hot breath teasing me.

"Red," I automatically reply, knowing that's basic protocol. I read that much in the entrance form.

"I'm going to pleasure you, Gwen. Do I have your consent?"

I bow my head once in acquiesce. "Yes, sir."

How does he know this is what I want? Can he tell? Part of me *should* feel bad, right? Where's the guilt? The self-loathing? The uncertainty? Yet, as I stand here, restrained, exposed to the world, I feel *relief*. Where did this come from? I have no clue, but I'm going to enjoy every touch, every minute, everything that Master Luca does to me. I need this.

Fisting his cock, he rubs the fat head to my inner thigh. A string of his pre-cum clings there, wetting my flesh. I shudder at the coolness. "I'm going to have so much fun with you, beautiful Gwen." He caresses my other thigh, repeating the process. It's like he's marking me. It's fucking hot.

Sweeping my tongue across my lips, I wet them. "May I speak?" I think I read somewhere this is the correct way to address your dom during play. Hell. I'm just winging it.

The smile I'm rewarded with is prize enough. I did well. "You may." He cups both of my breasts in his hands, lightly running his thumbs over their buds. Biting my inner cheek, I suppress a wanton moan, and he notices, glowering. "Now, now, female, you mustn't withhold from me, unless I ask. Give me all your sounds." And with that, he grips both of my nipples, twisting them firmly between his dexterous fingers. The heat it pools between my thighs is enough to make my knees weak. Trembling, I try to squeeze my legs together, to free some of this ache. They won't touch. I grumble in frustration.

Master Luca grins knowingly, the lines around his eyes showing his age. "Sorry, beautiful. Now ask what you were going to ask. Your pussy is mine to please. Your thighs can't help you." To cement his words, he cups my mound. "Mmmm … already so wet." He removes his hand and brings it to his nose, smelling me on him. It's sorta hot. "Your pussy is sweet. I love the smell and taste of a sweet pussy." Licking his lips as if he's picturing the taste, his hand travels back to my swathed bits, and he thrusts the tiny fabric to the side, slipping a finger through my drenched folds. This time, I can't control it when a guttural moan tears from my lips as he grazes my clit. "So, so wet. Now ask your question, Gwen." His ministrations linger. A finger slides through my slit until the tip circles my asshole then glides back through. My mind blanks, forgetting what I was going to ask. I … I can't remember. It was something about moving too fast … wasn't it? Oh, who cares, as long as he keeps touching me.

His lips press to the corner of mine. "You can't remember, can you?"

My mouth falls open, panting. I shake my head, shocked by sensations, by the overload, by everything. I can feel him. Sense him. The room. The electrical charge in the air. The eyes that shift toward us for but a moment then glance away. A man in the corner. I catch him staring. His dark frame shadowed, yet I can feel his impenetrable gaze. He's jacking his cock out of the flap of his jeans, watching me! *Oh, yes.* I throw my head back, moaning louder as Master Luca plays with my pussy more fervently. His fingers circle my clit, my center, my ass, never lingering, never penetrating. Only teasing, drawing me higher, turning me inside out. I sob my hunger, and he chuckles, prowling his massive form from my front to my back where he spanks me with his bare hand. A spike of pain radiates, soothing to a dull, ravenous ache. I try to squeeze my thighs again. Nothing. My pussy weeps from neglect and torment as liquid arousal drips down the inside of my legs. Another palm connects with my other cheek, and I wail, thrashing my head back. The sting travels to my core, and my knees buckle.

Master Luca seizes my waist. "Don't hurt your arms, beautiful. I've got you." His strong hand fastens around my stomach, as his other hand travels to my breast, playing, pinching, loving. It's unbelievable. I ... I've never felt anything like it. His cock head rubs along my ass cheeks, trailing his essence there. It helps cool the lingering heat.

"He's watching you," he whispers hotly in my ear before nibbling his teeth there. My nipples draw into sharper points. They need his mouth. They're begging for it.

Glancing to the corner again, I see the man pounding his cock. He's right. He's still watching. That's so fucking hot. Unable to speak, I nod, and Master Luca clucks his tongue. "No, no, beautiful one." His hand travels to my chin, turning it in the opposite direction, toward ... *Wes*. "He's watching. Can't you see his reddened face? He's angry. But those eyes tell us a different story, now don't they? He's turned on. Oooo ... watch him, beautiful. He's touching his dick just for you. He's hard, just for you. How does that make you feel?" he purrs.

Oh my god, Master Luca's right. Wes is watching us. He's watching *me*. Do you see it, too? A funny feeling ignites in my belly at the thought. He's rubbing himself as we stare at him, knowing full well what we're doing. He's so fucking sexy; hair a mess, cheeks flushed, his chest rising and falling. My heart slams into my ribs, agreeing with me, as my pussy clenches at the mere thought of how dirty this is. How much it turns me on. How much I love his eyes on me. His mouth parts across the room like he's expelling a silent moan. Jesus, he's... he's *perfect*.

"Yes," I breathe. "He's watching us."

Master Luca releases my chin to delicately trace his fingers down my front, between my breasts, and over my stomach until he's cupping my pussy. I whimper as he circles my clit over my thong. "Watch him, beautiful. Watch his need. Take it from him."

Obeying my Master, I intently observe Wes, powerless to tear my eyes away even if I wanted. His gaze falls upon me, raking my form like a thousand tiny fingers playing my body like a harp. I tremble when his baby blues settle between my thighs where Master Luca continues to circle my clit around and around. An orgasm swiftly unfurls, taking me over the brink of no return. My eyes lock with Wes's and I come, *hard,* my body flailing. A sudden palm connects with my ass and my pussy spasms harder, flooding juices down my legs. A murky haze of euphoria clouds the edges of my vision, as my throat belts sounds that I've never heard before. My arms yank on the chains as my other cheek is spanked, drawing my orgasm to a plateau I never knew existed. I wheeze heavily for breath between cries.

Wes's hooded eyes blaze across the distance as he whips his impressive erection out. His arm hooks around Amanda's neck, who's seated beside him. He shoves her to her knees in front of him. Like the good puppy she is, she obliges. With one quick thrust, he forces his dick into the back of her throat.

"Looks like he couldn't hold off. You're turning him on, Gwen. He wants you. He wants this. You're a beautiful screamer," Master Luca whispers to my ear, but I can't see anything but Wes. He's magnificent, as he fucks Amanda's mouth, watching me watch him. I love that he takes what he wants without question. If only I were brave enough to do that.

An audible rip resonates just before fresh air douses my soaked pussy. Blinking, I dial back into my body—where my core quivers with tiny aftershocks, and my legs finally stop shaking. I inhale a deep lungful of air. That was … amazing.

"You ready for more?"

Before I can reply, or take another breath, Master Luca magically elicits some of the most primal feelings deep from within my soul when he drops behind me, spreads my cheeks, and licks me—everywhere. His tongue delves into spaces I didn't know God created. My eyes burst wide when it encircles my clit, then dips into my core for a moment just before plunging into my asshole. Losing all of the air in my lungs, my body goes stiff at the strange, yet incredible sensation. Swirling there, he smacks both of my cheeks at once, and I flinch at the sexually charged pain, pinching his face between my globes. He groans, eating more of what should be dirty, but is one of the sexiest things ever discovered.

Across the room, Wes pounds Amanda's face earnestly. Visually, his body coils tighter when unabashed moans start to pour from my lips as I'm eaten alive. Master Luca spanks me again. Hot, ecstasy-induced pain explodes like a cannon through my limbs, driving me wilder. Fisting my hands, nails digging painfully into my palms, I scream toward the sky, jerking against my restraints. His tongue delves into my dripping center, relentlessly fucking my hole. Thrust-thrust-thrust-lick-thrust-thrust-swirl. He drives higher, winding me tighter and tighter until I'm ready to pop. Until my body is thrashing and begging for something, anything. Until my soul is torn open, gaping from my chest, aching for completion. My legs shake. More wetness floods my pussy. I'm on fire. I have to come.

Wes's gorgeous face twists into a snarl as he shoots down Amanda's throat, her hair wrapped around his fist. No sooner is he finished does Wes shove her kneeling form to the floor and stands. His eyes remain on me as he stalks across the room, leaving a pile of upset blonde in his wake. She calls to him, yet he ignores her. Our eyes lock, and I toss away the key. He stops two feet in front of me just as Master Luca sucks my clit into his mouth.

My eyes fly wide. "Oh fuck!" I scream. Suddenly, my world snaps in two as another orgasm sneaks up on me, barreling like a freight train to its destination. "Ahhh!" My body shakes like a fish outta water, as my eyes blank, mind blanks, and all I can feel is the sizzle of 100% proof bliss soaking into my every pore. *Yes!* Every inch of me focuses on a singular function—coming. More sucking of my clit has me rolling down another mountain. Air fires from my lungs in sharp pants. Sweat drips down the sides of my cheeks. I can feel everything. Every touch, every sound, every … Fuck! A hot mouth latches onto my nipple and my toes curl.

"That's it," Wes encourages, his tongue flicking my bud as his hand skims down my belly, between my legs. My eyes roll further into my head—into my soul. *Lord! Yes!* Master Luca's skilled mouth travels to my asshole, kissing, sucking, and fucking me there. What shouldn't be deliciously erotic *is*. Continuously, moans impart my lips between breaths. Wes's finger slips between my cleft and I hear him hiss. "Fuck, Kitten, you're so wet," he praises, and all I can seem to do is give him a faint nod before my head drops back for the count, since I can no longer hold it up.

Wes brushes atop my swollen clit before breaching my core with two eager fingers. They thrust in deep, curling just a bit to hit my sweet spot. He's no rookie. Thank God. "How many more orgasms?" he asks with a hint of humor. Is he asking me how many more I want? Master Luca swipes my asshole once more with his tongue before going upright behind me. His cockhead swings as he stands, colliding with my cheek. A spray of pre-cum covers my skin. He massages it in with his hand.

"I say we give her ten more," he replies.

Ten?!

I open my mouth to protest then quickly realize I can't speak. My throat is too raw from crying out as my body faintly quakes from spent orgasms. Yet, Wes's digits remain unmoving in my pussy like they belong there. Maybe they do. They feel so fucking good. I tighten around them so I can remember this forever. I inhale deeply to commit the mix of his scent, Master Luca's scent, and the scent of leather and sex to memory. I never want to forget this moment. Not when I'm eighty, sitting in a rocker, thinking about the good ole days. I want to draw this to mind, where two beautiful men took me to heights I've only dreamed about while shackled in a BDSM club. Talk about a story for the grandkids, right?

"Ten sounds fair," Wes hedges.

Wait. What? They can't be serious. I've only had a few and I'm already drained. My body feels like Jell-O. How can they expect me to stand that long? If I were lying down, sure. But I've never climaxed standing up like this before.

Then, he adds, "But I think fifteen sounds better. She came a lot just rubbing on me the other night. Fifteen is doable ... *for her*."

Are they seriously having this conversation with me standing here? Master Luca's finger slips between my ass cheeks, casually circling my damp rear hole. "I think that sounds fair. If she goes limp, we'll take turns holding her. Don't want her arms hurting *too* bad in the morning." He chuckles. He fucking chuckles!

"Me either. But you better keep your dick to yourself, if you expect her to walk anytime this week." Wes sounds so casual that it's disconcerting. Not that I doubt what he says. Master Luca is H.U.N.G.

Master Luca grumbles something under his breath, the tip of his finger pushing just a bit into my tight ring. It burns and feels amazing in equal measure. "I woulda put a condom on if I was planning to take her. But this isn't about me. This is about her and her experience. I'll use my hand or someone else for completion. And you've already come once, so your balls shouldn't turn too blue." He chuckles again, that deep baritone vibrating close to my ear. "Don't forget that I'm granting you permission to play on my scene, which is something I never do. But I can see that the female gets more excited with you around. Can't you hear her? She's still panting."

"Yes. I know. We have a unique friendship."

"Wes, baby, are you done?" Amanda's voice rings through, and I go stiff as a board at the sound. I almost forgot she was here.

Wes's fingers lightly massage against my sweet spot, and he leans in, brushing his lips over my exposed throat. "Calm down, Kitten." His tongue draws a sensuous line from my jaw to my ear. It feels so damn good that I nearly swallow my tongue as I suppress a moan, not wanting him to know how much I love it. "She was just a means to an end. I had to come from watching you. And I didn't wanna use my hand because of the mess I would've made. It would have went everywhere. *You're* the only one I want. So take a deep breath for me and let it out."

I comply with his tender, gravelly words, feeling a hundred times better. Warmth that has nothing to do with fantastic orgasms encases my heart.

"Wes," Amanda whines impatiently, sounding a whole lot like Kelly. If I didn't know any better, I'd say they were sisters. I wanna call her out, or snap her neck, but I can't. I'm too damn tired, and I trust Wes to handle it.

He grumbles against my neck, kisses me there just once, and then pulls away. But not entirely, as his fingers remain buried. "It's Master Wesley, Amanda. And can't you see I'm not done? If I were done, I would have my Kitten in my arms by now, and we'd all be going home, wouldn't we?" He's pissed. Dominant and pissed in some unusual Master mode. I almost feel sorry for Amanda. *Almost.*

"I … I…" she starts, and he cuts her off with a rumble in his throat.

"Master Geo, please escort Amanda to the dungeon and have Master Bane punish her." Wes is all bite, hard, and sexy, and it's turning me on even more. Which I didn't even think could happen.

Amanda squawks. "What-what? You can't—"

"I can, and I just did. Don't interrupt *any* Master in the middle of a scene. You signed the forms. You know the rules. You'll be awarded fair punishment."

"Consider it done," a man comments. "Do you want standard or stricter punishment, Master Wes?"

"Twenty paddles with Master Bane's choice of instrument and one lash with the whip."

"No! Not the whip!" Amanda screams in horror.

"Yes. The whip. You interfered with my Kitten's pleasure, and Master Luca's." Pausing a beat, he curbs his angry tone. "Are you still hard back there, Master Luca?" Wes asks.

"Yes, but I won't be for long," he grunts in response.

"Make that two whip lashes. You're wasting our time. If my Kitten doesn't complete fifteen orgasms because you interrupted us, Amanda, so help me. You'll be punished again. *Now go*." And with that Amanda starts to wail her distress. I can almost taste her tears, yet I don't seem to care one bit. If Wes thinks it fair, then it's an appropriate punishment. I trust his judgment.

It doesn't take long for her sobs to die down as she's carted to the dungeon, wherever that may be. "You still with us, Kitten?" Wes's tone is back to being soft and sexy, just the way I like it. Part of me wants to thank him for putting her in her place. Another part of me knows that's rude and out of line. So I keep quiet instead, loving this floaty feeling that has me drifting in peace.

"I think she's just about to hit a subby high," Master Luca notes with an air of amusement.

"Then I suppose we should make her higher. I didn't know she liked a little pain."

"Agreed," Master Luca says, and that's when it all starts again. My blood roars to life, leaving behind the peace as I'm thrown into the pit of unabashed ecstasy.

Tongues, fingers, lips, and teeth graze me from top to bottom, loving me, pleasing me, driving me utterly mad. With hard thrusts, Wes's fingers plunge in and out of my depths as Master Luca licks my ass cheeks and glides one slick finger into my rear hole. It burns, and I scream in exquisite pain as he breaches deeper. Once he's inside, I can feel both his and Wes's fingers dancing simultaneously, creating an otherworldly rhythm that leaves me a quivering mess.

"That's it, Kitten." Wes rakes his teeth over my nipples, one to the next and back again. "You're so fucking wet." He fucks me harder, sucking my pert bud into his mouth. Groaning around the tip, he seizes my pleasure. More thrashing and toe curling carries forth. My eyes daze completely, staring at the ceiling as I lose all ability to do anything but *feel*. They take every ounce of me away, stripping me bare for ecstasy and ecstasy alone.

Not in control of my body any longer, I come at their will, my pussy and ass clenching around their digits. "That's it, Kitten." Wes kisses my nipple, fingering my center into a state of constant detonation.

"Three," Wes groans in praise as I come apart again. Over and over, he calls them out, as I shatter to bits before their very eyes.

By number ten, I'm sinking, and Master Luca is holding me up, his finger never leaving my needy asshole as Wes laps my clit. "Oh yes, Kitten, come on. Come for me." He speaks around my bundle of nerves, his teeth nibbling it. And that's all it takes for me to lose myself in him, in everything. Wailing a hoarse cry, I tremble through the climax. Relentlessly, he continues to capture every last drop of my delight. Then carts me straight into another as he suckles me from one indulgent plateau to the next.

Eleven slips into twelve, then into thirteen, and by then, I can't even remember my name.

"You're doin' great, beautiful." Master Luca's hand around my stomach is sturdy, yet gentle. Those plump lips kiss my neck. "Just a few more."

Wanting to please them, needing to make them proud, I offer him a weak nod. "That's our girl," he praises. It feels amazing to be cherished like this. An even deeper warmth of happiness twirls around in my gut, dancing the tango with the ball of vibrant satiation that's taken up residency there for the time being.

Master Luca slides his pre-cum soaked dick up between my ass cheeks. "I'm gonna come on you, beautiful," he grinds out just before soaking my back in spurt after spurt of his release. It's enough to tip the scales, driving me into another fit of climatic elation. Riding his peak out with mine, he sucks on my neck, his hot pants matching the pitch of his slowing hips.

"So perfect. Now it's time for you to finish," he whispers, pulling away. "Thank you." One final kiss and he's gone, leaving my hot flesh cooled by his cum.

Before I can even process what's happening, Wes is standing at my front, cupping the nape of my tired neck, so I'm forced to look him in the eye. They're glistening with desire mixed with something else that I can't put my finger on.

Using the back of his hand, he swipes my juices from his face with a charming smirk. "You're done, Kitten. All fifteen. But you're gonna go for me just one more time, and you're going to look me in the eye when you do."

I want to fight and tell him that it's too intimate to watch him when I shatter. But all thought is lost when Wes leans in and claims my mouth *hard*. Shoving his thick tongue between my startled lips, he massages my essence into my taste buds, and we groan together. I fight against my restraints wanting to touch him. Stepping closer, his body molds to mine, tits to stomach, feet to feet. A firm palm grips my ass cheek for a moment before slipping between my parted thighs. Without pause, he delves two fingers into my dripping hole, and I wail into his mouth, my pussy throbbing around his digits. He smiles against my lips swirling his tongue with mine, his breath pumping in harsh spurts. *Fuck, he's incredible.* A concealed thickness jabs my belly. He groans once more, thrusting his hips to mine, driving his erection against my stomach. I whimper, desperate for him to release it. To use it on me. To replace his fingers with it. *I want him.*

Sensing my need, Wes deepens our kiss until I'm breathless and my brain is spinning. Then he sucks every last ounce of energy from me when his fingers begin their punishing pace, fucking my hole like they own it. His mouth swallows all of my cries, my whimpers, my moans, my everything as he kisses me, his tongue claiming this part while his fingers claim the other. I float into the sky, feeling lighter than air as my sensitive, sweet spot is massaged with masterful precision. Light bursts behind my eyes, riding on the razor's edge.

Wes tears his lips from mine, and we share a dual gasp. "It's time to come," he commands, curling his fingers just right to catapult me over the threshold. A violent orgasm rips me in two, and I nearly lose consciousness as I scream through it. Heeding his words, I evaporate into tiny particles of quivering bliss while keeping my eyes locked on his. Grunting, his hips thrust against my belly once more, and a roar that couldn't be conceived as anything other than *relief* erupts from deep within his chest, as his hips kick forward. A sudden dampness slickens my belly. Something clicks in my muddled brain. *He just came in his jeans.* The thought rocks a strange tremor through me; then everything goes limp. My arms drop, knees buckle, unable to hold myself up any longer. Everything feels like a million pounds. I need to rest. I need sleep. I need *Wes*.

"Whoa, Kitten." His fingers slip out, and he hefts me into his embrace as my head lulls onto his shoulder. He gently caresses my back. Out of nowhere, Master Luca appears and unhooks my restraints. Wes lifts my noodly form into his arms and carries me silently over to the couch behind the rope where he drops us, draping me over his lap.

"Here," the familiar voice of Master Luca says just before a warm, soft blanket covers my naked flesh. I curl my face into Wes's chest, inhaling his delicious scent as the Sandman beckons me.

Sprinkled kisses dance atop my damp hair. "Rest now, Kitten. We'll go home soon. You did beautifully." The weighted happiness in Wes's voice serenades me, warming me from the inside out. My eyes drift closed, and I cuddle his soothing warmth all the way into dreamland as he talks to Master Luca and others, never letting me go.

This is ... lo—happiness.

Chapter Sixteen

Day 12

Blinking my bleary eyes, a face resting on a pillow a mere foot from mine comes into focus. I gasp loudly. What is he doing in my bed? Covering my mouth, I yawn, taking in Wes's messy hair and soft bedroom eyes that are staring back at me. He really is too damn sexy, especially now with a crease on his cheek from sleeping and that scruff on his face. I wonder how that'd feel against my inner thighs this morning? Oh. Shit! I can't believe I just thought that. A flash of last night's events invade my mind for a millisecond. I had that mouth on my pussy, those fingers inside it. I clench, basking in the residual ache. You know you've had a life-changing night when you're sore in the morning. And damn, if I don't hurt everywhere.

A slow smile creeps into the corners of Wes's lips. "Good morning, Kitten." Leaning in, he brushes those lips over mine. My breath falters just before I start grinning like a stupid school girl. I re-cover my mouth with my hand, not wanting to knock him over with my dragon breath, and so I can hide this childlike giddiness.

For whatever reason, I'm blushing. Perhaps, it's because I've yet to wake up in bed with a man, for ages. A good five years, at least. And I know for certain I never had a magical night with any of those guys. Their sex was average at best. A few times, I never even came. I definitely can't say that about Wes. Although he did have the help of a talented Master.

"Ummm ... Morning? What are you—"

Wes shoves my hand to the side to kiss me again. I try to pull away, but he attacks my mouth with zeal, groaning his deprivation, hand cupping the back of my neck. My nipples harden between us. I moan in my throat at his soft, pliable lips shifting deliciously over mine, and the way his scent surrounds us in a cocoon of heat. His tongue sweeps across my seam, and I jerk to, snapping our connection before I climb on top of him and have my way. But he doesn't go too far, as his body slides closer and he grabs my thigh, hooking it over his hip. My breasts touch his chest. An obvious boner folds between us. The dampness beading on the head clings to my belly like a tiny kiss.

"I've wanted to do that for hours." He pecks the corner of my mouth. I'm not sure if he can help himself. He can't stop staring. It's both adorable and a little scary. I can feel the tethered connection between us now. It was there before, but now, the air surrounding us feels a lot different. Something's changed.

Seizing the moment, not letting our intimacy go to waste, I lay my hand on his side. His silky skin is firm underneath my palm. He shivers against my touch, and I feel it pass through his entire body as his eyes temporarily close. As if he's trying to retain control … or perhaps it's something else entirely.

"You've been lying here for hours watching me, haven't you?" I ask.

The sudden pink to his cheeks is answer enough. "I wanted to sleep with you. After last night, I couldn't help it. I … I've never come like that before. It was…."

"Sexy," I finish for him.

The pink cheeks swap to red, and Wes glances away, clearly out of his depths. "I was gonna say childish. What kind of thirty-eight year old man comes like he's seventeen all over again?"

"One who's turned on enough?"

Head slightly turned, Wes gazes into the distance, deep in thought. He shrugs. "Apparently so. You slept on me all night at the club. I felt you breathing. Even felt your heartbeat against my hand." His voice sounds different, like he's unsure about how he feels. "I've never held a woman like that … *ever*. Not even my wife. I loved her. But she was never one to let her guard down. Then, ten months to the day, after we were married, Garrett came and we never hugged after that. He had so many problems. We were both stressed. I was working two bartending jobs just to feed us." He chuckles humorlessly. "I'd forgotten how it was to truly hold someone. So when I carried you into the house last night, I brought you to bed. Then, I couldn't leave." He shrugs for the second time. "I don't know why. But I couldn't. I put you under the covers, took a shower, and then slid in next to you. It just sorta happened. I was hard the rest of the night. Barely slept a wink. So I watched you sleep instead."

Yep. It's official. These feelings between us are real. And right now, I'm melting into a puddle of pink gooey something. It's equally warm and hot. Soft and hard. Sweet and sexy. It's … *special.*

Wes keeps talking, and I keep listening as I bury myself deeper into him. "I hope that's not too creepy. I don't think I've watched anyone but Garrett sleep before. My employees don't stay the night. They complete their duties and leave. I'm not one for…" He trails off.

My body goes flush against his. Face tucked into the crook of his neck, I breathe him in. His erection kicks between us, begging for attention. So I give him just that as I wrap my fingers around his silken girth. My middle finger and thumb barely touch. Grinding himself into my palm, Wes groans. It's bottomless and erotic as hell. Heeding his call, my pussy quivers at the sound, growing wetter.

"You're not one for what?" Nuzzling my nose under his jaw, I prompt him to finish his thought. His palm skims over my side, sliding around my back where he holds me tight.

"I grew up a geeky loner, Kitten." Lost in thought, his fingers draw feather-light circles just above my butt. "I didn't have many friends. We were poor. My dad didn't even know I existed until I was four. My mother told me I'd met him once. He has an older son. One that he wanted. So I never saw him again. He's dead now. But I never knew him or my brother."

"Is your brother dead?" I whisper, not wanting to deter him.

He shakes his head. "No. He's the president of the club I just signed the gun contract with."

He's what?!

I couldn't withhold the shock from my voice if I tried. "Your brother is part of the Sacred Sinners?"

Holy cow.

Faintly, he nods. "Yup. His name's Richard. Apparently, they call him *Big Dick*. A few years ago, my mother passed. She'd begged me to reach out to him before she died, but I didn't."

He sounds sad. Maybe he regrets that decision. I know if I had a sibling floating around in this world, I'd wonder about them. I don't know how he's lived thirty-eight years without speaking to Richard. However, if he's anything like Nash or some of his club brothers, maybe keeping his distance is the right choice. Or was … considering he just got into bed with that club. A club my brother's in bed with, too, but in an entirely different way. Now that's crazy when you get to thinking about it. Wes and Nash are indirectly linked. I can't believe I hadn't thought about that sooner.

"What happened to her?" I ask, referring to his mother.

Frankly, I'm not even sure why we're lying in bed, naked in each other's arms, having a conversation this deep. Then again I kind of love it. I've never experienced pillow talk before. There's something sweet about it. Truthfully, I find myself wanting to know everything about Wes. And right now, he's showing me a part of himself that I'm willing to bet most people have never seen. That's a precious gift I'm not going to squander.

"Breast cancer," he grouses, as if the words leave a bad taste in his mouth. "Third time's a charm. She was first diagnosed when I was four. That's why I'd met my father. She needed to know that if she didn't make it that I'd be cared for. He blew her off. Said that he'd kill her or me if we ever tried to speak to him again. So I helped care for her from one remission to the next. Worked some sort of odd job since I was ten because she wasn't able to strip anymore. The diner's money wasn't cutting it, and her hours were scarce. If we were lucky, we could afford to eat once a day, sharing a can of beans, corn, or whatever. Most of the time, she went without so I could have that extra slice of bread. He never sent us a thing. Never helped my mother at all. I don't remember him, but I remember her. Every part of her. She was beautiful, even before she died." Love shines within his closing testament.

She sounds like she loved him very much. Too bad his dad was a complete asshole. Wes had a hard life. I can't say my life was a walk in the park, but I had two parents and a brother. I always had food on the table and a roof over my head. From the sounds of it, Wes was lucky to have much of anything. I had a few friends like that while growing up. They were dirt poor. They lived in houses that should have been condemned, and ate food that I wouldn't even feed my dog, if I had one. It's an unfortunate existence. I'm just glad that Wes has made something out of himself, even after all the obstacles he's had to overcome in the process. He's an inspiration.

"She was blonde, wasn't she?" I ask, genuinely wanting to know more.

Price, one of Nash's club brother's and a philosophy professor at Trish's university, has been known to preach time and time again about how men seek women who resemble their mother. While women want men who resemble their father. It's not always about looks. Maybe that's why both Nash and Wes appeal to me? Why I care for them both? It's not ideal, sure. But that's the way it is. Nash reminds me of my biological father. He was strong, defiant, a bad boy with a love for only one woman. I've heard the stories. Seen the pictures. Then there's Wes.

He's very much like Patrick, my step-dad. He's smart, articulate, charming, and in his own way, loving.

Wes smiles. It's not a happy smile. It's one that says he's thinking about his mother—nostalgic. He nods. "She was."

"So that's why you prefer blondes. Because of your mother," I remark, evenly. Trying to ignore the dull pain in my chest for voicing it aloud. I hate that he prefers blondes like Nash does. Some people don't have types. These men do. I can't lie and say it doesn't hurt. It does.

Wes's hand freezes on my back, and he shifts his head to look me straight in the eyes. The spot between his eyebrows is pinched, lips pursed into a thin line. *Shit.* He's irritated. "Before my ex, I *only* dated brunettes, which included her. Then she went and ruined them for me … until you showed up to the track years ago, wearing those purple racing boots with your hair in a ponytail. You were all fire and ice from the moment I laid eyes on you. Barking orders to your guys. Them falling in line. Yet, there was this softness to you when you hugged them. I got hard in an instant. Couldn't stop thinking about you the entire weekend. I fucked so many faceless holes, picturing you the entire time."

My mouth falls open as a burst of butterflies fill my soul. What did he just say? A boner? Fucking faceless holes while thinking about me? Oh. My. God. I can't… How does he remember that day? I barely remember that day. It was years ago. My first race on the circuit. I was nervous as hell. He was there with his blondes. There were a lot more of them back then. Ten, at least. He was parading them around in their bikini tops, kissing on them, fondling them. They were giving just as good as they were getting. It was a show nobody could miss, even though I wanted to. He was all money and ego. It made me sick.

"I remember you from then. I thought you were a dog." I did for years until I came here. Wes is different than I expected. Garrett changed that for me.

Without warning, he grabs a handful of my ass, and I jump, caught off guard. Though, my belly does a little twirl. "I am a dog." He grins devilishly.

My hand that's holding his dick squeezes, and I smile victoriously when his beautiful eyes light up at the pressure. So I do it again. This time, I'm rewarded with a low growl of appreciation. "Obviously, I don't think that anymore. Or I wouldn't be touching you here." My hand tightens once more to cement my statement, and he bucks his hips, fucking into my fist. It slickens with his pre-cum, making the perfect lube. So I jack him a few more times just because I can. It's a powerful thing, holding a man's dick, and owning his pleasure.

Wes's throat works. "You should." He sounds like he swallowed a bag of gravel.

"Why?"

I pretend that I can't feel his pulse racing through my fingertips. Or that his hand isn't gripping my ass harder and harder as I tug him a little at a time. Licking his lips, his eyes roll for an instant as I squeeze the crown of his member. His breath stalls, floundering before he inhales deeply. His frame shudders against mine. Jesus. I love this. He's so vulnerable right now. It's doing strange things to my heart and lower places, too. When was the last time I had this with a man? *Never*.

"Because ... I..." My thumb swirling around his cockhead distracts Wes for a beat. "Damn, Kitten. You're gonna make me blow if you keep that up."

Leaning forward, I scrape my teeth across his Adams apple, then I taste him there. "Blow? Really?" I tease, reveling in the addictive power. He controlled all of my orgasms last night. Turnabout's fair play, right?

"Fuck!" Wes roars, and before I know what's happening, I'm flipped onto my back, and Wes is thrusting into my pussy to the hilt.

Arching off the bed, nails clawing at the sheets, I wail through the sudden onslaught of rhapsody—the stretch, the burn, the connection. He takes my mouth, stealing my startled cries. Plowing his tongue inside, he deepens our kiss. Instinctively, I wrap my legs around his hips as he rocks into me ever so slowly. Detaching my fingers from the bed, I grab for him, my sharp nails raking his back, as my heels dig into his taut ass.

Flattening his palms on either side of my head, he gradually pulls away. Our lips stick together like glue before separating. I whimper at the loss. Wes's glistening blue eyes delve into mine. "Before you get upset, I'm not wearing a condom. And I always wear one. But I'm *not* wearing one with you." He's matter-of-fact.

I scowl at him for making that choice without my permission. Why didn't I even think of that? Oh, right, that's because his flawless dick is inside me. I can't think straight where he's concerned.

Wes grins, shaking his head, amused. "Don't give me that look." He pecks my lips once, then goes back to garnering eye contact. My face relaxes a little, only because of how adorably hot he looks right now. He withdraws his cock an inch or two before sliding home.

Happily, he sighs. "I've wanted to do that for years, Kitten. And I've wanted to kiss these lips for years…" Wes dips his head, claiming said lips for a brief interlude, before retracting. "Wanted to caress this skin." He runs his hand along my leg that's wrapped around him. Goosebumps surface in his wake. Fuck, why does he always feel so damn good?

A thought I probably shouldn't say aloud pops into my head, but I say it anyhow. "What happened to Master Wesley? Did he get sweet all of a sudden? How do you go from shoving your cock down some chick's throat, to this?" I crack a sassy smile.

His face twists into an imitation glare. "It's called lack of sleep, Kitten."

He's so full of himself. That's not it at all.

Exaggeratedly, my eyes roll so he can capture their full effect. "No, it's not."

A knock raps at the door. "Ms. Gwen, have you seen my dad?!" Garrett yells outside.

Oh. This is not good. This isn't good at all! Today's not the weekend. It's Thursday. Garrett will be expecting me to work. *Crap.* How could I have forgotten?

Wes must grasp how much I'm freaking out when he whispers, "Zoe already canceled your tutoring schedule with Garrett today. Calm down."

Is he crazy? Just because he tells me to calm down, doesn't mean I'm going to calm down. I'm hyperventilating over here. Isn't that taught in Women 101? Don't order her to calm down, because she most certainly won't listen. I can't do that. Garrett's outside my room. What if he has a key? What if dummy over here didn't lock it to begin with and he walks in on us having S.E.X? I can't be one of the blondes to Wes or to Garrett. They mean too much to me.

Before I get a chance to gather my bearings, Wes drops the fucking Atomic bomb in my bedroom. *Kaboom!*

"I'm in here with Gwen, Bud. Zoe's going to make sure you get some breakfast, then take you into town. Okay?"

I'm going to kill him! Then I'll dump his body in the pond so he can sleep with the fishes. I hope they feast on his eyeballs first.

"You're in there with Ms. Gwen?" It's not clicking. He sounds unsure. "Ms. Gwen, is Dad in there with you?" Garrett asks, and I can't help it. I smile. I don't want to because I'm freaking out. Nevertheless, that boy elicits another flippin' smile from me. What can I say? Garrett is special.

Grinning like a madman, Wes is the one to raise an eyebrow in challenge. *Asshole.*

Swallowing hard, I then reply, stammering, "Ye-yes, Gar-rett."

"Are you and Dad playing?"

Oh. My … God.

Coughing, I almost choke on my tongue. How do I answer that?!

Wes silently laughs, his entire body vibrating the damn bed and me. If I wasn't already peeved at him, I might actually find it kind of adorable. But I don't. Not at all. "Yes, Bud. We're playing," he answers with a hint of humor.

I slap his bicep, *hard*. It stings my palm, spiking pain into my shoulder. Ouch! What in the hell is he made of? Concrete? "You can't say that!" I whisper-scream, turning fifty shades of red. This is so fucked up. He shouldn't be in here. I shouldn't want him here. Last night should've never happened. I shouldn't have his dick in my pussy while we're talking with Garrett. This is wrong, wrong, wrong. To top it all off, the asshole is still chuckling. He's not taking this seriously at all.

"Are you bein' safe? If you're playing like I think you're playing, I don't want you hurting Ms. Gwen. She still has to teach me tomorrow."

He knows! He knows! Jesus! How am I going to face my pal tomorrow? Is he going to look at me strangely? Hate me? Ask me questions about it? Oh…

Wes doesn't give me much longer to prattle in my head when he drops Atomic bomb number two right on my chest. "Yes, I'm being careful with her. I'm not gonna hurt her, Bud. You know that." Wes's tone is oddly caring, like a sweet caress. I feel it all the way to my toes. My traitorous body shivers in delight. *Damn it.*

"Okay, Dad. Love her nicely."

So. Stinking. Cute!

"Will do, Bud. Have fun with Zoe today. I love you."

Involuntarily, my pussy tightens around Wes's mostly hard dick like it's hugging him for being a good dad. My body is such a damn traitor. Remind me to give it a talking to later. It's not right.

"We will. Love you, too. And Ms. Gwen?"

Wes peers down at me, waiting for me to speak. *Shit.*

"Huh?" I call.

"Love Dad nicely, too. And I love you."

I've melted into a big bowl of girly soup. That's me. Right now. Damn. I love that kid.

"I love you more. Now go have fun. Dad and I will be okay." I attempt to sound upbeat, when in reality, I'm on the verge of tears. He told me he loved me. Albeit, this isn't the most ideal time. But still, he said it. *To me!* I blink away the tears.

NOWHERE

We hear Garrett retreat, and when I know he's out of earshot, I lose it. All of it. "I can't believe you confirmed we were having sex! I mean, I know he's sixteen, and he has to know about sex, but he doesn't need to know about his tutor and his father getting it on! I ... Oh. My. God. Wesley. I can't believe that! *And* I can't believe you're still hard!" My stupid pussy clenches, again—checking. Yup. Rock solid. "I can't believe we did what we did last night! Or that you're so fucking hot!" I peer down his body, suspended above mine. *Fuck.* He's ripped, toned, and so yummy it has to be a sin to even look. Praise Jesus. "And I can't believe I'm sleeping with you right after you got your dick sucked by Amanda last night! And after you slept with her God knows how many times in the past week." My hands start to flail. "You sleep with her, and now I'm sleeping with you! That's sick! I haven't even fucked anyone in..." I pause to think back, but the numbers aren't computing right. They elude me. I give it an educated guess. "At least a month! Then you punished her last night! Even though she's in love with you. And I think you might be a little bit in love with her, too. I can—"

A mouth crashing down on mine forces me to stop talking. It growls to my lips just before thrusting its demanding tongue inside. I gasp sharply when it begins to battle. Then my brain short-circuits, and my pussy starts functioning on autopilot. The whore scratches the surface, clawing her way out, turning my nipples into sharp points. Wes slips his cock outta my pussy and slams it right back in. I squeal into our kiss, so he does it again.

Oh, fuck. Yes.

My nails dig into his back, holding on for dear life as Wes pounds me like a beast. Slam, slam, slam, slam! He fucks my hole until it's trembling around him. Grabbing my legs, he shoves them above my head, resting them on his shoulders. Then goes back to hammering my pussy into submission. Breaking our kiss, I throw my head into the pillows, wailing my need as his dick hits my sweet spot on repeat.

"That's it. You're so fucking beautiful, Kitten. So beautiful," Wes pants, thrusting deeper.

Moving one hand to my neck, he holds me there, fingers wrapping around my throat, adding the lightest of pressure. Sweat dampens his forehead as he smiles at me. It's soft and genuine, hitting me straight in the heart as it swells, sealing our connection. I'm never going to be the same again. Not after today. He's ruining me.

Wes's smile falters, and he grinds his teeth, jaw tight, nostrils flaring. His pupils blow, turning his eyes almost black. "You're gonna make me come." He strains, his body coiling tighter.

"Not, yet. Slow down." Reaching up to cup the side of his face, Wes's scruff tickles my palm. Gently, I run my thumb over his reddened lips. He bathes it in his rampant breath. "Slow, baby. Slow down."

Exhaling, Wes nods.

Unhooking my legs from his shoulders, he wraps them back around his waist, reducing his pace. It feels so much better this way. I don't know why, but it does. Folding my arms around his back, I pull him flush with me so that I'm supporting his weight. Dipping low, he briefly pecks my lips, combing his fingers through the side of my messy hair as he regards me with caring eyes. Then his gaze turns unexpectedly sad.

"I'm sorry." He pecks my lips again before burying his face in my neck. I hug him tighter, wrapping every part of me around him, including my heart. He feels so good in my arms. Hard against my soft.

"What are you sorry for?" I kiss the side of his head, my fingers caressing his shoulder blades.

Wes slides his cock out, then glides back in, slowly, unhurriedly, *perfectly*. I whimper when he bottoms out once more, right where he belongs. "For wanting to fuck you into the mattress."

I actually bark a laugh at that one, my body vibrating with humor. "I'm not. But if you don't wanna come, then we're gonna take it slow."

My neck tingles as he kisses me there, peppering sweetness from my jaw down to my collarbone then back again. "But you feel so good everywhere, I can't help myself."

"So do you." I squeeze my thighs around him, so he understands I really mean that. That I do care for him. That I do love the way he feels. Every part of me does. There's no denying it any longer.

"After this, Kitten, you have to understand I'm not gonna go back to keeping my distance." *Kiss to my throat.* "I'm not gonna be able to stop touching you." *Kiss.*

"Then don't," I breathe. That same gooey feeling takes over for the hundredth time.

"I won't. *Ever.*"

And with that, Wes makes love to me, like I've never experienced before. In and out, his dick hits deep, dragging over my sweet spot. Kissing, we rock against each other's bodies. Sweat slides between us as Wes stokes my fire from deep within. I moan, digging my nails into his shoulders as my first orgasm takes me, tossing me off a bridge into the unknown. My heart soars along with it, hitting the liquid bottom where sated bliss floats into heaven.

Tenderly, Wes kisses me, his tongue exploring every inch of my mouth. I cling to him, never wanting to let go. "That's it, Kitten. You like it right there, don't you?" Speaking to my lips, he shortens his thrusts to caress that spot that drives me insane.

"Yes," I cry.

"I'm gonna make you come again, aren't I, Kitten?"

"Yes!" My back arches, smashing my breasts against his rock wall of a chest, having no place to go.

Gradually, he continues the torture, his eight pack contracting atop my stomach. Ass firm beneath my digging heels. Snapping his hips forward, he drives into my pussy. Into that ... *spot*. "That's it." He does it again. "Time for number two. Tell me what you want, Kitten."

Eyes sliding into my skull, I sob against his mouth. "Please. Make. Me. Come."

Sharp thrusts explode from his hips as Wes flies me over the rainbow. Clenching around his thickness, my body convulses as light bursts behind my eyes. Lost in rapture, incoherent words slip off my tongue.

"I can't... Fuck!" Wes thunders alongside me, his body going rigid as he fills me with spurt after hot spurt of his cum. Just the thought of him losing it catapults my fizzling orgasm into another.

Panting together, heartbeats racing as one, my chest sticks to Wes's as we float down from our highs. Exhaling heavily, his body relaxes, becoming dead weight atop mine. Our foreheads connect. "You ... are ... incredible." He struggles, still catching his breath.

Internally, I dance a little jig at his compliment, and I tip my chin up to peck his top lip. "So are you."

Expelling a tired groan, Wes presses his hands into the mattress on either side of my head to detach his chest from mine. The sound of wet skin peeling apart is like Velcro separating. Gazing down upon me, Wes grins, his eyes now lax—sated. He kisses my nose, my lips, my chin, as he climbs down my frame, slipping his softening cock from my hole. I want to complain about our divide but don't as he continues his descent by kissing the hollow of my neck, one stiff nipple, the next, my sternum, my stomach, all the way down until his mouth is wafting steamy heat over my exhausted pussy. He nuzzles his nose in my cleft, audibly inhaling. "I can smell myself on you." One of his hands cups me there, holding his essence inside.

"What are you doing?" I'm all breathy.

Hand glued in place, Wes shifts his naked body over my legs, coming to lie his head on the pillow beside me. He yawns. "I'm bushed, Kitten. Let's get some sleep."

Out of universal habit, I yawn in succession. He's right—we could use some more sleep. After all the orgasms I've had in the past twenty-four hours, I'm zonked. Add the ones I just had to last nights, and I can't imagine how much pain I'll be in once we finally crawl out of our tiny bubble. I kinda love it here; the two of us and nobody else. It's serene. Although, sometime I've gotta take a hot shower and eat something. My belly grumbles at the thought. Of course, it does. I haven't eaten since we had dinner here last night. Thanks to the blondes, some fancy salads were prepared for us. They weren't very filling, even with the grilled chicken and pecans.

"I can't sleep with your hand between my legs." I turn my head to the side so that I can see his face square on.

"Try." He winks, although the rest of his enthusiasm doesn't hit his face. He's tired.

"Why?"

His cheeks pinken, going shy on me again. This is an unusual side to Wes. "Because I like knowing what I did there."

"That you came?" I clarify.

Biting his bottom lip, he nods. It's so innocent, coming from a not so innocent grown man. The admission itself makes those butterflies reappear tenfold.

I smirk. "You can say it, Wes. For being such a forthright guy, I'm surprised you're shy about something like this."

He shrugs like it ain't no thing. It dries his shyness right up. "I can't help it. You're right. I am a man who knows what he wants and says how it is. But I've never spoken about this kind of stuff before. It's new to me."

"You talk about sex all the time." It's true. He does. Out of all the men I've met, he's one of the most outgoing in terms of performing sex and talking about it. He could teach a class.

"Yes. But not about sex with a woman I actually care about. There's a huge difference between some faceless fuck and a beautiful woman that warms your bed."

Whoa. That's one hell of a statement. One that shouldn't be doing strange things to me like it is. *Very* strange things. Things that are making me smile like a blushing fool, among other oddities, internal ones.

"Now who's the shy one," he teases sweetly before leaning in to press an equally sweet kiss to my cheek. "You're special to me, Kitten. You have been for years. This is new for both of us. I don't know how you feel, and

I don't want to know right now. We have a few more weeks to let this sink in. But, in the meantime, I want us to get to know each other some more. That is, if that sounds okay with you? No rush. No pressure. Just two adults seeing where things might lead. What do you say?"

That sounds pretty much perfect. Just what I need. *No pressure*. How does he always seem to get that? It's like he's picking up Wi-Fi signals from my brain. He gets me. Understands things that most can't. I can be myself. It feels damn good.

However, there is just one little detail that we need to cover first.

"I'm in agreement, except … no more blonde blowjobs, no more blonde fucking, no more blondes groping you. Just no more blondes, period, where you're concerned."

"You do know they work for me?" he asks, not being shitty. If he were trying to pull one over, my gut would tell me. He's trying to make a point.

Nodding, I respond with firm dignity. "I know, and can handle that. But what I can't handle is seeing someone I'm growing to care about, fucking, or being sucked by some employee or otherwise. They can work for you without rubbing on your dick. The dick is off limits. If you agree with that, then we have a deal."

A sly smile spreads across his face, lighting it up. Even his eyes dance with amusement. "So what you're saying is, you own my dick? That my dick only goes in your pussy. Into your mouth." His eyes lock onto my lips, and he licks his own, clearly picturing a dirty fantasy in his head.

Playfully, I slap his arm, drawing his mind out of the gutter. "Yes. Your dick is mine, and so are your hands." I had to add that, too, just in case he thinks he can skate by and use his hands to play with them instead. Not that I think he would. But still, I have to cover all my bases. It's better to be safe than sorry.

"Oooo, kinky. Does that mean you're gonna hold my cock when I piss, too?" His eyebrows bounce with mischief.

Of course, the idiot would think that. What is it with men and that weird fantasy? Pursing a sour face, I slap his arm again just because I can. "No. I'm not holding it while you piss. You know what I mean."

Leaning closer, his smiling lips touch mine and linger there just on the surface, allowing us to breathe each other in. *Jesus.* I lo—like this man. "I know what you meant, Kitten." His tongue pokes out, sampling the seam of my lips. "And I agree. As long as you're mine, I won't need them, anyhow. They were only here to keep me from going crazy in your presence. It's difficult to tame a hard-on when you're horny 24-7 because you're living under the same roof with a brunette fox. I had to have something to take the edge off. But now that we've gotten this settled, I'll take the edge off using the fox's body instead. I just hope you don't get too jealous. She's fuckin' hot, and a firecracker in bed."

This man … he's too much.

Chuckling, with a huge smile, I grab the back of his neck and mold his lips to mine. "You're so cute sometimes," I mutter there, before kissing him with all I've got. It doesn't take long for the heat to build between us, and we're back to panting, hearts hammering. My brain swirls as he knocks me on my ass with yet another kiss. The man has one helluva talented mouth.

In the same moment, we tear our lips apart, gasping. We pause a beat, catching our breath. "My dick needs some sleep, almost as much as my brain does. We'll need our energy for later. Get some rest, Kitten."

Snuggling closer, I rest my cheek on Wes's chest, listening to the cadence of his heart pulsing against my ear. It's sort of romantic. The only other person I've ever done this with is Nash. *Gah!* Why do I have to go thinking about him at a time like this? Nope. Time to push him far from my mind. Wes is the one with me right here. Wes is the one I'm growing to care for. Wes is the one who actually wants me. *Wes is amazing.*

"Sweet dreams." I kiss his smooth, muscled pec.

Lips caress my forehead. "Sweet dreams, my foxy Kitten," they whisper there.

Here's to new beginnings.

Here's to Wes and me.

Here's to the possibility of love.

Here's to another seventeen days.

Sweet dreams everyone. See you when we finally crawl outta bed.

Wow, he really is sleeping with his hand smashed between my thighs.

Chapter Seventeen

<u>Still Day Twelve</u>

Bathed, and dressed in shorts and a tee, I'm ready for the day. Stepping out of my bedroom, and into the hall, I feel lighter than I have in months. This morning was good for Wes and me. I think we're actually moving forward into something great. I just hope it lasts and I'm just not a fun conquest. Although, the way my heart and gut feels about him says that he could be someone very special. Someone that could last. Who knows? Only time will tell.

When I'd woken about an hour ago, Wes was gone. On the pillow beside mine was a chicken scratch note that said he was working in his office for a few hours and didn't want to wake me. How cute is that?

Padding toward the living room, my stomach grumbles. I definitely need to grab something to snack on. It's already mid-afternoon. Hopefully, the cooks have something extra filling on the menu tonight. If not, I'll be starving by eight, and searching for chocolate. Well, I might search for some chocolate anyhow. It's a girl's best friend. I know, I know, you might not agree. Some people say it's diamonds. Well, they're liars. Diamonds don't comfort you. Chocolate does, and so do motorcycles, though in an entirely different way. Trust me.

Rounding the final corner, I slow my stride as numerous voices echo off the white walls. Another two tentative steps and I'm creeping closer to the living room's entrance.

"I can respect your position, but I don't agree with it." I can hear Wes clearly. He's all business. What if he's in the middle of a meeting? If he is, I don't want to disturb him.

Another two steps and I'm secretly peeking around the archway and into the vast room, just as someone remarks, "I don't give a fuck what you agree with. She shouldn't be here to begin with."

Motherfucker! You've got to be kidding me! This cannot be happening. Pinch me. This has to be a dream!

My eyes widen in shock and horror as they lock on the person speaking. Then I take a broad step, entering the room, my head held high. This is going to be interesting.

"Gwennie-bee!"

Nash is to his feet and across the room before I get an angry word in edgewise. His strong hands grasp my forearms at the same moment his mouth slams into mine, stealing my breath away. *Oh, fuck! This can't be real!* I stagger a step backward, but he keeps me going as he pushes us against the wall, pinning me there beneath his massive frame. I vaguely hear the heated shouts of men over the blood rushing through my ears. Taking a deep breath through my nose, my head spins like a top as Nash's heady scent hits me hard. My knees nearly give out.

Without consent, that familiar tongue invades my mouth, robbing me of my strength to push him away. Sweeping his tongue against mine, his hands frantically claw at my clothes, hips, breasts, ass, everywhere that they can touch. What's he doing here? Why is this happening? So many questions. So much tongue. So much Nash. *Oh God.*

Desperation clings to every action, as Nash growls into our kiss before grabbing my thigh and hooking it over his hip. A stout thickness prods my belly, and I groan at the feel of it there. I can't help it. Wrong or not, this is *my Nash.* My family. My ... Jesus ... *He's here.* What the ... Wait ... we're at Wes's. I was with Wes this morning. I can't do this. This is wrong. But ... *oh, so good.* I have to stop.

Go back to sleep, you needy whore! I scream inside my head. It does little good as my body not only betrays me but Wes, too. Mewling into our kiss, I slide my hands up Nash's shoulders to his neck where I slip my fingers into the base of his long hair. Damn. I missed him so much.

Nash groans his approval, palming my ass to jerk me closer.

Yes.

Lost in the moment, a wave of memories come tumbling in. Wes and I having pillow talk. Nash and I eating homemade pancakes with Trish. Wes and Garrett laughing together over breakfast. Nash putting Chapstick on Trish's lips before she went to play in the snow. Wes's hands curling around my belly just because he wanted to hold me. Nash ... never doing that because he always had a girlfriend. Always had someone else. I was always the sister with the fetish for kissing her step-brother. He never wanted more. Never expressed more. *Wes did* this morning. He wanted me for me. Not because we have some strange dependency with one another. No.

This is wrong. I can't do this. Not anymore.

Nash's lips moving over mine might feel like home. Every part of him does. From the way he smells. To the way his thick hair runs through my fingers. But he'll never be more than that. Not with Kelly around. He doesn't love me the way I love him, and he never will.

A special piece of my heart breaks off.

This is done.

I have to let go.

It's time to move on.

Grabbing Nash's shoulders, I shove him away. Our lips *snap* as they detach. He takes a staggered step backward. Those beautiful green eyes of his are glassy as they rake my wobbling form. I sag against the wall for balance, afraid that if I don't, I'll fall.

"I fuckin' missed you, Gwennie-bee." Nash comes at me again, except this time, I put both of my palms up to stop him. Thankfully, he complies.

Pausing a beat, I close my eyes to steady my breathing. I sweep my tongue over my engorged lips. Damn. He sure can kiss, too. One session with Nash and they're already swollen. Let's not forget about how turned on I am right now. If it weren't for my panties, there'd be a mess dripping down my inner thighs by now. They quiver in agreement.

As if my life wasn't already complicated and confusing enough with Wes, Nash is here. I glance up, scanning the room. So is Toa, Price, and four of their other brothers. Toa's standing beside a pissed off Wes, holding a shoulder to keep him seated in his chair. Wes's eyes are blazing as they glance my way, filled with pain and resentment. Here, I was talking about don't touch the blondes this morning, and I just finished playing tonsil hockey with Nash. What was I thinking? Moreover, what the hell was Nash thinking? A tsunami of guilt crashes forth. I'm such a hypocrite.

Ignoring Nash's disconcerting presence, I turn my pleading gaze upon Wes, seeking answers. "What's going on here?" With the flick of my wrist, I gesture to the room of antsy bikers.

Staring daggers in my direction, Wes massages the back of his neck, shrugging Toa's grip off his shoulder. Toa lets it fly when he gives him a wide berth. Taking a deep breath, his chest expanding, Wes releases it before responding. "Apparently, Kitten—"

Nash cuts him off. "Don't talk to him about this, Gwennie. Talk to me. I'm the one here."

Wes growls under his breath. "Show some fucking respect in my home and close your mouth. She's asking me. Not you. I have been respectful enough to talk with you when I could've kicked you out."

Nash whips around, glaring at Wes, his fists bunched at his sides, jaw tight. I know that stance. He's preparing to brawl. That's not good. "Whatever, motherfucker. I'd love to see ya try."

That cool, calm, badass exterior that Wes exudes most of the time shines through as he casually leans back in his chair, kicks his heel onto his knee, and regards Nash like he's a piece of shit. "You underestimate me, Mr. McQueen. Showing up here unannounced was disrespectful enough. Then you come in here, acting as though you own the place. No," he tsks, "I think not. I'm tolerating your presence because of my feelings for Gwen.

If you were smarter, you would have realized that I have this house under surveillance 24/7. By now, there are at least five of the highest trained men in the business surrounding the house. Including one of my drivers who lives on the premises. So I suggest you relax, and use your brain."

Wow. Nobody talks to Nash that way without getting a face full of his fist, except me. Typically, Nash is a fair man, but when his emotions are twisted, there's no telling what he'll do. I've seen him punch a dude in the face for smaller offenses. Call me crazy, but I don't feel all that worried, even if Nash is ready to let loose. Though, I don't know if he would with me here. At least the old Nash would never put me in harm's way.

A scary sound rumbles in Nash's chest.

Toa intervenes, taking a step toward him in warning. I can see the silent conversation passing between the two of them.

"Calm the fuck down," his eyes say.

"Fuck off," Nash returns.

Toa's eyes swap to me for an instant before relocking with Nash's. *"Do you want her to end up hurt?"*

The stare down must work, because Nash's shoulders deflate just before his fists unclench. I guess it's a good thing Toa and him are great friends. He can talk him down when I really don't feel like it. At this point, I'm not even sure if I like him being here or not. He wasn't invited. That's clear enough. Just looking at him in that leather cut, wearing a pair of dark denim jeans, with his dark hair loose, face unshaven- it's messing with my emotions. Part of me is happy to see him. While another is still trying to doctor the scab he just reopened the moment I saw him again. Sure, the last time we spoke things were a little better. He was sweet, even. But that doesn't excuse everything else. The distance. The brush off. Kelly. I have a wicked stubborn streak, and I'm not very big on forgiveness. Hey, don't judge me. I'm working on it.

Wes snaps his fingers, drawing the attention back to him. "As I was saying, Kitten, I was working in my office when I heard a bunch of motorcycles drive up. We've all been talking, and I guess our little strip club rendezvous wasn't as secretive as it should have been. One of the gentlemen at the meeting gave your brother a call to tell him that his sister was playing both sides."

I knew it! I knew something bad was going to come out of that. My orgasm show, I'm sure, didn't help matters. Oh well. Shit happens.

"I told Steel he was seein' things. I didn't believe him when he said he saw you with him." Nash lifts his chin toward Wes in disgust.

"I *was* with him. I've been with him for twelve days. What I don't understand is why you're here, and how this has anything to do with you. I called. You knew I was safe."

"Yeah. Real safe, Gwennie-bee; not using your cell and calling from more than a private number," Nash notes rudely, making my hand itch to smack his smug face.

Instead, I focus my energy on suppressing the urge to roll my eyes. It's bad manners to do that at a time like this, especially when the room is already full of too much testosterone to begin with. "More than a private number? Is there such a thing?" That came out nicer than I anticipated. *Score.*

"What he means, Gwen, is that Wes's number is encrypted. Gunz couldn't even crack it, when we asked for a favor," Toa, the voice of reason, answers politely.

Finally, one guy who's not being either a dickhead or acting like he's better than everyone.

"Thank you." I force a smile. The one he flashes right back is purely genuine. It dials my tension down a notch.

"The Sacred Sinners VP couldn't get a feel on you. He thought you were Crimson Outlaw property, so when he saw you humpin' this fucker," Nash does that chin lifty thing again, "he wanted to give me a heads up."

My hip cocks, hand hitching to it. Just because I can't eye roll does not mean this attitude isn't gonna come out, guns blazing. Why? Because these assholes are playing tattletale like a bunch of three year olds, when they could have… Oh … I dunno … *asked me*. It's not like I would lie. I'm not all about that.

"Now why would their VP think I'm Crimson property?"

I've never been anyone's property. This is the twenty-first century. Not the eighteen hundreds. I know that's club code. I'm a biker; not a club member.

Wesley scoffs, shaking his head in revulsion. "He thought you were Nash's old lady."

My eyes bug at that. He can't be serious. I swing my gaze to Nash. Yup. It's true. That's exactly what their VP thought. How do I know that? Because Nash won't look at me, and his feet can't stand still. He's antsy. And an antsy Nash is a guilty Nash. What the hell? I expected to have a great day after I took a long bath, then blow-dried my hair, and put on some light makeup. Sure, I was achy from all the orgasms. But pleasantly so. Now, I'm here staring at my step-brother, who just went and ruined my day by showing up to act like a barbaric asshole. I've still not grasped why he's rode all the way here. Nobody's talkin'. It's crickets up in this place.

"Why would he think that, Nathaniel?" I lift an irritated brow, chewing on my inner cheek to keep from kicking him in the shin.

I wanted to read comics with Garrett when he got home from town. Not argue with a bunch of bikers and Wes in the living room.

"Because, after you'd left that Friday, Steel asked me who you were and I told him."

He's looking at his feet, his tone no longer defiant. This is guilt-ridden Nash talking. I hate when his voice goes all vulnerable like that. It kicks my mothering needs into high gear, and all I want to do is hug him, kiss him, and tell him everything is going to be alright. But I'm not going to do that. Nope. I'm going to stand right here, at the front of the room where I can keep a keen eye on everyone. I don't need any more surprises.

"Told him what, exactly?" I ask.

"That—" Nash mutters under his breath but is cut short.

Wes intercedes, answering for him, "That you're his old lady."

"Shut the hell up, asshole! You don't know what you're talkin' about." Nash's anger is back in full force. Lifting his head, back straight, he takes a step toward Wes like he's about to pounce. Though Wes doesn't seem to care one iota as he remains seated—comfortable. Does he have a death wish or what? Or perhaps he's just that arrogant. I can't decide.

"Then why don't you enlighten us all? Including Gwen." Wes points to me. "Since your little, *poor me, I'm in trouble*, charade already started to steal the fire from her eyes. You sure know how to play her, don't you? Bet ya do it all the time to get your way. Use her need to nurture your own benefit. I have to admit, it's a smart move, but you're not going to do that here. I won't stand for it. So you sure as fuck better tell her what it is you came here for, or I will. You've already taken time out of our day. I'd very much like to get back to it. Now proceed."

Jeez, when Wes gets to the point, he pulls no punches. Is he right about Nash, though? Does he use me?

Nash turns his back to Wes, acting as if he's not even in the room. "Don't listen to him, Gwennie-bee. That motherfucker doesn't know shit about us. About our family. He's just tryin' to get in the way because he got a taste of your pussy. When Steel told me about ya bein' here, I had to come get ya. Now get your stuff. I'm takin' ya home."

"I'm not going anywhere."

Whoa. That came out without me having to think about it. It's true, though. I meant it. I'm not leaving here. Not until I have to. And it has nothing to do with Wes and everything to do with Garrett. I'm not about to abandon him. No way. Not when he's progressing so quickly. Not when I'm afraid my heart might break too much if I leave. I love that kid. Truly. He's like the son I never had.

Wes barks a laugh. "I told you she wouldn't agree to leave. She's here of her own free will. And I think you should show her more respect than that. Me having tasted her pussy has nothing to do with why she's here. That's just a new development. I'd call it a perk, on both of our parts."

It happens so fast that I barely see it coming. One second Nash is staring at me. The next he's linebacker tackling Wes to the floor. What's even more shocking is that Wes somehow anticipated this. So when Nash goes to slam his fist into his face, he blocks him. Toa takes a step back, and we meet eyes above the childish fight that's filled with grunts and nasty curses.

"I knew it'd come to this!' he hollers over the dumbasses.

I shrug in response. He's probably right.

An end table knocks over, and a lamp shatters. Nash slams his massive fist into Wes's gut, at the same time Wes is elbowing him in the face. Blood gushes from Nash's nose, and I have to hold myself back from getting in the middle of this. Boys will be boys. They will fight. I know they're both smart enough not to kill one another. At least, I hope so. It's good for them to let off some steam, even if it's painful to watch. It serves them both right for acting like fools.

A man in a black SWAT-like outfit sprints past me in a blur, headed toward the men. Just before he gets to Nash, to tear him off Wes, I grab his vest, tugging it. "Let them duke it out. They'll feel better later."

Luckily, he heeds my words and retreats a few steps to stand next to me. "Are you sure? I'm under strict orders not to let anything happen to Mr. King or his family."

That's sweet.

I pat the big guy on the chest. Wes wasn't lying. This man is, at least, seven feet tall, but agile as hell. I bet he's a former SEAL. "They're playing whose dick is bigger. Don't worry. Nothing major will come out of it."

"Okay, ma'am. Holler if ya need somethin'," the man comments before disappearing like a cloud of smoke.

Crazy.

"Fuck you!" Nash throws a punch at Wes's face.

NOWHERE

Just like a scene out of an action movie, Wes catches Nash's fist midflight, stopping the impact. Apparently, he's a helluva lot stronger than he looks. Bucking his hips, Wes dismounts Nash in one swoop, crashing his back into the wall-to-wall entertainment center. The TV shakes as a vase falls over on its side.

Aren't they about done? The floor is already covered in enough of their blood. By the time they're finished beating each other to a pulp, this room is going to need to be redecorated. Jesus. Do you see that smear across the rug? I don't think that stain's going to come out.

More cursing and fighting proceeds. It's almost comical to watch as they begin to wear each other down. Both of them are disasters. Wes's white t-shirt is torn, showing off his eight pack. Nash's hair is stuck to the sides of his sweaty, blood coated face. They're both heaving for breath with busted lips.

Laying belly down on the floor, Nash slaps the side of Wes's head that is lying a few feet away in the same prone position.

This is pathetic. I can't take it anymore. "Are ya done?" I scold, then turn my sights to Nash's club brothers who are standing on the side of the room, in front of the bay window, talking amongst themselves. "Boys, why don't you step out for a bit? Let me handle this. You can come back in two hours. Nash'll be ready to leave by then."

Toa kisses my cheek on his way out the door, as the rest of the brothers follow in his wake. "We'll be back in two hours. Good luck," Toa calls over his shoulder.

"Thanks!" I yell. I've definitely got my job cut out for me.

Shaking my head in exasperation, I wade further into the room, careful not to cut my feet on any broken glass. I nudge Nash in the side with my bare toes before I go and do the same to Wes, who groans when I touch his ribs. Yep. They're bruised. "I'm giving you babies two minutes to cut your shit and straighten up. I'll be right back with the first aid kit. By then, I expect you both to be sitting up so I can clean your bloody mugs." My most convincing disappointed tone comes out perfectly.

It works, too, because I hear them shuffling around, groaning in painful protest as I leave the room in search of the first aid kit. Not sure why I'm getting it. Probably because I'll feel guilty if I leave them to fend for themselves—especially if one of their cuts gets infected. Men aren't very smart about cleaning wounds. They'd rather run some water over it, and call it a day. It's not always that easy. I tried to tell that to Nash the one time he cut his arm working under a car. Five days later, it got infected, and I had to drain it twice. It was disgusting, oozing puss and green shit. He probably should have gone to the doctor's, but he refused. So I did it. He was lucky it didn't get into his bloodstream. It took three weeks to heal.

Five minutes later, kit in hand, I enter the room wearing a pair of flip flops. Wes has retaken his armchair while Nash is sprawled out on the couch, sans shirt and vest. I'd forgotten how delicious he looks bare-chested. All those tattoos and hair. It's … *yum.* For a moment, I don't even realize I'm staring, until he clears his throat, catching me red handed. *Shit,* I'm supposed to be all fire and ice. Isn't that how Wes described me earlier today? It fits. I'm going with it. No more ogling hot, sweaty dumbasses. It's time to get down to business.

"Nash, sit up." I use my thumb, gesturing the upward motion. "And Wes, sit beside him. I'm not going to walk back and forth across the room to clean the both of you babies."

They comply without complaint. Though they don't sit too close to each other. God forbid they get cooties or something. It's not like they don't already have enough of each other's blood painted on their faces.

Pulling up an end table, I sit on it then dole out the bandages and antiseptic. Back and forth, I wipe their faces and hands with fresh pads before getting to the harder stuff, like their lips, scratches, bruises, and so on.

"I don't know why you had to tackle him," I admonish Nash, dabbing his swollen bottom lip with a cotton ball.

"He was talkin' about your pussy," he mumbles, trying not to move his mouth too much.

That's not it at all. There is no need to fight over that. Why would there be? It's not like he was defending my honor.

"I've fucked most of your club brothers, Nash. You're not *that* sensitive." We're not getting into this conversation. It's pointless. They were both willing participants. They're both guilty. He needs to stop lying. "You know what, I don't care. It was stupid. You are both adults, as am I. If I told you I didn't want to leave, you should respect that. You shouldn't have come in the first place. Did you think I'd listen and go with you? I have seventeen more days here. I made a commitment that I'm going to follow through with." I move to Nash's forehead, cleaning the oozing gash in his eyebrow. It'll need some butterfly stitches. Beside us, Wes is relaxing on the couch with his eyes shut.

"Don't go to sleep, Wesley. I don't know if you have a concussion or not," I remark.

Eyes still closed, he grins that same charismatic grin that makes me feel all funny inside. "Thanks, Kitten. I'm fine. No concussion. Just giving you two some privacy."

Awe, that's sort of sweet.

Nash snorts. "Privacy. Sure. Whatever you say. You've already won."

Alright, I'm lost here. There were no winners in this match.

I meet Nash's beautiful eyes. One of them is partially swollen shut. "Won what? There were no winners here. You're both banged up dumbasses."

"Not like that, Kitten. Nash thinks I won *you*. That you staying here means you're mine. Not gonna lie and say it doesn't feel good. But I know that's not the case. What we have is too new, so I know you're only staying because of Garrett."

See? Like I've said a million times, Wes somehow gets me. And to top it off, he doesn't sound disappointed that I'm staying here for his son. That's reassuring.

Jerking away from my touch, Nash groans in defeat, leaning back into the couch. "There's another guy? Who the fuck is Garrett?"

"My son," Wes answers.

Evidently, Wes didn't fill in the blanks for Nash and neither did that Steel guy, because he didn't bother to ask. All this fighting and drama, and for what?

I color in the details. "Wes made a bet with me at a race a few weekends ago. I took it and lost. I don't need to go into details about it, except to say that I'm now tutoring Garrett, Wes's son. That's why I'm here, to begin with. *To tutor*. We hadn't even had sex until this morning."

That confession must get Nash's blood boiling again, because one second he's sitting and the next, he's pacing the room. So much for honesty. I should probably keep my mouth shut on an occasion. "Get him cleaned up, Gwennie, and then we're going home." His hands are tugging at his hair, face staring at his feet.

"I'm not going anywhere. I thought I told you."

"I don't give a fuck! I'm not gonna let you stay here for another seventeen days with this guy." He points to Wes, still doing his step-step-step-pivot-step-step-step. What is it with the men in my life and pacing?

"Why?" I snap.

"Because, I forbid it. You shouldn't be here, to begin with. And since when do you date men when you race?"

Wait? What? Back the truck up here. He's forbidding me? And he knows about my racing? Oh. Hell. No.

He stops to look me in the eye. "Don't look so shocked, Gwennie. Yes. I knew about the racing. Can't say I was thrilled about it at first. But I knew it was something ya needed to do. Do you really think Trish keeps anything from me?"

I'm going to strangle my daughter. Of course, she'd tell him. Why am I so surprised? I shouldn't be. So much for mother, daughter confidentiality. Jeez, this day just keeps getting better and better. Fuck!

Taking a page out of Nash's playbook, I cross my arms over my chest and leer at him. "You're not the boss of me, Nathaniel. I still haven't forgiven you about Kelly and the blow off. Why in the world would I listen to you now? Right ... *I'm not*. There is no real reason for me to go. So why would I? Wes is nice to me. I'm fed. Clothed. I have a lovely bedroom. And I get to help a boy out that I love to pieces. I'm not abandoning him. I'm not like his mother, and I'm not *your* mother." That perks his ears right up, now doesn't it.

I'm not done. "Now, tell me why you're here, Nathaniel. I'm done playing this wishy-washy, back and forth."

"I broke up with Kelly after I found out you were here," he blurts.

"Why in the hell would you do that? I thought you were in love with her." I'm not upset in the least by this. Sayonara, bitch.

Nash shrugs, indifferently. "I can't be in love with a woman who's not all mine. I cared for her, sure. But her boss over here," he flicks his eyes to Wes then back to me, "could fuck her anytime he wanted, along with any of the high-paying customers at the strip club."

Note to self: Murder that two timing slut when I get home.

Then again, that's too much to deal with right now. At least, he knows, though. I guess.

Poor Nash.

My family mode kicks into high gear. "I never liked her, anyway. You're too good for her. She was a slut." *So am I. Don't hate me,* I tack on in my head.

Nash ignores my words when he commands, "I'm not staying another second in this house, Gwen. So go pack your things. We're leaving."

Does he really think that's going to work? I sincerely hope not. If so, he doesn't know me at all.

Holding my head high, I straighten my spine to square off against him. "I'm not going anywhere with you. Get it through your thick skull, Nash. I'm tired of this fighting. You want to kick each other around like babies. Fine. Do it. But I'm not going to be dragged away from Garrett because you've decided you want to be in my life again. Wait your damn turn." With that, I stand and amble toward the exit.

"Now where in the hell do ya think you're goin'?!" Nash booms so loudly his voice echoes off the walls.

I peer over my shoulder. "Where does it look like, Nash?" I raise a cocky brow. "Away from you. You can see yourself out. I'll be home in seventeen days. *If* I fucking feel like it. Now, if you'll excuse me, I have some sunbathing to do." Whipping my head around, hair flying, I walk straight out of the door, leaving Nash and Wes in my dust. Does it feel good to stand up to them? Hell yes, it does. At the same time, I can't help but wonder if I'm making a huge mistake. That's the beautiful thing about my pride. It's keeping me afloat right about now, because if I didn't have it, I'd probably be bawling like a baby on the floor from all this stress. Yep, I really do need to throw on my bathing suit and soak up the sun. Maybe that'll relax me. If not, I dunno what will.

"I'm not leaving here without you, Gwen! You're coming home with me one way or another. Even if I have to drag you kicking and screaming," Nash growls to my retreating back.

Wes barks a laugh in response. "Go put your bathing suit on, Kitten. I'll take care of this." As always, he's as cool as a cucumber. One of the things I'm growing to love about Wes.

"You'll take care of jack shit, motherfucker. She's leaving with me, or I'm not going at all!"

"Do you always act like such a child? It makes me wonder what she sees in you at all." I can sense his eyes rolling from here as I slow my strides on my way down the hall.

"Go fuck yourself, Wesley!"

"No thanks. I got plenty of that this morning."

Uh oh...

There's a thunderous roar, and then the sound of more glass breaking. Jesus. Nash really needs to get a handle on his anger issues. I don't remember him being such a loose cannon. Oh well. I guess it's time to catch some sun. I just pray they don't kill each other in the meantime. That'd be a shame. They're both amazing men that I happen to care a lot about. Hopefully, they'll come to their senses. Or Nash will. Wes seems to keep his most of the time. Remind me to thank him later for handling this for me. I think I'll give him a blow job as payment.

I'll see ya later.

It's time for me to grab myself a snack and catch some rays. Maybe Garrett will be home soon so we can read together. That'd be nice. I already miss him.

The End... For now...

Made in the USA
Lexington, KY
01 October 2017